The Seaside Detective Agency

THE CASE OF THE BRAZEN BURGLAR

THE ISLE OF MAN COZY MYSTERY SERIES
BOOK TWO

By
J C Williams

You can subscribe to JC Williams' mailing list and view all his other books at: www.authorjcwilliams.com

The Seaside Detective Agency: The Case of the Brazen Burglar

Copyright © 2020 J C Williams

All rights reserved. No part of this book may be reproduced in any manner without written permission except in the case of brief quotations included in critical articles and reviews. For information, please contact the author.

All characters appearing in this work are fictitious. Any resemblance to real persons, living or dead, is purely coincidental.

ISBN: 9798558342437

First printing November 2020

Cover artwork by Mikey Nugent

Interior formatting & design by Dave Scott

CONTENTS

Chapter One – Forest of a Thousand Trails 1
Chapter Two – All About the Busts 11
Chapter Three – Millionaire's Shortbread 25
Chapter Four – Big Fish 39
Chapter Five – Code Red 51
Chapter Six – Hand Sandwich 59
Chapter Seven – A Three-Horse Race 65
Chapter Eight – A Barrel of Hogwash 73
Chapter Nine – A Song and a Dance 83
Chapter Ten – A Mist Rolls In 95
Chapter Eleven – Brighter than the Sun 105
Chapter Twelve – Greensleeves 111
Chapter Thirteen – The Plot Thickens 127
Chapter Fourteen – A Little Bit of Elvis 133
Chapter Fifteen – Another Chocolate Teapot 139
Chapter Sixteen – A Load of Bollocks 147
Chapter Seventeen – Three Peas in a Pod 159
Chapter Eighteen – No Bloody Signal 171
Chapter Nineteen – A Funny Place to Take a Nap 183
Chapter Twenty – A Thief in the Knight 195
Chapter Twenty-One – Shift It! 203
Also by the Author 209

CHAPTER ONE
Forest of a Thousand Trails

Archallagan Forest, known by many as the Forest of a Thousand Trails, was a diverse landscape of trees, rough moorland, and marshy bog. Popular with mountain bikers and walkers alike, the tranquil surroundings were the perfect antidote for folk eager to cast aside the shackles of the daily grind to explore and embrace the great outdoors.

Corsican pines towered high into the sky, carpeting the rolling Manx countryside. During daylight hours, the forest floor offered its visitors a fairyland of discovery and adventure. But, as darkness approached, however, the warm welcome shifted to a somewhat more forbidding climate.

Creaking tree trunks, dancing shadows, and the flutter of wings unseen could play havoc with your senses, especially if you were of a nervous disposition. Something the Isle of Man's preeminent PI, Sam Levy, most certainly was.

"Who... who... who's there?" Sam said in response to the sound of a breaking twig, but the precision beam of light from his torch revealed nothing untoward. Only row upon row upon row of uniform tree trunks.

"I'm armed," he said, lying, his voice dripping with fear. Sam pivoted around with his torch trained in front of him, gripped firmly in his shaking hand. "There's six of us," he added, lying once more. "And we all know judo," he said, lowering his voice an octave or two in an attempt to radiate his rugged and manly presence. "Get your gun out, Troy," Sam instructed, loudly, to one of his fictitious colleagues.

"Roger that," he replied on Troy's behalf, altering his voice to impersonate how the imaginary Troy could likely sound. "Want me to get the dog from the van?" asked Troy.

"The gun should do," Sam suggested, happy with his voice acting talents. Sam moved slowly in a circle, casting the beam of light into the gloomy abyss and, fortunately, the only noise he could now hear was his pulse in his ears.

Sam's breathing returned to normal once the cracking noise stopped. There was silence as Sam stood rooted to the spot. The threat from his elite armed judo squad appeared to have done the trick in scaring off any potential assailant. Either that or Sam himself was, in actual fact, the source of the noise in the first place. A point confirmed when he ventured forth, once more, and the cracking recommenced each time his feet pressed into the mossy undergrowth. "Noisy feet," he muttered, taking a deep breath and making every effort to soften his step.

With his right hand still employed on torch deployment, Sam raised his spare arm, flicking his arm smartly forward to reveal his Casio digital watch and moving his wrist closer to the radiance so he could view the digits. *Ten past four,* he observed silently, working out in his head how long he had until the blanket of darkness would give way to sunrise. Sam came to a halt, crouching down, and then coming to a rest on one knee. "Stay alert, Sam," he said softly, removing his backpack and placing it on the ground in front of him. He lifted his chin in the direction of the dense canopy overhead, hoping for a glimpse of daylight. "Not long now," he said when no natural light was visible, assuring himself that the darkness would soon lift.

With his torch now trained on his bag, he unzipped it as quietly as he could, reaching inside to retrieve his flask. With the mystery noise identified as himself, he felt confident he was alone and figured a caffeine fix would lift his mood and, perhaps, settle his frayed

CHAPTER ONE — FOREST OF A THOUSAND TRAILS

nerves. As he twisted the metallic lid, he felt a flap of paper in his palm and reached for his torch to investigate further. It was a Post-It note, which he peeled off, placing it under the torchlight to read the handwritten note aloud:

Love you. Be brave.
Oh, wear your hat. Bloody midges!
Abby xx

"Aww," Sam said, buoyed on by that simple gesture. And, Abby was right, of course. She often was. Even sat alone and scared in a forest, a note in her handwriting brought an immediate smile to his face. He did as the message instructed, placing the knitted bobble hat over his baldy bonce. It was summertime, and warm... too warm for a hat, but as he'd discovered the day before, the midges — or flying bastards as he'd taken to calling them — were particularly fond of nibbling him. He needed to protect his scalp, which was already a sea of painful red lumps. He folded the note, placing it into his trouser pocket with a warm smile.

"Coffee time," Sam said, giving his head a quick scratch.

It was day three of his current mission which he'd codenamed *Cher Ami*. He remained hopeful that today would be more fruitful than the previous two, as he'd not had a sniff or glimmer of success, despite long and arduous hours spent in the great outdoors.

Sam had no particular desire to trudge through the forest in the dead of night, but, in doing so, he'd be where he needed to be at first light and able to maximise the daylight time available to him. Abby had suggested he was crazy to even consider taking the case he was working on. Still, the prospect of a five-thousand-pound finder's fee was sufficient temptation to endure the midge-based assault and early alarm calls.

Sam sipped his coffee, planning his strategy for the day ahead, but his sensitive ears were playing cruel tricks on him. He stopped slurping, certain he'd heard something creeping in the darkness. He raised his torch, placing his cup down on a fallen tree trunk beside him. His heart raced as he fanned the beam of light over the area in front of him, certain he was going to be greeted by a demonic face staring back at any moment.

The sound of wood snapping resulted in Sam sitting bolt upright, like a meerkat. He took a firm grip of his torch in case it would soon be required to double up as a weapon.

"Hello?" Sam said weakly and slightly high-pitched owing to his shattered nerves. He stood, slowly, clearing his throat. "Hello," he said once more, a little gruffer and more manly this time. But further visual inspection of the area revealed nothing of concern.

"Pesky shadows," he said, sitting once more to regulate his breathing and slow his racing heart.

Fortunately, at least for Sam's anxiety levels, the dawn chorus soon erupted into life. Also arriving with the uplifting birdsong were the first of the sun's rays piercing the thick coverage of leaves, rendering Sam's torch redundant.

Sam was confident that he'd caught a glimpse of the target the day before and so centred his search parameter on this location. He retrieved his spyglass from his bag, extended it to full length, placing it to his right eye. The purchase of the spyglass had been an oversight on his part. He had intended to order compact binoculars for this operation — easy to carry and lightweight — but inadvertently ended up with a spyglass instead. His online shopping error was much to the amusement of Abby who'd taken to calling him Jack Sparrow as a result.

Of course, he didn't mind the pirate comparison, and although the purchase was a red wine-induced error, he far preferred using one eye in surveillance mode as opposed to both as would be required to operate binoculars. He reasoned he could now be more efficient and use his free eye to monitor for trip hazards and such. And as he hadn't yet fallen, his plan appeared to be working, for now.

Sam rotated a full 360 degrees, purposefully, shifting the aim of the spyglass between the partially illuminated trees. He paused each time his eyes fell on each new branch, meticulously examining every inch. It was extraordinarily time-consuming and monotonous as the trees looked identical, relatively speaking. Progress had been quicker

CHAPTER ONE – FOREST OF A THOUSAND TRAILS

on the first day, but constant twisting around at speed had caused him dizzy spells from which he had to sit down for five minutes each time. Slow and steady wins the race, he reminded himself.

"Where are you, Douglas?" he whispered, commencing another rotation like a rotisserie chicken on a spit.

Two frustrating hours later, and Sam had a crick in his neck, the onset of heatstroke from wearing a bobble hat in the middle of summer and, sadly, no actual sign of what he'd been in the forest for three days attempting to locate. He couldn't even phone Abby to cheer himself up as he'd forgotten to fully charge his phone the night before. He sat with his head in his hands, dejected, questioning what the hell he was doing there. And just then his ears tuned into the sound of a bird calling that piqued his interest.

He must have listened to several thousand birds singing since dawn, but he just had a feeling about this one. From his seated position, he pressed the spyglass to his eye, easing his stiff neck skyward, using his ears to triangulate where the call originated. He shifted his attention between several trees before spotting the feathered owner of the delightful noise, resting there, on a branch, like he didn't have a care in the world.

Sam took a sharp intake of breath as he grabbed the poster from inside his jacket pocket, all the while keeping his eye on the bird as he did so. He unfolded it with one hand, allowing his eyes to fall down onto the printed page, darting his attention between the poster and the bird.

"Striking red eyes. Check," he said, getting excited. "Vibrant green and pink stripes on the neck. Check," he said, beginning to hyperventilate. "Purple ring on the right leg," he added. "Check," he said, scarcely able to believe his eyes. He raised the page to his lips where he kissed the image of the pigeon printed on it, just below the statement in bold lettering: *Missing, £5,000 reward!*

"Don't make a sound," Sam whispered, reaching behind him for his rucksack. He moved with the silent, deft agility of a cat hunting a mouse. He eased the zip open, removing a small packet of a grain mix that Douglas's owner said he'd find irresistible.

Ever so gently, Sam tipped the contents of the plastic pouch onto the bed of leaves by his feet. He crouched down, creeping slowly backward, leaving the culinary delight for Douglas to hopefully swoop down and claim for his breakfast.

All Sam could do, for now, was stare at the branch and pray that Douglas hadn't eaten since he went AWOL and would be famished once he caught a waft of the grain on the breeze.

Douglas Bader was a strange name for a racing pigeon, Sam reckoned. Well, until it was explained to Sam that Douglas was named after the famous WW2 pilot who was also exceptional in the air.

What was even stranger to Sam was the desperate chap who was willing to pay five thousand smackers to have the bird safely returned. When Sam first received the phone call, he assumed it to be some sort of joke, perhaps Abby-inspired. Until, that is, the owner explained just how much Douglas could earn racing and, in turn, what his offspring could be worth. Sam most certainly didn't fancy pigeons, but the money for its safe return would be most welcome warming the company bank account. Sam really couldn't understand, however, how this homing/racing pigeon was so valuable when the dozy bugger found himself lost on the way home. Not much of a homing pigeon, Sam figured.

Sam flexed his muscles involuntarily in reaction to every slight movement by the bird. "Come on," Sam said, willing the bird to come to him. Twenty minutes turned to an hour, and Sam now had no feeling in his feet due to the restricted blood flow from lack of movement.

Sam clamped his teeth down on his fist, such was the anticipation from the money at stake. Douglas had extended his wings — having a pleasant little stretch — peering down in Sam's general direction. "Come on, you little..." Sam whispered. "Come to papa."

The imploring words from Sam the bird whisperer must have registered. And, in a glorious, wing-flapping instant, Douglas swooped down from his branch with the elegance of an Olympic diver, coming to a rest inches from the grain mix that Sam had laid out for him.

CHAPTER ONE – FOREST OF A THOUSAND TRAILS

It was now or never, Sam thought. If the bird took to the wing, Sam didn't have the time or inclination to continue, and the pursuit would be over. Douglas's owner had provided Sam with a butterfly net, recommending it as the safest way of capturing the animal without inflicting pain or damaging its precious feathers. A loop on Sam's rucksack had held the net securely in place until its deployment was required, as it was now. *Had*, being the operative word in this case. Because it was at that precise moment when Sam realised he'd left the net lying on the back seat of his car when he packed his bag in a sleep-deprived state.

"Please... God... no!" he said through gritted teeth, searching the area around his bag, which was futile, and he knew it.

Sam was now motionless, face-to-beak with the creature he'd spent the last three days painstakingly searching for. Douglas was in touching distance, snaffling up the grain, and Sam didn't have anything to catch it with. It was like going fishing without a rod or cycling without a bike — utterly useless!

Sam could feel the reward money disappearing before his eyes. Well, in this case, flying away, the instant the bird had filled its belly. Sam had invested too much time and effort to simply give up now.

He toyed with the notion of just diving on it — grabbing Douglas in his hands — but the likelihood of collateral damage was too high. Exceptionally so, and Sam figured Douglas's owner wouldn't want to cough up for a handful of blood-splattered feathers.

My coat! Sam thought in a eureka moment, wondering if he could use it to trap the bird.

With one eye trained on Douglas, Sam unzipped his jacket as silently as possible, tenderly easing open the zip with the consideration of a gentle lover. Sam hadn't yet figured out what he'd do if and when he managed to remove his jacket without scaring the bird away in the process. Would he simply throw it over Douglas to prevent escape? Perhaps it might work. But, whatever he was going to do, he'd need to do it smartly. For Douglas had now raised his beak and was doing the avian equivalent of unfastening a notch on his belt after a rather sumptuous, Sunday lunch. Feeding time was over, and Douglas was unlikely to hang about for pudding.

Sam removed his left arm from his jacket and then his right, then stretching the fabric out like a sail, ready to release and, hopefully, prevent the bird's departure once deployed.

Douglas glanced over in Sam's direction, extending his wings, almost as if he knew what was coming and appearing to ready himself to take to the skies. "I don't think so," Sam declared, arching his back to acquire the appropriate thrust to propel his makeshift trap.

However, even before Sam could release the coat, a flash of camouflage tore through the air with an audible whoosh.

"Gotcha!" announced a confident male voice, whose owner performed an elegant forward roll before coming to a rest on one knee in front of Sam, with Douglas flapping furiously in his net.

Sam recoiled in terror, unsure if he were, perhaps, under attack. He raised his jacket like it were some sort of protective shield, like Batfink's wings. When no assault commenced, he cautiously lowered his jacket, peering over the top, where he could now clearly see the man dressed head to foot in combat gear.

"What the hell?" Sam said. "What are you doing with my bird?"

"Lovely day for a stroll," came an immediate, cheery reply.

Sam could do little to disguise the contempt written on his face. "I might have soddin' well known it was you," Sam said, slamming his coat to the ground. "Drexel Popek," Sam continued with a sneer. "What brings you all the way out here?"

"I love the great outdoors," Drexel replied, with a giggling snort, dangling the captured pigeon for Sam's benefit.

Sam reared up, raging, shaking his head and offering up a firmly pointed finger. "That's *my* bird, Drexel."

Drexel smiled in response which only served to rile Sam further. "Who's a pretty boy," Drexel cooed, grinning inanely. "You're a pretty boy, that's right," he continued, though it wasn't exactly clear if this sentiment was directed towards Sam or Douglas. "You're a pretty boy who's worth an awful lot of money to me," Drexel continued, this time directly to the bird. "That's right, isn't it handsome."

CHAPTER ONE – FOREST OF A THOUSAND TRAILS

"That's my bird," protested Sam. "I've been out in this forest for three days tracking that pigeon, so..."

Drexel laughed. He was enjoying this. "*Whose* bird?" he asked. "It very much appears to be in *my* net right about now, Levy."

Sam couldn't argue with the logic of that statement. "You followed me," Sam asked, "didn't you? Was it you I heard creeping through the undergrowth earlier?"

"Would I?" Drexel said, with a sarcastic smile indicating he'd done exactly that. "Well, okay... guilty as charged." Drexel struggled to contain his delight, swaying the net gently to soothe the agitated bird. "When this pigeon recovery job came into the office, I wasn't particularly interested as I'm *just so busy*," Drexel said, rolling his eyes as if this were some terrible imposition.

"And yet you're still here?"

"Well... five grand is still five grand, and I knew that you'd be all over this case like fleas on a stray dog. So, I thought I'd just leave you to do the legwork for a couple of days, make a few enquiries and get the scent, as it were, and then I'd swoop in at the last moment to secure the prize," Drexel explained. "Come on, Sam. You have to admit that it's a great blooming plan?"

Drexel stared intently, looking for a flicker of admiration for his genius, but he'd have been waiting a while judging by the steam coming out of Sam's ears and possibly nose.

"How did you know where I was?" Sam asked dejectedly.

Drexel narrowed his eyes. "Sam, you do know I'm a PI, don't you?" he asked with a sneer. "It's kinda what I do for a living, you know, finding out about things. Well, at least it's what a *competent* PI does."

Sam briefly considered the option of fisticuffs, but it wasn't worth getting arrested for a pile of feathers, no matter what they might be worth. Also, Drexel appeared as if he might work out, so Sam reasoned that walking away in a huff was the best approach, all things considered.

"I hope the little bastard pecks your eyes out," Sam offered as a parting shot, collecting his belongings before trudging back towards his car, alone, with no pigeon.

Sam was now exceptionally tired, sweaty, and bitten something rotten. But despite this, what annoyed him the most was his begrudging admiration for Drexel. The guy had a full ghillie suit with netting dangling from his cap. He even had an accessory belt to store his torch and who-knew-what-other goodies, which meant Drexel didn't have to go rummaging around for in his backpack when called into action like Sam did.

"I should have worn a camouflage suit," Sam said, kicking a fallen pinecone in frustration. "Bloody pigeons!"

CHAPTER TWO
All About the Busts

Business and life in general at the Eyes Peeled detective agency had been brisk these last six months. Building on their success in the well-publicised case The Art of the Forgery, the agency had gone from strength to strength with their services very much in demand, resulting in a healthy bank balance.

Sam had even fulfilled his dream of becoming his own boss when the former owner of the agency, Harry, called it a day, deciding on early retirement in Spain. Of course Sam and Abby, being the first and only winners of the employee of the month award, were offered the opportunity of a management buyout. It didn't come cheap, however, and involved the remortgage of Sam's house, but, by Jove, it was too great an opportunity to let pass them by.

And so Sam and Abby were now partners in the business sense as well as the relationship sense. Life was good, with money coming in thick and fast. The agency was expanding and on the up — nothing could get in their way of the good life that they felt confident lay ahead. Well, that is until a great big spanner in the works arrived that could very well scupper their dreams of a utopia.

"Goddam Drexel Popek!" Sam shouted, emerging from the bathroom with his paper tucked under his arm. "Honestly, everywhere I turn or look at the moment, he's there, looking back at me with a smug grin," Sam said, slapping the paper down on Abby's desk.

"Hey, Ace Ventura, what's up?" Abby asked with her face pressed up to her computer monitor.

Sam opened the well-thumbed newspaper to the page where he'd poked his finger through in anger. "Look," Sam said, jabbing his finger down on the photograph of Drexel receiving an honour from the Isle of Man Pigeon Fanciers Society. "They're even referring to him as a hero," Sam added, reading from the paper. "A hero, no less... That should be my photograph receiving a statue of a golden pigeon, Abby. Not him. He stole that feathered rat from under my nose."

With the feeling that Sam wasn't going to let her continue doing what she was doing, Abby spun round in her chair to face him. "What would you even do with a statue of a golden pigeon anyway?"

Sam lowered his head, clearly disappointed judging by the angle his lower lip was pressed out. "I'd have put it on the shelf in our meeting room," he said, throwing his thumb over his shoulder. "That's the sort of thing that impresses clients."

Drexel Popek had been Sam and Abby's first new employee when they took control of the agency. Drexel was a new arrival to the island, having relocated after enjoying several visits to the Isle of Man TT races and taking the bold move in making a permanent move. Fastidious, affable, and with an insatiable desire to sniff out a case like a bloodhound, Drexel was the ideal addition to complement their close-knit team of investigators. His unrivalled success rate with complex and remunerative cases resulted in the cash flowing in. After only four months, he was bringing in more commissions than anyone else on the team.

It was likely about that time that the new arrival realised how much of that cash could be warming his pocket if he ventured out and set up in business on his own. In doing this, he also poached a significant portion of the Eyes Peeled client list in the process. Sam and Abby were devasted about the breach of trust when he left.

Fortunately, the portion of clients that Drexel nicked was the lower end of the book — only choosing to move for a significant discount on the services received. For this reason, Drexel had to supplement his income by taking on the sort of work that Eyes Peeled

CHAPTER TWO – ALL ABOUT THE BUSTS

simply weren't interested in. That work being the investigation of missing pets, for example — arguably the lowest of the low for any professional, self-respecting private dick. But credit where credit was due as Drexel steadily carved out a niche for this unique service. On a little island in the middle of the Irish Sea, it was quite remarkable how many pets actually went missing. Cats, dogs, and the occasional livestock were his new bread and butter. In time, as he established himself further, his caseload became more rare and exotic creatures and that, in turn, resulted in larger finder's fees. Social media was soon rife with images of Drexel reuniting grateful owners with their prized animal. As his presence grew, so did the calibre of the workload coming his way, resulting in his pet recovery business taking something of a back seat, to a large extent. He was becoming something of a minor celebrity, was Drexel.

Fairly soon after, Eyes Peeled inevitably began to feel the pinch as their regular work started to dry up. Previously loyal clients were now eager, it would appear, to acquire the services of the hottest new investigative genius in town — Drexel Popek.

Sam had little desire to become a pet detective, but in the absence of much other new work coming in, his options were somewhat limited. Infuriatingly for Sam, Drexel wasn't content with just his newly acquired workload. As Sam recently discovered, Drexel was still eager also to pursue the occasional animal-related case when the mood took. Likely when there was a whopping great reward on offer, such as the missing Douglas Bader.

Ten minutes of a Drexel-inspired tirade continued, with the throbbing vein in Sam's forehead in real danger of exploding. "I don't understand it, Abby," Sam ranted, pressing his hand to his head. "I've just experienced, first-hand, how difficult it is to capture a missing animal that doesn't want to be caught. Yet Drexel has been finding them at will and likely pocketing a fortune in the process. I just don't see how it's possible?"

Abby loaded up Drexel's Facebook profile on her monitor, scrolling through the images of him next to a menagerie of animals he'd reunited with their grateful owners. "Blimey," Abby said, continuing to navigate through the array of photos. "I knew he was doing well, but I didn't realise just *how* well."

"I know!" Sam replied. "He could have opened a zoo with that lot."

Abby moved her chair around, taking Sam's hand, giving it a gentle squeeze. "We'll get through this, Sam. We've been through lean spells before and will, likely, again."

Sam appreciated her confidence in the situation, but couldn't help being less bullish. "The last lean spell we had, though," he reflected, "we didn't have an eye-watering business loan, or the worry of funding the payroll for four full-time staff as we do now."

"Sam, there's still work coming in," Abby said. "Suzie's out working on an insurance fraud investigation," she added, pointing to Suzie's empty chair. "Tom's working on the theft of a tractor. Investigating, that is... not planning," she said with a laugh to lighten Sam's mood.

Sam grinned. Abby could always find a way to make him smile. "Aww, I know you're right, Abby. I'm probably just still grumpy about spending three days scared and tired in the forest for nothing."

"Well, I for one thought you were fearless, Sam Levy," Abby said, blowing him a kiss. "Also, this might interest you," added Abby, returning her attention to her monitor. "This email came in when you were... well... in there," she said, pointing to the bathroom.

Sam lowered his head, placing his chin on her shoulder and reading the email there on the screen.

"Mmm," Sam offered, reading along, raising one eyebrow, his interest piqued. "Could be very interesting..."

"Should I tell them you're on your way?" Abby asked, happy to act as his temporary secretary, fingers hovering above her keyboard, ready for action.

"Sure," Sam replied. "Why not? It'll be a pleasant change to investigate something that doesn't have feathers or four legs," he said, grabbing his jacket from the back of his chair. "You can say I'll be there within the hour!"

CHAPTER TWO – ALL ABOUT THE BUSTS

Sam adored any opportunity to get out and about on the Isle of Man. Aside from the occasional traffic jam, driving around the island was an absolute joy. Winding tree-lined country roads opened up to introduce unspoiled, rolling countryside with a glimpse of the seaside never too far in the distance. His chariot remained his trusty thirteen-year-old silver Ford Fiesta, resplendent with sporadic rust spots, and now a recurring issue that resulted in his exhaust pipe sounding like a Harrier Jump Jet taking flight. Sam liked to suggest to Abby that these little foibles added to the car's overall character. He'd considered upgrading his transport a few months earlier when the company's bank balance was in rude health. After recently binge-watching two series of *Ray Donovan*, Sam toyed with the idea of buying an angry-looking black Mercedes — just like Ray's — which he felt sure would, somehow, complement his investigative prowess. Fortunately, he talked himself out of it as another monthly expense, right now, was the last thing they needed.

Sam drove towards Castletown, the former capital of the Isle of Man. A town steeped in history with a medieval castle at its heart. It was a popular destination for both tourists and locals alike, and somewhere Sam and Abby could happily spend the day, idling through the ancient streets lined with stone-built fishing cottages and a wonderful place to purchase a nice pint of bitter.

Approaching the address indicated on the email, Sam slowed, looking for the property, which wasn't too much of a challenge as it was like a royal palace.

"Sheesh!" he said, driving through the two stone entrance columns with an imposing lion sat atop each one. He slowed to a crawl, marvelling at the length of the driveway stretching out in front of him as far as the eye could see with fastidiously tendered gardens running either side. "Sheesh," he said, once more, as the sheer scale of the place was simply staggering. He half expected to see a herd of antelope go galloping by any moment. He wondered if he should have pressed a buzzer, or something, to announce his arrival, but the sound of his exhaust would likely announce his arrival long before the occupants of the house actually clapped eyes on him.

Soon enough, a pristine white gravel driveway guided him to the main residence. Sam drove the final hundred or so metres with his jaw swinging loose, feasting his eyes on the magnificent house. Mind you, to call this merely a house would be like referring to the *RMS Titanic* as a dinghy. The handsome Edwardian mansion had a generous coating of ivy, with an ornate fountain in the middle of the turning circle outside the main entrance. Slowing up for a moment, Sam took the opportunity to capture a photograph to show Abby later. She was an ardent viewer of *Downton Abbey* and would undoubtedly have appreciated it, he thought.

Outside the property were no visible visitor parking spaces, so Sam came to a halt next to the fountain. He took a moment to appreciate the intricate carving of some marbled fellow with a washboard stomach and an impossibly small penis. Sam was happy to consider himself the polar opposite of this chap, what with his slight paunch and a considerable—

A-ha, Sam said to himself, glancing to the gentlemen who'd appeared by the weathered oak front door. Sam figured this mature chap to be the owner of the property on account of his impeccable dress sense and air of regal authority. His grey slacks had a razor-sharp seam down the front, perfectly complemented by his navy double-breasted blazer. All finished off with a black and red paisley cravat. Sam could immediately tell he was in distinguished company on this assignment and as he climbed out of his car, he rather wished he'd polished his shoes in advance of the meeting, or, at all.

Sam walked across the drive, offering his hand with a cordial smile. "Hello, I'm—"

"What's the meaning of this," demanded the agitated man frostily. He pointed at Sam's car, struggling to articulate his absolute disgust for the disaster parked on his driveway. "That-that-that," he stuttered with his cheeks wobbling. "Move that bally travesty out of my drive!" he commanded, caressing his manicured moustache. "What on earth would people think if they happened upon that heap, parked there."

CHAPTER TWO – ALL ABOUT THE BUSTS

Sam shrugged, taken aback but eager to please his new client. Looking around for an alternative parking spot that wouldn't offend his host, it wasn't immediately clear where he should move his heap to, exactly. "To where?" asked Sam.

"What?" asked the man, cupping his ear. "Speak up, man!"

"To... where...?" Sam said again, only louder, clearly enunciating each word.

"Over there!" came the harsh response, followed by a firm finger-pointing to where Sam's car should now be. "Around the side of the house, man. Where nobody could possibly hope to set eyes on... that... monstrosity."

Sam smiled politely — always the consummate professional — before jumping back into his car to immediately shift it, as instructed. Only Sam's car had an occasional nasty habit of taking a couple of attempts to start, and this was one of those occasions. The engine turned over but wouldn't burst into life at the first time of asking, or the second for that matter. The frustrated owner of the house had climbed down his steps and was now stood over Sam's car — pointing furiously — appearing increasingly impatient with the situation. On the third attempt, the engine gloriously fired with the resulting explosion from the faulty exhaust causing the man to wail and clutch his chest. Sam popped the gear stick into reverse and slowly distanced himself, taking care not to increase the noise pollution in the process by only gently applying the accelerator.

"Please, God, no," Sam pleaded through gritted teeth as he reversed. He leaned forward, looking over the steering wheel, continuing his prayer. "No," he offered to a higher power as a line of engine oil now sullied the formerly immaculate white gravel driveway, leaving a dirty brown snail trail. Sam turned the wheel, heading to the area he'd been directed and hoping beyond hope that it wasn't his car causing the offending stain. But a glance in his rear-view mirror confirmed that the oil trail was indeed following him and his car was the culprit. Although the guilty party was likely never in doubt.

Parked up with his leaking vehicle at a suitable distance and now immensely flustered, Sam took his anger out on his car, cursing and threatening it with the crusher. The oil was like a path of breadcrumbs from Hansel and Gretel directing him to where he'd just left. He attempted to disrupt the stones with his foot, discreetly, but his attempts were futile, and his efforts simply made him appear like he had some form of nervous tic as he walked towards the fountain.

"I'm ever so sorry!" he shouted, apologising in advance of his arrival, as this chap appeared to be the sort who may own weaponry of some variety. "I'm Sam Levy," he said, extending his arm, once stood before the man. "Are you Barrington Hedley-Smythe, by any chance?"

"Sir!" came the barked reply.

Sam was impressed by the formality of the reply. "I know I'm a private investigator, but there's no need to call me sir," Sam suggested, but secretly rather appreciated it.

"What?" the man snapped, cupping his ear once more. Sam was starting to deduce that his hearing may not be the most acute.

"I was saying you don't need to call me sir," Sam said. "Well, unless you insist, then—"

"Not *you*, you blithering idiot. *Me!*"

"Excuse me?" Sam asked, worrying he'd not made his finest first impression. In fact, this level of annoyance was a new record for Sam, surely. He'd not even shaken the man's hand and was already in danger of being shot, assuming he had access to a firearm, of course.

"I'm *Sir* Barrington Hedley-Smythe," he said, shaking his head at the terrible imposition of having to speak with someone such as Sam.

"Ah," Sam cordially replied. "A pleasure to make your acquaintance," he added, in his politest tone. Unfortunately, Sam's offer of a handshake was promptly ignored as Sir Barrington headed back towards his palatial home.

Sam remained rooted to the spot as it wasn't entirely clear if Sir Barrington had simply had enough of him and wandered off, or if he expected Sam to follow his lead.

"Don't stand there like a bloody statue," Sir Barrington called over with an audible tut. "What sort of man has a name like Pam, anyway?" Sir Barrington called out over his shoulder.

CHAPTER TWO – ALL ABOUT THE BUSTS

"No, sir," Sam replied, in hot pursuit. "It's Sam... Sam Levy," he said, but suspected his explanation fell on deaf ears. Literally.

"This is the dining room," advised Sir Barrington once inside. "This is where you should focus your investigation."

"I should," Sam said, agreeably, and then, "I should!" he added, with a degree of certainty even though he wasn't exactly sure about what he should be investigating. Abby had printed the original email for him but what with the oil slick and everything, he'd not as yet read it. He knew something had been stolen, but what exactly remained a mystery.

Undeterred, Sam retrieved a pen from his pocket and used it to push cutlery around on the polished mahogany table as he began his investigation. "You could play a game of tennis on this," he remarked. "What with it being so large," he added with a laugh which, once again, fell on deaf ears. "Anyway..." Sam pressed on undaunted and now looking for clues. With nothing appearing untoward on the surface of the table, he continued with his preliminary investigation underneath, pulling back a chair and inspecting the carpet.

"What have you dropped?" Sir Barrington asked in a brusque tone that a sergeant major would be happy with.

"Nothing, sir," Sam replied, standing tall, returning the chair to its original position. "I was just commencing my investigation as you wisely suggested," he said, tapping the bridge of his nose for no apparent reason.

The echo of approaching heels clicking off the wooden floor distracted Sam for a moment. "So sorry," announced a breathless female voice moving through the door to the dining room at pace. "Sir Barrington, the gentleman about the roof repairs is waiting in your study," the female owner of the voice announced. Sir Barrington appeared relieved for any reason to take his leave, throwing Sam a derisory glance as he departed. "Pam indeed," he muttered as he walked by.

"Forgive me," she said, once Sir Barrington had left the dining room. "I'm Olivia," she explained, offering a friendly hand. "I'm Sir Barrington's private secretary and the person who made the appointment with your office." Olivia removed her cream suit jacket, making a fanning gesture with her hand. "Awfully hot from running around this place. I had an emergency call from our janitor to attend to. He said there was a god-awful racket a few minutes ago and was concerned the boiler had blown up. Fortunately, it was a false alarm."

Sam smiled, suspecting the offending racket may have, in fact, been his exhaust pipe issue, but he kept that to himself. "Sam Levy, at your service!"

"I didn't mean to inflict Sir Barrington on you, Sam. He's an acquired taste to the uninitiated."

"I hadn't noticed," Sam said, stretching the truth.

Olivia removed her glasses and propped them on her head, rubbing the tension away in her forehead. "It's been quite the week," she said, with a forced laugh. "Anyway, what are your thoughts?"

Sam chewed that question over for several seconds, narrowing his eyes, deep in thought. "About?" he asked eventually.

"About the robbery," Olivia replied as if this should have been perfectly obvious.

At this point, Sam held his hands up, choosing to come clean. "Cards on the table, Olivia. I'm not entirely sure what this case is all about," he confessed. "You see, I was just so eager to get here that I didn't get all the details from my... ehm... secretary," he said, bravely, knowing Abby would castrate him for actively referring to her as such.

"Oh," Olivia replied, impressed it would appear at Sam's desire to make haste. "Well, how about I fill in the blanks, then?"

Olivia then pointed Sam in the direction of a five-foot-tall stone column stood near to the door she'd just arrived through. "That's the first one," she said. "There's also one in each corner of the room," she added, helping Sam by pointing to each corner in turn.

Sam nodded along with each new introduction. "They're very nice," Sam said, unsure what else he could say.

"They're also empty," Olivia said, walking Sam to the nearest column.

"They are!" agreed Sam.

CHAPTER TWO – ALL ABOUT THE BUSTS

Olivia wiped the polished surface of the stone with her hand. "They shouldn't be," she said despondently.

"No?"

"No! That's why you're here today, Sam. On each of those stone columns should be sat a very expensive bronze bust. This one was home to Sir Winston Churchill."

"Stolen?" Sam asked, leaning forward for a closer inspection of the empty surface.

"Stolen," Olivia confirmed. "Along with Queen Victoria, Sir Isaac Newton, and William Shakespeare."

Sam felt a tingling sensation coursing through his veins. It was either angina or, as he hoped, the prospect of a proper, bona fide investigation he could sink his teeth into with not a pigeon in sight.

"I see," Sam said thoughtfully. "And you've reported this to the police?"

"Of course. They're still investigating but have so far drawn a blank. Sam, these items are of great importance to Sir Barrington and, as you can imagine, are exceptionally valuable. Because of the value, the insurance company have requested we also engage the services of a private detective." Olivia loaded up a picture of the stolen items on her mobile phone for Sam's benefit. "We're also willing to pay a generous finder's fee for their prompt and safe return. We called you in again after the marvellous success you had with Sir Barrington's missing peacock earlier in the year."

"Excellent," Sam replied, reaching for his notebook from inside his jacket and eager to commence his investigation proper. He allowed Olivia's last statement to digest for just a moment longer. "Peacock?" he said after a few seconds, assuming this to be the start of a joke. Sam appreciated a good joke and stared back, awaiting the punchline.

Olivia looked over her shoulder, trying to ascertain where Sam's eyes were directed and why he was looking decidedly vacant.

"Yes, peacock," Olivia said when Sam didn't blink. "After your team successfully reunited Sir Barrington with his stolen peacock," she added, uncertain why she was receiving the reaction she was. "It wasn't that long ago!"

Sam had absolutely no idea what Olivia was talking about. Before his lips parted to ask, however, he suddenly had the recall of an image he'd seen back in the office earlier. And that's when it hit him. Oliva must have been referring to the peacock Drexel had plastered all over his social media.

"Ahh," Sam said, playing it cooly. "Yes, that's right. If I recall it was my colleague, Drexel, who recovered the stolen peacock?"

"Shaven-headed chap who looks like he goes to the gym," Olivia said.

"That's the chap," Sam said, barely able to contain his glee. "He's one of our very best investigators."

Sam had now twigged that Eyes Peeled had been phoned in error for this new case and Sam didn't care one jot. It was karma as far as he was concerned following the Douglas Bader situation. Knowing that this new job should have been assigned to Drexel made it taste that little bit sweeter.

Sam wandered casually around the dining room, making the occasional encouraging noise for Olivia's benefit. "I'll need to speak with all the staff," Sam said, "and also review your security arrangements and CCTV."

"Of course," Olivia replied. "I'll make arrangements for anything you need. So, you'll take the case?"

Sam paused for a moment to show he wasn't overly eager. "I'll just need to check in with the office first," he said, "as we've a lot on at the moment." (This was a lie.) "But, I'm confident we can move things around for you. What with you being a returning customer, after all."

"Excellent!" Olivia said, pleased to have hopefully secured the services of her man. Or so she thought. "I'll leave you to look around," she said, handing him a slip of paper with her phone number written on it. "It's a large house, so if you need me, it might be quicker to phone me rather than shouting or wandering around aimlessly."

CHAPTER TWO — ALL ABOUT THE BUSTS

Olivia excused herself, leaving Sam to do what he needed to do. As soon as she was out of earshot, Sam took out his phone and hit the speed dial button for his beloved, Abby.

"Hi, sweetheart," he said quietly, taking a quick look to make sure he was still alone. "Abby, I can't talk for too long, but I wanted to tell you that I'm going to be at this place for at least a couple of hours. Yes, yes, we've got the case, oh… and we've had a right result with this one at Drexel's expense."

Sam proceeded to fill Abby in on how the case erroneously landed in their lap. He also explained, in detail, about how he'd managed to leave a humungous skid mark on the white gravel driveway. "I might also need your expertise on this case, Abby," he suggested, and then listened to the response. "That's right, there are four of them in total and are worth a fortune by all accounts. Anyway, I need to go. I love you!"

Sam retrieved and then placed his notepad onto the surface of the table as he took a seat. He rattled his fingers, tilting his head as he glanced around the wood-panelled walls, narrowing his eyes, deep in thought. You'd be forgiven for assuming that Sam, sat there, was a diligent investigator, planning his strategy for the speedy repatriation of the stolen items.

In actual fact, Sam was trying to figure out a name for the case by utilising the word *bust*.

He scribbled several down but dismissed them as quickly. "The Case of the Magnificent Busts," he mused, figuring it to be the best of a bad bunch. Abby was always creative at this sort of thing, so he'd text her later and get her thoughts on this vital matter.

For now, however, the hunt for the magnificent busts was very much on!

CHAPTER THREE
Millionaire's Shortbread

Working at Eyes Peeled was more than just a job for Sam and Abby — it was a calling and their passion. Fortunately, this was a sentiment also shared by the other permanent members of staff, Tom and Suzie. The increasing competition from Drexel's rival business had significantly eaten into their overall workload, and none of them was naïve enough to realise that a dwindling caseload would eventually result in reduced income and potentially pay cuts, or, heaven forbid, worse. For that reason, when a meaty new case did present itself, the gang were ready, willing and able to double their efforts and burn the midnight oil, if and when required.

"Okay," Suzie cheerily announced, stood in front of the whiteboard, marker pen in hand for their regular nine a.m. team briefing. She always added colour to any meeting on account of her psychedelic-themed clothing. The youngest in the office but with a penchant for the swinging sixties, she was the ultimate hippy chick. Suzie was someone who'd dropped through a portal to a time gone by and then catapulted herself back into the present.

"Tom, what do we have?" Suzie asked, poised and ready to add any response to the list she'd already started writing.

Tom was a thinker. Someone who considered each and every response, sometimes a little too much. Newly retired from the police force, his investigative tenacity was admirable as were the contacts garnered in his Rolodex over a thirty-odd year career. The others in the office, particularly Sam, were willing and eager to learn from him, even if he did take his sweet time, on occasion.

"Well..." Tom replied, shuffling in his seat, tapping his pen on the table. "I've done the rounds with the auction houses, both physical and internet-based..." he added, trailing off as he placed his pen behind his ear. He rubbed the stubble on his chin like he was considering his next words.

"And?" Suzie asked, ready to scribe his considered response.

Tom shook his head. "Zip... zilch... nada!" Tom then pointed to the printed image of the stolen busts which Suzie had pinned to the wall. "I wasn't expecting to find anything anyway, if I'm honest. Those busts are simply too hot to move on, and there are likely only a few people who'd be in the market for them. I also spoke to some of my old police colleagues, and they don't hold out much hope of finding them."

"They are investigating, though?" Abby asked.

"Of course," Tom replied. "Chances are, though, that they'll have already left the island, and it'll likely be left to the insurance company to cough up."

"But why just steal the bronze busts?" Suzie asked with a shrug. "I mean, that mansion must have been stuffed with priceless items, so, why just them?" she asked, also now pointing at the printout. "It just doesn't make sense."

"Stolen to order?" Tom suggested. "That would at least explain why just those specific items were nicked."

Sam, who'd been listening intently, was also quietly reviewing the photographs captured from the crime scene the previous day. "That house was like an episode of the Antiques Roadshow," Sam said. "Heirlooms, precious furniture, and exquisite paintings wherever you turned. I'm with Tom on the stolen-to-order theory. Most of the other valuable items in that house would take several men and a removal van to shift. Those busts are relatively portable and exceptionally expensive, so it does make sense why they were targeted."

CHAPTER THREE – MILLIONAIRE'S SHORTBREAD

"How expensive?" Suzie asked.

Sam rubbed his thumb and forefinger together at this point like he was counting out a pile of banknotes. "Sir Barrington originally bought them at auction for eighty-five thousand!"

"Damn!" Suzie said, writing that down. "It's amazing what crap rich people will spend their money on."

"Each, that is!" Sam added. "So, not too bad a day's work for someone. His secretary told me they've gone up in value over the years and now have a combined insurance valuation of over one million pounds!"

"What if...?" Tom entered in, but then trailed off as he often liked to do.

"Yeah?" Abby pressed. "Go on, please. Remember, no idea is a bad idea around this table."

Tom narrowed his left eye, tilting his head to one side. It wasn't clear if he were still contemplating his idea, or, merely building the tension. "What about an inside job? The old fellow, perhaps?" Tom suggested, eventually. After all, no idea was a bad idea.

"Sir Barrington?" Sam moved to clarify. "I'm not so sure on that one to be honest. Judging by his house, money doesn't appear to be an issue."

Tom shrugged. He had nothing further on his hypothesis at this stage.

"What do we know about the staff?" Suzie asked, eager to move the investigation along.

Sam opened his leather binder which had been sat on the table in front of him. He licked his thumb, removing several pieces of paper. "Here they are," Sam said, sliding one copy to each of those around the table.

"Impressive!" Abby said, examining each of the mugshots with a name and brief job description listed below them.

"Suzie helped me," Sam confessed, not wanting to take all the plaudits. "There's thirteen full and part-time staff working on the estate," Sam confirmed. "I went through their personnel records last night, and all but two have been employed there for over five years."

Sam held up his copy, pointing at the two images at the bottom of the page. "Only those two are relatively new. Kim and Theodore Rankin, who were taken on six months ago to tend to the gardens."

"Want me to call in a favour and have all of these names run through the system?" Tom asked.

"Please!" Sam said. "Also, see if you can dig up anything on Kim and Theodore. It can't be a coincidence that they share the same surname."

"Are they not maybe married?" Tom asked, circling their images with his pen.

Sam took a gulp, wondering why he hadn't thought of that himself. "Good work, Tom. And as Abby said, no idea is a bad idea, or, a question for that matter."

"Okay," Abby said, moving on to spare Sam's blushes. "Tom and Suzie, you're going to see what you can come up with on the employees, yeah? Do a bit of digging around to see if any skeletons are hiding. Sam, what are you thinking? You look deep in thought."

"I was just thinking about what Tom suggested regarding an inside job."

"You think it's likely?" Suzie asked, adding this as a new bullet point on the board.

Sam pressed his finger down on the smug-looking image of Sir Barrington. "It's probably nothing," he began. "But, when I first turned up, Sir Barrington had to leave me for another appointment. I assumed he just didn't want to be in my company as I'd defiled his driveway, which was fair enough. Anyway, during my preliminary investigations, I later heard him raising his voice in what I assume was his study."

"With who?" Suzie asked.

"He was having a heated conversation about the roof. Well, in particular, rotting timbers. He referred to the quote he'd been given previously as a travesty."

"A new roof is a costly affair," Tom suggested.

"Exactly," Sam said. "Especially when the roof is the size of a small country."

CHAPTER THREE – MILLIONAIRE'S SHORTBREAD

"Mmm," Suzie added, "perhaps Sir Barrington is feeling the pinch?"

"And a timely little insurance pay-out could be just what the doctor ordered," Sam said. "I think it might be an idea to tail Sir Barrington and see what he gets up to."

"Be careful, Sam," Abby offered immediately. "And please don't get yourself in any… any… *Sam* situations!"

Suzie popped the cap on her marker pen, which was in danger of drying out. "It sounds like we have a plan of action, so, meeting adjourned, in that case."

Sam hadn't been out on a surveillance operation for months, and he did miss the thrill of the chase. It wasn't for everyone, however. Sat patiently in your car for hours on end, often hungry and in dire need of a wee, wasn't everybody's idea of a good time. Fortunately, being in the last few days of April meant he wasn't going to be freezing his nether regions off at least, as he'd still not attended to the temperamental heater in his car. Sam had also retired his surveillance wig (as used on the Art of the Forgery case). On reflection, he did — as Abby suggested several times — have a passing similarity to Lloyd from the film *Dumb and Dumber* when wearing it.

With a successful trip to the local garage, Sam acquired his vital surveillance equipment for the day/possibly night. Consisting of a packet of sandwiches, a can of Diet Coke, a Double Decker, and a motorbike racing magazine to help him while away the hours, he was all set to go. It wasn't just the prospect of a juicy case that'd presently lifted Sam's demeanour, oh no. This time of year also meant it was only a few short weeks away from the most exceptional sporting spectacle on earth — the Isle of Man TT races. Sam would often drift into a daydream where he was one of the heroic riders, rolling his machine towards the start line ahead of a race. It wasn't just the racing action that Sam adored, however. It was also the atmosphere on the island when nearly fifty thousand race fans invaded the ordinarily sleepy little island. Parked up in a layby near to Sir Barrington's palatial home, Sam was happy to settle down, have his lunch, and soon drift off into a pleasant little daydream when...

"Bugger!" Sam said, just as his hungry lips caressed the bread on his tuna and sweetcorn sandwich. He placed his spyglass to his right eye, focusing in on the vehicle emerging from the driveway up ahead.

Sam stuffed the sandwich back into the plastic container, dropping several chunks of tuna onto his new camouflage suit (a gift from Abby). "Where are you off to?" he said, turning the ignition key once he'd visually confirmed Sir Barrington was at the wheel.

Sir Barrington's gold-coloured Rolls-Royce glistened in the spring sunshine, purring down the road oozing an elegant charm. Like its owner, it was no spring chicken either, but its attractive lines still drew an appreciative glance from those pedestrians watching her glide by. The same, however, could not be said for Sam and his spluttering rust bucket, following behind at a safe distance. Sam felt confident that Sir Barrington would be unlikely to recall what he even looked like, let alone what kind of car he drove, but it didn't hurt to remain cautiously distant.

The Rolls-Royce headed out of Castletown and in the direction of the airport, leaving Sam to wonder if he was, perhaps, planning a little trip off-island. This wasn't the case, however, confirmed when Sir Barrington continued his leisurely pace, driving in the direction of the island's capital, Douglas.

Sam was in his element out working on a live case. He felt the glorious adrenalin pumping through his body, taking a moment for an appreciative glance at the rural beauty all around and then to the red light flashing intermittently on his dashboard. No matter, a firm application of his fingernail tapping on the plastic cover offered a temporary reprieve from the distracting warning light. A mechanic may have been a preferable option, but Sam was content he'd solved the issue at least until the next time the bulb activated again.

Twenty or so minutes later, the right indicator of the Rolls-Royce was followed a moment later by the application of the brake lights.

CHAPTER THREE – MILLIONAIRE'S SHORTBREAD

"Interesting," Sam observed, following suit. Interesting, as this was a destination that Sam was particularly familiar with. Kirby Garden Centre was Abby's absolute favourite destination on a Sunday afternoon, wandering aimlessly, admiring the floral explosion. It was because of this place that Sam's car had a permanent layer of topsoil in the boot from transporting flowers and such home for Abby's next green-fingered project. The latest being a veggie patch which was currently at the planning stage and had been for about two years.

There were several available parking spaces near to the entrance, but Sam drove past Sir Barrington — who was reversing into his space — opting instead for a secluded section of the car park. Sam waited, watching as Sir Barrington climbed out of his car, scanning the area as he enjoyed a little stretch. Sam took this as his cue to turn his surveillance operation to one conducted on foot. He brushed off an errant tuna chunk clinging to his new trousers, popped a baseball cap on his head (for additional cover), and casually strolled behind, mirroring Sir Barrington's pace to maintain a suitable gap.

Sir Barrington didn't strike Sam as the type to spend an afternoon tending to his geraniums as he'd likely have people to attend to such matters. So, it was no surprise to Sam that he headed directly through the medley of alluring blooms towards the cosy coffee shop. This presented Sam with an issue as he and Abby were regulars in the establishment and known to most of the staff. Not ideal, then, when you're on a critical undercover operation.

Sam initially headed for and then took up position in the wooden hut opposite the coffee shop, hoping it would offer him a suitable view to confirm where Sir Barrington was seated. This hut was often Sam's sanctuary when Abby was in her lengthy "flower mode," as he referred to it. Sam had forged countless friendships in this place as it was here that the goldfish swam in large tanks hoping to attract a new owner and a new home.

"Hey, guys!" Sam said cheerily, waving to his favourite variety, the clownfish (although he never told the others who his favourite was). "Can't stop and talk today," he added, "as I'm on a mission."

Sam flicked his attention to the coffee shop windows, but it was useless, as the glaring sunshine bounced off the panes of glass, making a view inside almost impossible. He shifted between several different spots, but the result was the same from each. "I'm going in," Sam whispered for the benefit of circling fish. "Wish me luck!"

Sam crossed over the walkway, head bowed, and eased open the coffee shop door taking the opportunity to run his eyes around the interior. Sam caught a glimpse of Sir Barrington sat next to the window, facing the direction of the entrance. Fortunately, he was engaged in animated conversation with his companion and so paid Sam no attention.

Without hesitation, Sam headed to the rear of the shop to a vacant table next to the fire escape. From this location, Sam had the perfect vantage point over the entire area, but was, unfortunately, too far away to hear what was being said on Sir Barrington's table.

His associate was unknown to Sam. Mid-thirties, sharp pinstripe suit, and a fluffy head of black hair. Sam took out his mobile phone and, on the pretence of writing a text, captured several photographs of the man for future reference.

Overall, so far, Sam was jolly pleased with his abilities to blend into his surroundings without being noticed. Until...

"*Sammy... Sam... Sam*," sang an approaching cheery female voice, causing several heads to turn in Sam's direction in the busy shop. "How's my favourite Magnum?"

Gail, the merry proprietor of this fine establishment, had been busying herself cleaning a nearby table when Sam crept in. She was always good value, was Gail, often enjoying a joke or two when Sam and Abby dropped by. She liked to refer to him as Magnum, with Sam taking this to be a reference to the moustachioed PI as opposed to the delicious ice cream. "No Abby?" she asked, leaning on the empty chair opposite Sam.

Sam shuffled awkwardly. "You need to lower your voice," he said through gritted teeth.

"No Abby?" Gail repeated at precisely the same volume, only this time in a more resonant, throaty voice that Barry White would have

CHAPTER THREE – MILLIONAIRE'S SHORTBREAD

been pleased with. "I lowered my voice," she declared, laughing at her own comic genius at a raucous level that attracted even more attention to them.

"Gail!" Sam admonished. "I'm serious. I'm on an undercover mission," he added, pressing a finger to his mouth. "Although, that was an impressive gag," he conceded with a discreet grin.

"Oh! Is that why you're wearing the camouflage?" she whispered. "That'll be why I didn't see you come in, you know, because of..." she explained, pointing to his outfit.

"I get it!" Sam said, getting it. Sam leaned over to his right, looking around Gail to check if Sir Barrington was still there and also that he hadn't been disturbed by all of the frivolity. Fortunately, Sam remembered that the old chap's hearing wasn't the most acute, and the two of them were, fortunately, still engaged in deep conversation undisturbed. Unlike the rest of the patrons in the shop.

"Is that who you're following?" Gail asked, turning and pointing with little appreciation, it would appear, of the term *undercover*.

"Yes, but *shh*!" Sam said, encouraging her to take a seat before she completely destroyed his cover. "Gail, these could be dangerous criminals, so you just need to be a little less... obvious."

"Him?" Gail asked with a sneer. "Nah, he comes in here every now and then. I think he's a lord or something?"

"A knight," Sam replied.

"Ooh, like the chess piece?" Gail asked. "Well rook me," she added, unable to stifle the laugh that followed. "Does it smell of fish around here?" she asked, flaring her nostrils.

"It's my new trousers," Sam explained. "I dropped the contents of my tuna sandwiches on them."

"Why would you do that?" Gail asked, turning up her nose.

"Well, I didn't do it on purpose, now did I?"

To Sam's considerable frustration, Gail spun around for another lingering gawp. "What's the case, anyway?" she asked. "Oh, I've always wanted to say that!" Gail turned back to face Sam, clapping her hands in excitement. "Can I help?" she asked, deadpan. "I'd be wonderful at this undercover work."

Sam leaned across the table. "Gail, the only way you could possibly be any more obvious is if you were riding an elephant with a brass band following you around in full swing. So, thanks but no thanks," he said. "Also, I'm not happy with you!" he added, moving the direction of the conversation.

"Me?" Gail clarified, her cheery demeanour souring.

"Yes, you! Since you put that millionaire's shortbread cake on the menu, I've had to go down a notch on my belt. Or is it up? Whichever means I'm putting weight on."

"The ultimate compliment," Gail said with her mood lifting to previous levels. She briefly glanced over her shoulder. "Have you bugged them?"

"What? No, of course I've not bugged them," Sam replied, secretly wishing he could do precisely that. "I just wanted to see where the knight was headed to, and now I'd very much like to know who that chap he's talking to is."

"Go and ask them," Gail suggested, matter-of-factly.

"I can't just wander over there and ask, Gail! Don't talk crazy."

"I can, though!" Gail advised, pushing her seat back, then proceeding towards the counter situated at the front of the shop.

"Gail," Sam said, but it was too late as she was evidently a woman on a mission. She turned to offer Sam a confident wink and a raised thumb.

"Enjoy!" Gail said to the couple paying her colleague for their coffee and cake. She waited a moment, allowing them to move away before she reached over for a small glass bowl sat by the till. Contained in that bowl were a dozen or so business cards sat inside. She held it up for Sam's benefit indicating this was a crucial element of the plan she'd just hatched in her head.

Sam flapped his hand with a shake of his head. "Gail," he mouthed, urging her to stand down, which, it would appear, she had absolutely no intention of doing.

Offering a further wink for Sam's benefit, Gail sidled over to within earshot of Sir Barrington, busying herself by cleaning the table adjacent to them. The very same table she'd cleaned only a few

CHAPTER THREE – MILLIONAIRE'S SHORTBREAD

minutes earlier and one that had not been dirtied since. Add to this the fact that she didn't have a cloth in her hand, either. She was basically just rubbing her bare hand over the surface of the table, with her ears tuned into the conversation happening behind her.

She continued to clean the table with her imaginary cloth, but her acting skills were average, at best.

The chap talking with Sir Barrington pushed his chair back, offering his warm gratitude and a generous handshake. Although Gail couldn't see this happening behind her back, from the tone of the conversation she correctly surmised they were both preparing to leave. If she wanted to be successful on her debut mission — a mission she wasn't asked to or invited to participate in, it should be pointed out — she figured it was now or never.

She spun on a sixpence, holding out the glass bowl in front of her like Oliver Twist asking for a second helping. "Gentlemen," she said to the two men who were now stood, with Sir Barrington putting his blazer on. "Would you care to enter our weekly competition to win afternoon tea for two?" she said, giving the bowl a gentle shake, jiggling the business cards inside. "To enter you just need to throw your business card in the bowl and a lucky—"

"I don't have a business card," Sir Barrington replied, likely wondering why he was being bothered in such a fashion.

Undeterred, Gail edged the bowl under the nose of his associate. After all, she already knew who Sir Barrington was, so his refusal mattered not.

"I'm afraid I'm not local and only flown over for the day, so the prize would be wasted on me," he explained, in a more courteous manner.

Gail had no intention of falling at the first hurdle on her debut mission, however. No sir... not a chance. She stood there, smiling, maintaining eye contact without blinking. The man shifted his weight with an expression that said *why-are-you-still-stood-there*, but Gail was unwavering. Likely suspecting that this woman before him was going nowhere and that it was probably easier to just throw in his business card. So, he did precisely that. "I guess I'll need to come back if I win," he joked, retrieving a business card from his wallet, dropping it into the glass bowl with the others already entered into the prize draw.

"Thank you for coming to Kirby Garden Centre," Gail said, taking a pace back, clutching the bowl close to her chest. "Good luck!" she added, tapping the bowl in a spirited fashion.

The moment the two men had left the building, Gail couldn't contain her excitement, skipping over to Sam's table with a cheesy, broad grin.

"What was all that about?" Sam said, returning the smile.

Gail took a seat, placing the bowl on the table in front of Sam. "I was improvising, Sam. It's what all us investigators do."

"Did you hear what they were talking about?" Sam asked, leaning closer, eyes widening in anticipation.

"Not too much," she said. "But, I did manage to catch the tail end of their conversation," she added, teasing a hopeful Sam.

"And?" Sam asked. "What did you hear?"

"Sir Barrington thanking the other chap for coming," she said.

Sam leaned back to the position he'd started from. "What about before that?" he asked, with his enthusiasm waning.

"Oh, not too much," Gail said, enjoying herself. She paused for a moment or two to build the tension, puffing out her cheeks, playing with the salt cellar on the table. "There... was... one thing, though," she added.

"Yeah!" Sam said, leaning forward, again. He was in danger of making himself seasick with all this motion. "Well?"

"The chess piece man said something about needing a speedy transaction and discretion assured at all times. The other fellow then said he could guarantee it." Gail placed her finger on the rim of the glass bowl. "Oh, and using my extensive talents, I also managed to obtain the other man's business card for you," she said, tipping her head in the direction of the bowl. "Oh, and the chap is not local, having flown over for the day. Or so he said."

"Bingo!" Sam said, slapping his hands together. "Gail, if you ever decide to hang your apron up, you'd be a fine addition to the agency."

CHAPTER THREE – MILLIONAIRE'S SHORTBREAD

Gail dropped her hand into the glass bowl, stirring its contents like a seasoned bingo caller jiggling their balls. She gripped the newest addition and whipped it out, handing it over to Sam.

"Thanks," he said, studying the name on the black card with embossed gold lettering.

"Well?" Gail asked. "Was it worth tailing him?"

Sam gripped the card between his thumb and forefinger, fanning it in Gail's direction. "This," Sam said, "is pure gold dust to our investigation. With your help, Gail, I think we're on our way to solving the case of the... the... *shit*. I forgot to get Abby involved concerning the name of the case. She's brilliant at coming up with them, and my effort wasn't the greatest if I'm honest. Tell you what, I'll phone you when I have it."

"Ooh, how exciting, my heart's racing!" Gail said. "I should buy a gun for my next mission," she added as a statement rather than a question which was concerning.

Sam smiled but wasn't entirely sure if she was serious or not due to her far-away expression. "Anything else I can do?" Gail asked once she'd returned to the present.

"There is one thing," suggested Sam with a twinkle in his eye.

"Yeah?"

"Yeah!" Sam said. "I could murder a slice of millionaire's shortbread," he said, patting his stomach. "I might just need to buy a larger belt."

Gail took her glass bowl, returning to the counter area with a spring in her step. "One slice of millionaire's shortbread coming right up, partner!" she called over her shoulder.

Sam took another lingering look at the business card in his hand. "Quentin Thrumbolt," he said, reading the gold lettering.

Sam narrowed his eyes, processing the events of the day. "Meeting a mystery man who's flown over for the day and then demanding discretion just days after a major theft," Sam said, happy to sit there having a conversation with himself, it would appear.

Sam could feel his mouth watering. He wasn't clear if this was a result of the cake soon to be heading his way or the fact that they were a step closer to solving the case in record time. "Sam Levy always gets his man," he said, a broad grin appearing on his face. "Sir Barrington Hedley-Smythe... Gotcha!"

CHAPTER FOUR
Big Fish

A young lad, no more than six or seven years of age, wrestled with his fishing rod, squealing in delight, waging a furious battle to wind the line in. An older man — possibly the boy's grandad — watched on, offering words of encouragement, but eager, it would appear, to leave the little tyke to claim his eventual prize all by himself.

"Come on!" yelled the boy, his arms shaking and cheeks reddening under the considerable strain.

The older man moved forward a pace, glancing over the metal fence to the water below. "I can see it, lad. You're nearly there, Charlie. Just a little more effort and you've done it."

The lad dug in for a final, valiant effort, winding furiously with all his might. His efforts were soon rewarded, however, by the introduction to a feisty gurnard thrashing around on the end of his line. Charlie could barely contain his joy. "I did it, Grampy. My first fish and I caught it all on my own."

"Well done, Charlie!" Grampy said, offering an experienced hand to remove the hook. "Here," Grampy said, handing the fish to the cautious boy. "He won't bite, Charlie. But be careful of the spines which can dig in a little."

Grampy took his phone from his pocket. "Hold it up, Charlie. Your gran will love this picture."

"Cheese," Charlie said, keeping a cautious eye on the irritated fish. "Is this a big fish, Grampy?"

Grampy nodded his head, sucking in air through his teeth. "Big?" he said. "Any bigger and we'd be calling it a whale," he suggested. "Now let's get this chap safely back in the sea," he said. "See, Charlie. I knew you could do it."

Watching the drama unfold over on the harbour wall was Sam, sitting atop a weathered barrel in his front garden with a nostalgic smile. He could feel a lump in his throat, watching the young lad having the time of his life as that was exactly what Sam did in the very same spot, with his grandad, many years earlier.

He'd been awake for hours, unable to sleep with his brain working in overdrive. Rather than disturb Abby, he'd headed outside to his sanctuary. There was no more magical place to sit and appreciate the sun come up on a spring morning than in their garden. The house Sam inherited from his grandparents was nestled in a prime location within the Port St Mary harbour where his neighbours consisted mostly of fishing boats and hungry seabirds. Sam could drift away for hours listening to the sea washing up against the pebbled shore.

"I had a feeling you'd be out here," Abby said, stood in the doorway of the cottage with a tray of tea. "You were up bright and early," she said, moving to join him in the garden. "Everything okay?"

Sam gratefully accepted the cuppa on offer. "Oh, I just feel like I'm growing up, Abby," Sam said with a heavy sigh. "And it scares me."

"How so?" Abby asked, rubbing his shoulder.

"We own our own business, and I'm living with a girl," Sam explained.

"And that's a bad thing?" Abby asked with a laugh. "Should I take offence at this point?"

Sam replayed his previous sentence in his head, smiling at Abby. "No, of course not," he said. "I was just watching the young chap fishing over there, and I suppose it got me to thinking," he said, drawing Abby's eyeline in the direction of his own. "I used to fish

CHAPTER FOUR – BIG FISH

with my grandad on that exact spot," he said, before blowing on his steaming drink.

"What's really up, Sam? You're not yourself lately."

"You know me too well," Sam said, taking a sip of his tea, running his eyes around the garden. "It's this place, Abs. This wonderful seaside cottage was their dream home, and I'm in danger of throwing it all away."

"Is this about the remortgage we took out to buy the business?" Abby asked, receiving a nod in the affirmative. "Sam Levy," she said, staring intently, "Sam, we own the finest detective agency on the Isle of Man, bar none! Sure, it's a little quiet at the moment, but things will pick up."

"Drexel Popek doesn't appear to be too quiet at the moment," Sam suggested, lowering his head like a scolded puppy.

"Sam Levy! Are you comparing yourself to that disloyal oaf? Is that why you've been down in the dumps? Don't forget, you're twice the detective he is. Drexel is nothing but a snivelling... snivelling... *wazzock*."

"Wazzock?" Sam said, impressed by the schoolyard vocabulary.

Abby's eyes drifted away for a moment, with her appearing deep in thought. "Oh, I've just remembered what I was dreaming about?" she said, in giddy fashion.

"What dream?" asked Sam. "You dreamed about calling Drexel a wazzock?"

"No, silly, the name of the case," she said, skipping through multiple subjects in her head at the same time it would appear.

"Yeah?" Sam asked, spirits lifting. "For the stolen bronze busts?"

Abby cleared her throat, preparing for the grand unveiling with Sam hanging on her every word. "The Seaside Detective Agency, in The Case of the Brazen Burglar," she announced, pleased with herself for recalling her dream.

Sam nodded his head, chewing over the suggestion but with no immediate response.

"You like?" Abby asked.

"Mmm," Sam replied, continuing to chew the suggestion over for a moment longer. He took another sip of his tea. "I like where you're going with it, Abs. But I can't get the image of a thief in the night with a massive pair of—"

"Sam!"

"No, no," Sam ventured further. "I'm not saying it's an unpleasant image... I'm going to shut up now."

"Ah, it'll do for now until something else comes up, yeah?" Abby suggested.

"Yeah, it'll do for now. Thanks for cheering me up, Abs."

"We'll be fine," added Abby. "Don't forget, you've just nailed a major case this week while Drexel's probably out there looking for a missing kitten, or something."

"I know, Abs. I suppose I'm just worried about money at the moment. Work is certainly less stressful when it's someone else's responsibility to pay you each month, you know what I mean?"

"I do," Abby said sincerely.

"Also," Sam continued, "the size of the loan secured against the house is just giving me a few restless nights, I suppose," he said with a sigh. "And I doubt we're going to get paid for the time spent working on the stolen busts, either."

"Eh? You solved the case, didn't you? The bronze busts get nicked, and a short while later, Sir B has a cosy tête-à-tête with an antique dealer who was heard to guarantee discretion. Sounds like case closed to me."

Sam kicked his heels back and forth off the wooden barrel. "I don't doubt Sir Barrington's guilt, Abby. But as he's the one who employed us in the first place, I suspect he won't be overly eager to pay us for pointing the finger of suspicion in his direction."

"Oh," replied Abby. "I don't suppose he will, now you mention it. What about the insurance company? If they don't have to pay out on a substantial insurance claim, then they might consider a reward for any useful information received?"

"I suppose," Sam said, with an air of optimism. "I'm certainly going to give the insurance company, and the police, an update on my

CHAPTER FOUR – BIG FISH

surveillance yesterday. Hopefully, they'll be eager to speak with Sir Barrington and Quentin Thrumbolt."

Sam pushed himself off the barrel, smiling as he noticed the young lad casting off, once more, from the harbour wall. "Thanks, Abby," he said. "Thanks for making me believe in myself."

"Come here," Abby said, placing the two cups on the tray before administering a warm cuddle. "Don't forget, Sam Levy. You're twice the detective that Drexel Popek will ever be!"

A little later that same morning, Sam attended Douglas police station to present his suspicions against Sir Barrington Hedley-Smythe and Quentin Thrumbolt. Granted, Sam could only provide them with circumstantial evidence which was, however, compelling, Sam thought.

The team at Eyes Peeled enjoyed a positive working relationship with the local plod and a general willingness to collaborate when the opportunity presented itself. Sure, some reward money would be nice, but Sam didn't hold out too much hope in that regard. At least in providing the police with what was, in essence, a solved case, Sam figured he'd be able to bank a favour he could redeem at a future date. Additionally, Sam hadn't forgotten how Sir Barrington had wasted their time in hiring Eyes Peeled for a spurious investigation to find what he'd nicked in the first place. For that reason alone, Sam certainly wouldn't lose sleep in aiding in his conviction.

Before heading back to their office in Peel, Sam realised he'd skipped breakfast, as his rumbling belly was pleased to audibly testify to.

"Ah," he said, happily, admiring the magnificent golden arches up ahead. "Yes, still time," he added, glancing to the dashboard clock to confirm there were at least six minutes until the breakfast serving time ended.

Sam headed towards the drive-thru giving serious consideration to what would best satisfy his hunger. Fortunately, there were only two vehicles in the queue ahead, so plenty of time to place his order.

He feasted his eyes over the breakfast menu posters, strategically placed to tempt the famished driver. "Something healthy," he said, pulling up to the magic machine where the orders were collated.

"Double-sausage-and-egg McMuffin with an orange juice," he said when prompted, with the healthy option, apparently, discounted in the two metres he'd driven since making the decision. Still, at least the orange juice contained oranges.

"Window one," came the crackled and curt instruction through the intercom.

"Thank you," Sam said, marvelling at the technology in the magic machine that fed him without even having to step out of his car.

Sam glanced in his rear-view mirror before moving away, as all good driving instructors recommended. He did a double-take, as the driver in the car behind appeared to be reading a broadsheet newspaper which must have obscured their view entirely. Sam liked to relax with a newspaper, but in a drive-thru, while in the driver's seat, well, that was just a touch odd. Each to their own, he thought, before pulling away.

Sam drew up to window one, as instructed to by the voice, reaching into his wallet for his card.

"One pound twenty-nine," announced the young lad with a small head once he'd opened up the glass screen separating his workspace from the waiting public. The lad was able to speak to Sam at the same time as processing another order he was receiving via his headset. The ability to multi-task was impressive, Sam thought.

Sam placed his debit card up against the payment machine, smiled, then drove the short distance to collect his order at the next window.

"Hello," Sam greeted the familiar-looking lad with an unusually small head. Sam stared at the lad for a moment as that pinhead was not one you saw every day, and now Sam was sure he'd seen two of them in quick succession. Sam could, on occasion, get a touch lightheaded when hungry, so wondered if he'd even moved to the next window to collect his order. Sam looked back over his shoulder, then to the lad opposite, and then back over his shoulder.

CHAPTER FOUR – BIG FISH

With a sense that this could go on for a good while longer, the lad moved to explain. "That's my twin brother," he said, throwing his thumb in the direction of the other window. "In case you were wondering?"

"Ah," Sam said, relieved he wasn't having some sort of funny turn.

"There you go, sir," the lad said, handing a small bottle of orange juice to Sam. With a practised smile, he then returned his attention to the monitor displaying the next order to be collected.

Sam dropped the bottle in the cup holder on his dashboard and smiled back, saliva pooling in his cheeks in anticipation of his breakfast.

After a good fifteen seconds, the lad looked back out at Sam with an expression that translated as *why-the-hell-are-you-still-sat-there*. After several more awkward seconds consisting of Sam and the lad having a staring competition, Sam felt the need to speak and break the tension.

"My breakfast?" Sam said with raised eyebrows.

The lad screwed up his face in return. "I just gave it to you!"

"No, you didn't," Sam replied, offering a cordial laugh.

The lad checked Sam's original order on his monitor then returned his attention to Sam. "I can see it there," he said, leaning out of his window, pointing at the contents of Sam's cup holder.

"It's just an orange juice," Sam said, holding it up for inspection.

"Well... yeah."

"Where's the rest of it?" Sam asked with a shrug.

The lad returned to his screen, once more. "You only ordered an orange juice," he confirmed. "So, you have an orange juice," he added, pointing to the bottle in Sam's hand.

Sam shook his head in dismay, taking note of the lad's name badge displayed there on his chest. "Barney, do you honestly think I'd come all the way to McDonald's for an orange juice and nothing else? What sort of sick individual would even do that?"

"It happens," Barney suggested sagely. "Anyway, that's all you've paid for," he added. "Did you not think to query the fact you were only charged..." he said, looking to the screen again, "one pound twenty-nine."

Sam gripped the steering wheel a little tighter now. "Look, if I'm honest, I was distracted by the teeny size of the guy's head and how his headset drowned him."

"*Ha-ha-ha*," offered Barney, slapping the countertop in appreciation of Sam's genius observation. "He does have a peanut for a head," he continued, laughing heartily at his brother's expense. That brother being his identical twin and by virtue of this close relationship, sharing the same sized head as he did. A point Barney appeared happy and willing to overlook.

"Look," Sam said, once the laughter died down. "There's clearly been some confusion as I didn't order just an orange juice. I'd like my double-sausage-and-egg McMuffin, please. Then I'll be on my way."

"Sure thing," Barney said, still chuckling away. "Unfortunately, I can't take payment from this station, so you'll need to go to..." he said, popping his head out of his hatch like an inquisitive horse, and now pointing to where Sam should go. Which was precisely where he'd started off, minutes earlier, at the magic talking machine.

"So, you're saying that I need to drive all the way around, place my order, pay peanut-head, and then come back and see you again? That's what you're saying, right?"

"Smashing!" Barney said, swerving or at least ignoring the frustration in Sam's tone. "See you soon," Barney added, and with that, the shutter was closed over. Well, at least until the next hungry punter appeared to collect their order.

Hungry, frustrated, and realising further dialogue with Barney would prove fruitless, Sam drove a rapid loop of the building, ending up, once more, at the ordering booth. Waiting for the voice to take his order, Sam glanced in his rear-view mirror and sat there, once again, was a driver with their face obscured by a broadsheet newspaper.

"Can I take your order, please?" asked the familiar crackling voice.

CHAPTER FOUR – BIG FISH

Sam kept his attention fixed on the car behind with an increasing sense of déjà vu. Another newspaper-reading driver was too much of a weird coincidence, he thought.

"Can I take your order, please?"

"Eh, yeah... I'll have a double-sausage-and-egg McMuffin meal, please. Don't worry about the orange juice as I've already got one."

"Sorry, sir," came the immediate reply. "You're too late for breakfast."

"What?" Sam snapped back.

The intercom crackled back into life. "Breakfast stops at eleven a.m."

"Yes, I know," replied an increasingly exasperated Sam double-checking the time. "But your colleague sent me back around as my order was... well, there was... I've only got an orange juice, and I'm hungry!" Sam declared.

"Breakfast stops at eleven a.m." repeated the robotic voice which Sam assumed to be owned by the chap with the peanut-shaped bonce.

"Yes... I know. It's just that... You know what, forget it!" Sam conceded, clenching his fist.

Sam climbed out of his car, grinding his teeth with the vein bulging in his head. It was like a remake of the film *Falling Down*, where some other unfortunate was refused their breakfast in similar circumstances and with grave consequences. Rather than taking his angst out on the staff, however, Sam wandered to the car behind. As Sam approached the open driver's window, the angle of the newspaper inside also shifted, continuing to obscure the identity of the person behind it.

"Are you following me?" Sam asked, tapping the newspaper with his finger. "Only I've done two circuits of this building this morning, and you were behind me both times. That's some coincidence otherwise."

"*Moi?*" replied a surprised voice from behind the newspaper.

"I bloody knew it was you!" Sam said, now using his same finger to ease down the paper, revealing the face behind it. "Popek! What are you following me for?"

"I'm only here to buy my breakfast, Sam," Drexel replied, pointing to the bag of delicious-smelling food on his passenger seat.

"Bollocks!" Sam said succinctly. "Then why did you follow me around for the second time?"

Drexel rolled his eyes. "Okay, okay," he said, waving his hand in submission. "You've got me bang to rights. Look, Sam, I was just following you to see what you're up to, is all. Take it as a compliment, yeah? Also, I did hear on the grapevine that you're working for that crazy old dude with the large house."

"That's already solved!" Sam replied with a sniff.

"Oh, well done," Drexel said like he was appeasing a child. "And there was me hoping to let you do all the running around, again, so I could swoop in at the last moment."

"I've not forgiven you for that pigeon farce, either," Sam added. "So start doing your own homework and stop following me, you devious... devious... wazzock!"

"It's business, Sam. Don't take it too personally," Drexel said, and then, "So you've solved that case, you say?" Drexel asked rhetorically as he'd just been told as much. "So, who's in the frame for it? Theft, wasn't it?"

Sam ignored the question, instead walking around to the other side of Drexel's stationary car, offering an apologetic wave to the hungry patrons waiting behind in the queue. Now positioned next to the open passenger window, Sam lowered his head inside the car, so he was looking directly at Drexel. "None of your bloody business who's in the frame," Sam said. "You can read about it in the newspaper you appear so fond of."

Sam reached inside the vehicle, taking a grip of the brown bag sat on the passenger seat. "As payback for the pigeon incident and for also following me, I'm taking your breakfast!" Sam said, maintaining eye contact with Drexel all the while.

CHAPTER FOUR – BIG FISH

"Enjoy," Drexel said. "We should do breakfast together again soon."

Sam offered a further apologetic wave to the queue, then returned to his car with Drexel's breakfast now his own.

Now seated with one hand on the steering wheel, Sam was interrupted by... "Can I please take your order," asked the exasperated voice from the booth, who must have been asking, in vain, since Sam had wandered off.

"No thanks, peanut-head," Sam said, patting the bag now sat on his passenger seat. "I'm sorted, but cheers!"

CHAPTER FIVE
Code Red

Standing over two metres tall at the shoulder, the dramatic skeleton of a giant deer cut an imposing figure. It was difficult to comprehend that such magnificent animals once freely roamed the open tundra landscape of the British Isles.

Alongside and keeping the deer company, was the Bronze Age Man display, where a bearded chap with questionable oral hygiene stood precariously in his coracle. With his eyes fixed firmly on his fishing net, he appeared hopeful of a generous bounty.

"Good evening, Boris," Adrian said to the deer with a warm smile. "Looking good tonight, Eric," he continued, with his greeting now directed towards the optimistic angler.

No response was expected nor received, however, as they were both museum displays, after all. Still, it didn't prevent Adrian from offering a cordial greeting as he commenced his first security sweep of the evening.

The illumination levels in the building were dimmed by ninety percent overnight, so Adrian's giant torch — a birthday present from his mum — was his trusty companion for his eight-hour shift. It was ordered to his exacting specifications and was bright enough, if required, to be seen from another planet, probably. Another advantage of requesting this exact specification — knowledge which he didn't share with his mum — was that it was perfectly weighted to double up as an effective weapon, should the need arise. Adrian spent hours in his bedroom (and a fair few at work) honing his fighting skills so he could dispatch a knockout blow, if and when the requirement presented itself. What nunchucks were to Bruce Lee, the flashlight was to Adrian Fitzherbert, and he was a master of all he surveyed. Well, from eleven p.m. until seven a.m., that is.

The uninitiated may refer to Adrian as a night watchman, but he was so much more than that. Well, in both his and his mum's humble opinion, at least. Each evening, Adrian was charged with protecting the cultural heritage of the Isle of Man, no less. For the princely remuneration of nine pounds and twenty-three pence an hour (with a pound an hour extra for weekend work), Adrian maintained order at the Manx Museum. Something he did with an iron fist. The law would be maintained at all times when he was on duty. That was also the tagline he'd employed on the business cards he'd had printed along with his self-appointed job title:

Adrian Fitzherbert
Law maintained at all times
Guardian of history!

Adrian was eager to promote his job title as being a guardian of history, as was his mum. He was confident the ladies would also be impressed when he eventually plucked up the courage to speak to a few. For now, however, he had no time for such distractions as the security of this fine establishment landed firmly on his narrow shoulders. Shoulders that were drowning inside his dad's nylon suit jacket that he'd borrowed eighteen months earlier and not yet returned.

Confident that all was as it should be in this section of the museum, and the residents were settled in for the night, Adrian continued his rounds in the direction of the Isle of Man TT Races exhibition. For some, the reduced lighting and isolation would be disconcerting, but not for Adrian. His eyes had adjusted, like an owl, and he had his torch on standby should additional illumination be required.

"Strangers in the night," he sang, followed by a whistling melody that echoed through the corridors.

CHAPTER FIVE – CODE RED

Being something of a motorbike racing fan, the current exhibition of Isle of Man TT machinery, trophies, and various racing nostalgia was a popular and welcome addition to the museum-going public and to Adrian himself.

Ordinarily, nobody was permitted beyond the confines of the yellow velvet rope surrounding the bikes on display. Not even Adrian's security clearance allowed the removal of the sacred barrier, but, it had been too great an opportunity to miss while he'd had the chance. His phone was now filled with selfies of him astride the HM Plant-sponsored missile that'd propelled John McGuinness to the first 130 mph average lap speed around the famous circuit several years earlier.

Star of the exhibition, however, even amongst such esteemed company, was the Isle of Man Senior TT Trophy. First awarded to Charlie Collier in 1907, the trophy is considered by many to be the most prestigious in any sport. Presented to the winner of the blue-riband event, the Senior TT race, it was the reward for winning arguably the most formidable challenge in motorsport.

There were only a small number of riders who had and would lay claim to this magnificent prize. Over a metre tall and featuring the winged messenger from Roman mythology, Mercury, the insurance value alone was said to be over one point five million pounds. But in terms of sporting heritage it was considered by many to be entirely priceless.

The exhibition was an annual event, held in the run-up to the year's racing festival. It gave locals and those visiting the opportunity to get up close and personal to a superb collection of motorsport memorabilia.

Sadly, at least for Adrian, a photo opportunity with him lifting it would elude him, what with it being secured behind a one-inch thick glass presentation case. He could look, however — something he did, at length, each time he walked by during the night. Well at least, that is, until the trophy was required for the actual race.

Adrian pushed on with his sweep of the building, walking through the collection of stuffed Manx animals and into the exhibition of tourism through the decades. Adrian always chuckled at the selection of saucy postcards hung from a rack outside the recreation of a seafront shop. It was a nostalgic homage to a bygone time when the Isle of Man was a mecca for tourists eager to walk in the sand, enjoy an ice cream and, perhaps, for those braver souls to enjoy a dip in the Irish Sea.

Once satisfied there was nothing amiss and everything was as it should be, Adrian returned to his office which was, in reality, the staff canteen doubling up as his operational nerve centre each evening. Adrian brushed away the remnants of someone's egg sandwich from his favourite chair and completed his inspection sheet, confirming that his mission was accomplished. At least, that is, until his next circuit in precisely one hour.

"Ooh baby," he whispered, leaning back in his chair so it came to a rest on its back legs, his feet now propped on the surface of the table. He pressed down on the remote control, and the wall-mounted fifty-inch screen burst into life. "Show me what you've got," he said, increasing the volume.

"Gotcha!" he said, flicking his index finger and connecting sweetly with another bit of discarded egg that'd fallen from the table, landing in his lap. He took a mental note to reference the scruffy conditions in his daily security report. He'd also be sure to escalate this lapse in discipline with the day supervisor to take swift and immediate action as standards had to be maintained.

Clear of lunchtime crumbs, Adrian returned his attention to the TV. "Show me what you've got, baby!" he said again, teasing the television with a seductive wink. Lesser men would presently be enjoying Netflix or similar, but not Adrian. Such was his complete devotion and utter professionalism, that unless he was out on foot patrol or using the loo, then his attention would remain fixed on the security camera footage broadcast on the wall-mounted screen.

Six live video feeds covering the interior and exterior of the museum, streamed for Adrian's viewing pleasure. It wasn't exactly the sophisticated surveillance operation you'd find, say, in a Las Vegas casino, but for a small rural museum, it was perfectly adequate. The

CHAPTER FIVE – CODE RED

cloud-based technology even offered him the ability to log in remotely as he often did when struggling to sleep on his night off. He found it soothing, and knowing all was well at work usually resulted in a good night's sleep.

Several completed inspections later and everything was still as it was and as it should be. Well, there was a minor situation when Adrian had been spinning his torch like a baton twirler, catching the corner of an antique desk when it slipped from his grasp. There was no visible damage that he could see, but he'd still spent the previous twenty minutes considering if he should complete a detailed damage report. He'd leave it for now and check for damage again in daylight, he reasoned. Considering the hefty weight of his torch, he knew he'd had a lucky escape, this time. For that reason, his baton twirling days were now at a premature end.

Three a.m. meant it was lunchtime for Adrian. In the canteen, he unwrapped the sandwiches his mum had prepared for him. "Ham, again," he said, disappointed, lifting up one corner of the bread for further inspection. He'd had ham four days running, so he'd have to have a word with his mum later on. "Not even that fresh," he said with a sigh, jabbing the bread with his finger.

He lifted his lunch to his mouth, but before his lips made contact, his eyes were drawn to section three on the TV screen.

"What the...?" he said, dropping his sandwich on the table and moving towards the TV. He wondered if the movement he'd seen on the screen was just a fly that had landed on the lens of the security camera. Adrian stared intently without blinking. He moved back slowly, and without breaking his attention from the video feed patted his hand on the table to take hold of his torch in case it had to be deployed as a weapon. Adrian swallowed hard, his heart racing. This is why he was paid the big bucks, he thought.

"Wee-waa, wee-waa, wee-waa," bellowed the security alarm that burst into life, sending Adrian at least two feet into the air as it did.

"Code red!" screamed Adrian, but as he was alone, it was unclear whose benefit this was for. "Code red!" he continued to call, checking on the monitor to see which section had actually triggered the alarm.

THE SEASIDE DETECTIVE AGENCY BOOK TWO

With no concern for his own safety, Adrian sprinted from the canteen towards the Isle of Man TT exhibition which he identified as the source of the alarm. The entire building was now flooded with light — an automatic feature when the security system triggered. "I've got you surrounded!" Adrian shouted, which was a lie as he hadn't even arrived at his destination by this point.

The alarm system continued to scream and would have by now, hopefully, notified the Isle of Man constabulary that there was a situation unfolding that required their presence. Adrian, however, had absolutely no intention of waiting for backup as this moment was one he'd dreamed about all his adult life.

"Code red," he repeated, once more, and while his brain was fogged with panic, he knew he had to remember his training. Advanced training garnered from watching hours of close protection and self-defence videos on YouTube and various Facebook groups.

Sprinting towards the hall housing the TT exhibition at breakneck speed, his dad's trousers were starting to come loose under strain. At home, his dad sported a generous paunch, so the pants Adrian had inherited were a few sizes too big. As such, his belt was struggling to keep things where they were intended. "Shit," Adrian said, but it was too late to take remedial action. His pants slid down under the exertion, and with the sudden restriction in movement for his legs, Adrian was sent tumbling to the floor, sliding the final few metres on his stomach.

"Freeze!" Adrian commanded as he came to a gradual halt. Pulling his trousers back to their intended location, he leapt up with his torch at the ready should a threat present itself upon his person.

The incessant wail of the alarm bore deep into Adrian's skull, making rational thought a challenge. "Who's there?" he asked, his head darting around the room. "Show yourself."

But apart from the exhibits who lived there, the area appeared empty of intruders. Had he somehow imagined the movement on the security footage? Lack of sleep, maybe? But, if so, why had the alarm activated at the same time? These thoughts ran through his mind as he moved around the room in a heightened state.

CHAPTER FIVE – CODE RED

"What the…" he said, lowering his torch as he approached the Senior TT presentation case in the far corner of the room. "No… no… no," he added, afraid to believe what his eyes were telling him. He reached for his phone, dialling 999, with his feet crunching the smashed glass strewn all over the floor.

"Yes, police please," Adrian said when prompted to by the operator. As the call was transferred over to the police control room, he looked up in case the intruder had come in via the skylight, Tom Cruise style, and was still dangling there, like a spider.

"Hello, police," Adrian said with a shaking voice. "If you don't have officers already dispatched, then I must request immediate backup!" Adrian spoke clearly and concisely as his YouTube training recommended. "Yes, my name is Adrian Fitzherbert, and I'm the head of security for the Manx Museum," he confirmed, giving himself a promotion in the process. "I regret to report that we've been robbed."

Adrian paced in a circle, keeping one eye out in case the perpetrator was still on the premises.

"Yes," Adrian replied to the question presented to him over the phone. "As far as I can see, only one item has been stolen," he said solemnly. "Yes," he added when questioned. "I regret to advise that the item in question is the Isle of Man Senior TT Trophy. Please, send back up! Code red… code red…"

CHAPTER SIX
Hand Sandwich

Tom puffed out his chubby cheeks, shaking his head like a dog fresh out of the bath. "You should probably take a look at this, Suzie?" he suggested, pointing at his computer screen with a heavy sigh.

Suzie dug her heels into the carpet, propelling her chair over to Tom's desk. "Bollocks!" she said as a considered response. "Do you know if Sam or Abby have seen this?"

"Nope. Well at least I don't think so. It's only just been published on the Government's Twitter feed and I suspect Sam's going to have a fit when he does."

"He doesn't appear to be having a particularly good day as it is," Suzie suggested, looking across the office in the direction of the Eyes Peeled client suite. With the blinds open, Sam could be seen with his head buried in his hands giving the impression that his meeting with the police wasn't going in the direction he'd hoped. "Don't show him," suggested Suzie. "It could be the final straw, you know... tip him over the edge."

Tom raised one eyebrow as his initial response. "Better he hears it from us, Suzie?"

A few moments later the meeting drew to a close with Sam standing first, holding the door open for their guest, Detective Inspector Rump.

THE SEASIDE DETECTIVE AGENCY BOOK TWO

"You win some, you lose some," Sam suggested, escorting their guest through the office.

DI Rump shrugged his shoulders in sympathy. "I'm sorry it's not better news, Sam. But, I thought it'd be better to pop around and tell you in person," he said, offering a cordial nod in the direction of Tom, a former colleague in the force. With one foot through the front door, DI Rump looked over his shoulder. "Don't forget that I'm always available for consultancy work," he added.

"Of course not," Abby replied with a gracious smile. "We'll let you know if something crops up," she said, closing the door behind him.

Sam dropped to his knees, placing his head on the surface of his desk like he was having a nap at primary school.

"Sam..." Abby said, rubbing his back. "It's not all bad. Sam..."

"The meeting didn't go well?" Tom ventured, reasonably confident he already knew the answer to the question.

"No," Sam replied, his voice muffled by the desk. "Not good at all."

Abby left Sam where he was and fell back into her chair. "We didn't quite crack the case of stolen busts," she said by way of explanation for Tom and Suzie.

"Oh?" Suzie said, standing so she could see over the computer monitors dividing the two of them. "I thought that was all but nailed down?"

Abby rolled her eyes. "We all did, Suzie," Abby said. "DI Rump was kind enough to drop by and confirm that Sir Barrington has been cleared of any wrongdoing."

"What?" Tom chipped in, his ordinarily calm demeanour faltering. "What about the cloak and dagger meeting with the high-end antique dealer that Sam witnessed?"

"All coincidence... apparently," Abby said. "DI Rump confirmed that the police spoke to both Sir B and Thrumbolt. Both of them gave the same account of the meeting, which was merely arranging for the sale of two valuable grandfather clocks. Sir B further confided that he didn't want all and sundry knowing his cashflow was currently an issue, hence arranging the transaction with an off-island antique dealer at short notice. So, it appears Sir B was just selling

CHAPTER SIX – HAND SANDWICH

some assets to pay the bills, such as the cost of the roof repairs, I imagine."

"Well," Suzie said, attempting to restore some much-needed cheer with her happy demeanour, "we'll just need to redouble our efforts to find the actual thief now we know it wasn't Sir B. If he didn't do it then someone else must have and so we'll—"

"No," Sam moaned, cutting across Suzie's rousing speech. "Sir Barrington has fired us from this case and doesn't want us... well... me in particular, to darken his door ever again. Spoiler alert, he didn't take too kindly to being falsely accused of stealing his own belongings or being followed by me."

Abby nodded as confirmation. "Yeah, Sir B wasn't overly complimentary about us."

"You mean *me*," Sam said. "You're just trying to spare my feelings."

Abby nodded, conceding that point. "We're a team, Sam. Always a team. Anyway, DI Rump also mentioned that Sir B was aware of his error in employing us in the first place. For that reason, he's now made alternative arrangements and employed the person he was supposed to in the first place."

"Drexel sodding Popek!" Sam said, his voice dripping with anger. Not that this point really needed clarifying for a room full of experienced private investigators.

Tom glanced over to Suzie, unsure what he should do with the information displayed on his monitor. He raised the palms of his hands. "Should I say something?" he asked, mouthing the words.

Suzie nodded her agreement. After all, he'd find out soon enough, and as they'd referenced, it was preferable that the unfortunate news was delivered by them.

Tom wiggled his finger at Abby, inviting her to come around to his side of the desk. Abby could read the concerned expressions on both Tom and Suzie's face, heading around without hesitation.

With the office having fallen silent, Sam peeled his face off the desk, looking up to see if anybody was still there.

"What's up?" he asked on seeing the three others huddled around Tom's computer wearing grave expressions. "Guys!" he added when no response was offered. It was clear from Abby's face that it wasn't going to be good news.

Abby cleared her throat. "Well, you know about the theft of the Senior TT Trophy and how we were hopeful of being contracted to investigate?"

"Nooooo!" Sam replied, clenching his fingers into a fist, shaking it to the heavens. "Don't tell me Drexel's been appointed to that case, also?"

Sam received no response, which confirmed all he needed to know. "I don't believe it. Which insurance company has employed that treacherous git?"

Tom glanced at his screen and then back to Sam. "Tower Royal," he replied.

Sam lowered his head. "Tower Royal," he said. "They'll be offering him at least a ten percent finder's fee for this case. That's fifteen thousand pounds we've potentially lost out on and money we could really do with."

Abby didn't have the heart or desire to correct him that ten percent of the insurance value was one hundred and fifty thousand, rather than just fifteen thousand. What with his present fragile state, and all.

"Sod it," Sam said, clapping his hands together with a sudden change of demeanour. He straightened himself up. Chest pressed out, shoulders back. "We can still investigate it!" he said.

"We can?" Suzie asked.

Sam walked around the desk to see what the rest of them were actually looking at. "Sure we can! Technically, the insurance company won't give two hoots who's been officially appointed if they get it back promptly. If we can find that trophy before Popek or the police, then that fifteen grand finder's fee will be ours. All the insurance company will be interested in is not paying out on a claim of one point five million."

Sam continued reading the press release down to the part where Drexel was referred to, in rather glowing terms, as the island's primo private investigator.

CHAPTER SIX — HAND SANDWICH

"Come on," Sam said. "Who's with me?" he asked, laying his palm out flat. "Let's show them all who the island's *primo* private investigators are, yeah?"

Tom went first, laying his hand on top of Sam's, followed by Abby and finally Suzie. Sam then placed his other hand on the top of the pile, completing their hand sandwich.

"We've got this, people!" he said, throwing his eyes around the cosy circle they'd now formed. "Let's get to work, guys. We've got a bloody great big trophy to find!"

CHAPTER SEVEN
A Three-Horse Race

The theft of the Senior TT Trophy was front-page news, globally. Even if motorsport wasn't your thing, you'd likely heard of the Isle of Man TT races. The audacious crime was likened to the magnitude of stealing, say, the Jules Rimet Trophy or, perhaps, the Vince Lombardi. Media commentators simply couldn't understand why somebody would be daft enough to steal something so instantly recognisable. The scrap value alone simply didn't warrant the potential jail time if caught, and any likely buyers in the black market would have been few and far between as it wasn't exactly something that could be displayed on your mantelpiece. It was simply too hot to handle.

The security arrangements at the museum weren't exactly cutting-edge, it'd be fair to suggest. But even then, to execute the theft still required a certain level of criminal sophistication. The perpetrator had scaled the exterior wall of the building to gain entry via a lift shaft — opening and progressing through several locked doors in the process. That was all before the actual challenge of removing the trophy from its display and then having it away on their toes without being seen. This was not the modus operandi of a two-bit novice thief. This was the work of a master criminal who knew exactly what they were doing and precisely what they were looking for.

The theft had also cast a long shadow over the year's TT festival, which was due to commence shortly. For those competing, the thirty-seven point seven-three miles long circuit represented the ultimate test for both man and machine. The majority of which weren't in this game for the prize money, which, compared to other sports — such as football — was peanuts, relatively speaking. Those brave enough to venture over the start line on Glencrutchery Road were there to experience and enjoy the ultimate challenge in motorsport. And there was no more incredible honour than standing on the top step after winning the blue-riband race — the Senior TT — to lift the Marquis de Mouzilly St Mars trophy. That, at present, was sadly looking like an unlikely outcome unless the perpetrator could be apprehended, and quickly!

The Isle of Man government were beside themselves over the incident. After all, the trophy had been stolen on their watch with the resulting publicity not overly complimentary. This was a national crisis. An unmitigated disaster that needed resolving before the start of the TT races where even more eyes would be upon this sleepy little island in the middle of the Irish Sea. Sure, the TT would continue, regardless, but, like a child seeing Santa getting dressed at the shopping mall, drinking whiskey, the magic would wane, somewhat.

One significant advantage for Drexel being formally appointed to investigate the theft was access to the ongoing intelligence from both the police and insurance company. Powerful resources that, unfortunately, Sam and co wouldn't have direct access to.

Meanwhile, back at Eyes Peeled HQ, Sam was feeling the onset of a migraine from banging his head against a brick wall, figuratively speaking.

"I don't know what the hell Drexel's up to," Sam said, removing his coat, throwing it to the floor. He stomped down on it like it was on fire such was his frustration. His rowdy entrance, however, was largely ignored on account of the others in the office being occupied on the phone. Sam collapsed into his seat, rubbing his temples, practising his new yoga breathing techniques, designed for a moment of stress, such as this.

"I owe you a large one," Tom declared into his phone, nodding happily. He paused for a moment, listening further to what was

CHAPTER SEVEN – A THREE-HORSE RACE

being said. "Sure," Tom replied. "I'll have a word, but just make sure to keep us updated, yeah?" he added, bringing the call to a conclusion with a smug grin on his chops. "That was DI Rump," Tom explained for the newly arrived Sam. Tom left his chair and parked his right bum cheek on the corner of Sam's desk before adding, "Rump's more than happy to share any police intel with us!" he said, offering and receiving a fist pump from his boss.

"Amazing!" Sam said, his stress appearing to ease.

"I know what old Rump's up to," Tom said. "He's getting close to retirement and is probably thinking about his measly pension."

Sam's jaw swung open. "I'm not bribing him," Sam replied immediately. "No way, José!"

Tom waved away the suggestion. "It's not that, Sam. He's probably seeing himself working with us when he retires. You know, top-up his pension a little. Also, he confided that the police department is getting it in the ear from the Chief Minister, big time. They want this case sorted post-haste. By utilising us, also, they're getting four extra investigators at no additional cost to them."

"That also puts us on a level playing field with Drexel," Abby, who'd concluded her own call, chipped in.

"So, anything useful we can use?" Sam asked, hopeful and perking up somewhat.

Tom nodded in the affirmative, referring to the scribbled notes he'd taken. "Sure," he said, trying to make sense of his own writing.

"Okay," Tom began, taking a breath. "In no particular order. The CCTV in the museum has given them nothing concrete to go on. There were no fingerprints left behind anywhere at the crime scene. All vehicles leaving the island are now being stopped and searched. They've had several phone calls from the public with various lines of enquiry ongoing. Rump confirmed he'd keep us appraised of and updated in that regard. Oh, and one caller advised they were awoken by a misfiring car engine shortly before the museum alarms sounded. Finally, Rump did confide that the police have regular catch-ups with Drexel and he's apparently also completely in the dark, at this stage." Tom wiped his brow with an exaggerated sigh.

"Great work," Sam said. "Drexel being no further forward at least clarifies what I saw him doing all morning."

"And was that also the reason you were jumping on your coat when you came in?" Abby asked, entering into the conversation and blowing Sam a kiss.

Sam grabbed the air kiss floating in his direction and, once caught, placed it against his cheek. "It's that bloody Popek," Sam confided, lowering his head in frustration. "I've been following him all morning and—"

"Following Drexel?" Abby asked, in a tone suggesting this was something he'd promised he wouldn't do.

"He did it to me first," Sam said, with the assured logic of a stroppy six-year-old child. "Anyway, it was a complete waste of time and turned out to be a wild goose chase. I'd hoped he might be following up on some decent leads which we could benefit from. But it appears he's still working on his pet detective business rather than actually looking for the missing trophy."

"And you know this, how…?" Tom asked.

Sam opened up the camera roll on his mobile phone, handing it over for inspection. "When Drexel went to the bakery, I snuck up and took some photos through the rear window of his van," Sam explained.

"Is that a…" Tom asked, moving his head closer to the screen. He screwed up his eyes, pinching the screen to the maximum magnification. "Is that a… parrot?"

"I dunno," Sam said. "It had wings and made a bloody racket whatever it was. I'm also guessing that it was probably worth a chunky reward from whoever lost or misplaced it. More money heading into his back pocket, no doubt. I almost considered breaking into the van and nicking it."

"This is positive news," Abby said, eager to lift spirits.

"What? That I didn't kidnap a parrot?" Sam asked.

Abby shot Sam a look. "No, silly. Think about it. The police, so far, have nothing to go on, and Drexel doesn't appear to either. Otherwise, he wouldn't be working on missing parrots, now would he?"

CHAPTER SEVEN – A THREE-HORSE RACE

"Go on," Sam ventured, eager to hear more.

"Well, that's about it," Abby said. "But, we've got just as much chance of solving this case as Drexel has. Including the police, there are currently three horses in this investigative race, and we're all neck and neck at the moment."

"Not quite!" Suzie said, removing her headset as she stood. It was remarkable that the hippy-inspired daisy chain she'd painted on her forehead remained unsmudged. "Eyes Peeled is now ahead by a nose in this three-horse race," Suzie announced with a confident smile and a snap of her fingers. "Yours truly," she said, introducing herself with her hand, "has just uncovered someone with a solid motive to steal our missing trophy."

"Who?" Tom asked.

Suzie deliberately held onto her response, building the tension. She whistled a happy tune, taking a moment to inspect the chipped yellow varnish on her index finger.

"Suzie!" Abby said. "Spill it!"

"Okay, okay," Suzie conceded, moving to the printer to collect what she'd printed. "Sam, I suspect you'll recognise this chap?" she asked, holding up the printout for all to see.

"It's the antique dealer, Quentin Thrumbolt," Sam confirmed. "But, the police already gave him a clean bill of health?"

"Correct," Suzie said. "The police didn't suspect his involvement in the stolen bronze busts. However, just look at what he's standing next to in this photograph I found online."

Suzie received three blank faces in return as the rest of the office moved in for a closer look.

Abby was first to offer up a suggestion. "A vase... no... maybe a... sorry don't know," Abby said, looking to her colleagues for a more educated guess, which didn't arrive.

"That," Suzie began on her big reveal, tapping the page in her hand. "That is a diamond-encrusted horse racing trophy from the eighteenth century. This photograph was taken for the catalogue of an auction coordinated by our friend, Quentin Thrumbolt. Quentin's firm has brokered the sale of dozens of precious and valuable artefacts, including... rare trophies. So, the police are satisfied that Quentin wasn't involved in the stolen bronze busts, but..."

Sam took a sharp intake of breath, digesting this revelation. After a few seconds, he slapped his hand down on the table. "I bloody knew there was something shifty about that bloke."

"Mmm," Abby entered in. "The Senior TT Trophy gets nicked about the same time that Quentin appears on the scene. That cannot be a coincidence? Great work, Suzie."

"Why thank you," Suzie replied with a dainty curtsy.

"Thrumbolt didn't strike me as a professional cat burglar," Sam said. "A bit of a puss–"

"Sam!" Abby said, cutting him off mid-curse.

Tom had been mulling over the suggestion of Quentin being responsible for the theft of the trophy. "You know," he entered into the discussion, "there's one thing on my mind," he said, caressing his chin.

"Which is?" Suzie asked.

Tom narrowed his eyes deep in thought. "If Quentin nicked the TT trophy then it's also likely he lied to the police about him buying grandfather clocks rather than the stolen bronze busts," he put forth.

"Which would also confirm why Sir Barrington didn't want us near this case," Abby replied. "If they were in cahoots all along, they wouldn't want Sam getting too close for comfort."

"It's the first time I've been fired for being too efficient," Sam remarked.

"Okay," Suzie said, wheeling in the whiteboard, quickly retrieved from the meeting room. In an impressive flurry, she summarised their discussion in note form. Suzie did like to be organised. "So," she said, pointing to the two caricatures she'd drawn at the top of the board. "In *The Case of the Brazen Burglar*, we still think we have two potential suspects, even if the police don't. Sir Barrington Hedley-Smythe and Quentin Thrumbolt," she added, this time writing the word suspects beneath each head that she'd drawn. "Also," she continued, tapping her pen on Quentin's image. "Mr Thrumbolt

CHAPTER SEVEN – A THREE-HORSE RACE

is now also in the frame for the stolen Senior TT Trophy, yeah?" she added, drawing a crude picture of a trophy beneath his head.

Sam couldn't contain his grin in response to Suzie's summary. "Yeah! You know, this also means there's still a chance of a finder's fee from the Brazen Burglar case if we can pin it on the two of them."

"And also the Senior TT case!" Suzie added, with a confident tap of her marker pen on the whiteboard.

Sam walked over to retrieve his well-trodden coat, then extended his arm like he was inviting Abby to dance. "Shall we?" he asked, with the hint a bow.

"Lead on," Abby said, grabbing her own coat. "To where, exactly?"

"I'm not entirely sure," Sam said. "But we could start at Hedley-Smythe's house. I know I shouldn't take work so personally, but I would take great delight in seeing that pompous old duffer behind bars for insurance fraud!"

CHAPTER EIGHT
A Barrel of Hogwash

Each year, around late May, the Isle of Man went through something of a metamorphosis. Nearly fifty thousand race fans were soon to invade these magnificent shores as the Viking raiders had done a thousand years earlier. This time, fortunately, there were no axes, and pillaging was, for the large part, unlikely. The arriving cohort would be armed only with their beer money for a couple of weeks, a giddy sense of apprehension, and for the more optimistic of the bunch a generous supply of sunscreen for the hours they'd be sat trackside.

With each arriving boat, the island's population swelled a little further as did the decibel level. The scent of engine oil and sound of exhaust pipes filled the air and, soon, ordinarily sedate country roads would evolve to create the most famous race track on earth.

It was remarkable, then, to consider that the island's infrastructure had to cater for normal everyday life one minute, and then at the flick of a switch, transform into a racing circuit. To describe it as a logistical challenge was something of an understatement, all things considered.

The first week of the fortnight-long festival consisted of qualifying practice sessions each evening, ahead of a full week of races. Roads were required to be closed each time, with thousands of marshals deployed the length of the track, emergency services coordinated, and the public still had to have the ability to conduct their everyday lives while all of this was going on.

The weight of this considerable burden was, for a large part, absorbed by the Isle of Man's Head of Motorsport, Sidney Postlethwaite, a career civil servant approaching the twilight of his distinguished career and who was, desperately, trying to avoid being remembered for one unsavoury incident...

"Found your trophy yet?" another comic genius heckled, as Sidney made his way through the paddock at the rear of the TT Grandstand.

Sidney bit his lip, close to telling the witty observer to sod right off. But, he was a public servant, after all. "We've got our very best people on it," he replied instead, in a more tactful fashion. Unfortunately, at least for Sidney, it was a challenge to pass through a crowd unnoticed, on account of his being at least six foot six inches tall with a generous covering of snow-white hair. Ordinarily, he immensely enjoyed the attention he received at this time of the year, but not now. Not with every joker eager to take the piss at his expense.

"No respite, boss?" enquired his personal assistant, Catlin, once inside his office.

Sidney fell into his chair, placing his feet on his desk. "Honestly, every bugger is a comedian at the moment, Caitlin. I've only walked from my car to here. What's that? Three hundred metres or so, and I must have had twenty smart-arsed remarks already. If that trophy doesn't show up soon, then heads are going to roll over this."

Sidney was also acutely aware that his scalp was likely the first to be claimed if heads did begin to roll as he suggested. As the man at the helm of the TT operation, Sidney had signed off on the trophy being released for display in the first place as he'd done every previous year without incident. Additionally, he'd rubber-stamped the security arrangements at the museum. No one man was bigger than the TT and the powers that be wouldn't want anything to tarnish its reputation. Something that the stolen trophy was currently doing on a global scale. The same powers that be would soon require a

CHAPTER EIGHT – A BARREL OF HOGWASH

scapegoat and Sidney knew they wouldn't be looking too far beyond his office door for a suitable candidate.

"Anything from the police?" Sidney asked, running his hands through his hair.

Caitlin shook her head. "No, sorry, Sid. The Chief Constable did offer his assurances that they're doing all they can. Pulling out all the stops, he said."

Sidney puffed out his cheeks. "Wonderful! They're doing all they can to find it. This being the same Chief Constable who couldn't even find his way out of a broom cupboard without getting lost. So, forgive me if I don't hold my breath. Caitlin, this is a bloody disaster. We're now the laughingstock of the sporting world, and if that trophy doesn't turn up in time for the Senior TT, then we may as well pack our bags."

"*We*?" Caitlin asked, glancing up from her monitor.

Sidney appeared wounded by the question. "We're the dream team," he suggested. "I didn't think you'd want to carry on without me? Solidarity and all that, yeah?"

Caitlin tilted her head, giving the outward appearance that she was, at least, mulling the decision over. "Mmm, I kinda need the cash, Sid. See, I've just taken out a loan for my new hot tub, so... you know," she explained, returning her attention to her computer so as not to invite further discussion on her career choice or hot tub purchase. "Oh," she added as an afterthought, "don't forget that you're hosting the delegation visiting from the Isle of Wight at eleven."

"I'm bloody not!" Sidney snapped back, swinging his legs off his desk and sitting bolt upright at the very suggestion. "I told the Tourism Minister at the time that he could bugger off if he thought I was going to host that lot around here." Sidney turned on his monitor. "I'll even show you the email where I told the minister what a daft idea it was." Caitlin didn't appear particularly enthusiastic or bothered, either way, now hiding from view behind her screen.

"Honestly," Sidney continued, now several steps up his soapbox. "Why on God's green earth would we want to show another island how we run things when they're hoping to set up their own race in direct competition with us? It's ludicrous, is what it is!"

Caitlin didn't appear overly convinced by his vigorous protests. "Sid, it's all about fostering relationships with another island and promoting mutual tourism. Oh, and a whacking great consultancy fee, apparently. Besides, It's not exactly a competition, Sid. I mean, the Isle of Wight TT is going to operate at a completely different time of the year, and it's not really on the same scale."

"For now," Sidney said. "But do we really want them snapping at our heels, actually helping them in the process? It's taken us over a hundred years to get this place running like a well-oiled machine, and—"

"Apart from our missing trophy," Caitlin ventured, with a grin.

"You can have that," Sidney said, before continuing, "And don't forget, there are only so many advertisers, sponsors, and competitors to go around. The Isle of Wight might not be a competitor at the moment, but, you mark my word, they'll have designs on what we've spent a century perfecting. For that reason, the Tourism Minister can kiss my—"

"Good morning, Minister," Caitlin said, cutting Sidney off mid-sentence.

Sidney spun around in his chair, ashen-faced. "Magnificent, Caitlin," he said, relieved to see there was nobody stood in the doorway. "You nearly had me then," he added, with a nervous grin.

"Nearly?" Caitlin scoffed. "I thought you were about to start crying for a moment," she said, laughing. "Anyway, it doesn't matter why the Tourism Minister made an agreement with the Isle of Wight, does it. If he wants us to collaborate, then that's what we need to do, no? Look, Sid... no disrespect, but I'm not sure you want to be pissing off the minister further, you know, especially after the stolen trophy situation?"

Sidney replied with a series of petulant grumbling noises. He knew Caitlin was correct, of course. His relationship with his paymasters had often been frosty, but, of late, it was approaching the

CHAPTER EIGHT – A BARREL OF HOGWASH

Ice Age, so he consigned himself to doing what he needed to in hosting the Isle of Wight contingent.

"I'll tell you one thing, Caitlin," Sidney said, once he'd finally stopped whinging. "I'll toe the party line on this one, but if the minister thinks I need to be cordial to that stuck-up tart running their committee then he's got another—"

"Hello, Minister," Caitlin said, again cutting Sidney off mid-sentence.

Sidney was starting to wish he'd now closed the door behind him.

"Sidney," offered the gruff voice of the Tourism Minister stood in the open doorway with a stern-faced woman on his right. "I'd like to formally introduce you to, *ahem*, Tamara Urquhart. Chair of the Isle of Wight road racing committee."

"A pleasure," Sidney advised, jumping out of his seat with his hand extended. "I hope you had an enjoyable flight over?" he asked, receiving a thousand-yard death stare in return.

"Have you found your trophy?" Tamara asked, with no attempt to conceal her contempt.

After a long and, on occasion, distinguished career, old Sidney was well versed at working with cantankerous, hairy-arsed politicians. Often, to survive in this game for this long, elbows had to be at their sharpest in what was often a dog-eat-dog world. Dealing with Tamara Urquhart was, however, an entirely different proposition altogether. Simply put, she was terrifying. Of modest build, in her early thirties, with an impeccable understated dress sense, she was sharp as a tack and fiercely imposing to boot.

To make amends for the earlier stuck-up tart reference, Sidney had turned the charm dial up to maximum and was performing the role of obliging host, admirably. Tamara was cordial enough, but it was clear to Sid that she was there for one thing and one thing only. This was her golden opportunity to learn from the masters about the art of operating a successful road race on a global scale.

The Isle of Wight was the new kid on the block in racing terms. Their aspirations were wildly ambitious and such projects, inevitably, didn't come cheap. A consortium of financial backers, including Tamara, had according to press reports pumped an eyewatering amount of cash into ensuring their project was a commercial success. It was no wonder, then, that Tamara embraced the opportunity to grill Sidney on every operational detail throughout the day.

Her desire for the minutia was quite remarkable. She was a sponge, and there was no time or inclination for small talk on her part. The rest of her loyal delegation followed behind her, like ducklings. The casual observer could indeed be forgiven for thinking this was a royal visit such was her regal aura and general grovelling from those around her.

To give Sidney his due, he equipped himself flawlessly throughout. He was equal to all of the questions posed to him, and with the educational tour drawing to a close, Tamara even appeared to be thawing in her attitude to him.

"You know," Tamara said, taking a further walk up the pit lane, "there's not much about racing that you don't know. Well, apart from how to find a trophy." She added this with the merest suggestion of a smile that Sidney was relieved to see.

Tamara stopped to appreciate the famous TT scoreboard across the road from where they stood. It was easy to drift away and imagine the hopes and dreams that it'd been a witness to for over one-hundred years. After a period of quiet contemplation, she turned, looking up to the exceptionally tall Sidney.

"Why don't you join us?" Tamara asked with a deadpan expression.

Sidney smiled awkwardly like he had a touch of wind. He assumed he'd drifted off and missed the first part of the question. "For... dinner?" he asked, unsure what else she could be inviting him to.

Tamara narrowed her eyes, glancing down to her watch. "No, not for dinner," she replied. Tamara looked over her shoulder to the suited chap stood diligently behind her. That simplest of glances

CHAPTER EIGHT – A BARREL OF HOGWASH

enough for him to know it was time to leave and that he should open the door of the black BMW that'd pulled up. Tamara returned her attention to Sidney. "We need a director of operations," she said. "To run our Isle of Wight TT festival," she added, handing him her business card.

"Wh-what?" Sidney stuttered in response. "You're serious?" Sidney asked. "Even after the stuck-up tart thing, earlier? And also the missing trophy?"

"Come and work with us, Mr Postlethwaite," she said, happy enough to overlook both of those points. "You'll be part of a new adventure, in on the ground floor. We need the best on board," she added. "What we're doing is one of the most significant investments in motorsport for a generation. Join us, and you'll be a pioneer."

Tamara didn't wait for a response to her proposition. "I appreciate your hospitality," she said, climbing into the car.

Sidney waved to her, open-mouthed, and somewhat taken aback by the surreal events of the day. The rear passenger window wound down to reveal Tamara staring dead ahead. "I heard your present contract is under strain. So, don't take too long to think about it," she said, before giving her driver a nod of the head and with that they were away.

Sidney watched the BMW disappear from view, presumably heading towards the airport. The day had left him drained yet intrigued. The short walk back to his office meant navigating hordes of people enjoying the party atmosphere at the rear of the grandstand, many of whom would be well lubricated by this time of day. Sidney didn't even react to the several trophy-based jokes hurled in his direction for his mind was, right now, elsewhere.

"How'd it go?" Caitlin asked him, once back inside.

Sidney shrugged his shoulders, pressing out his lower lip. "It was an experience," he replied, taking a seat.

"Oh?"

"Tamara is certainly an acquired taste, but exceptionally astute. When I first heard about this Isle of Wight initiative, I thought it was all a barrel of hogwash."

"And it's not?"

Sidney considered his response for a moment before replying. "I don't think so, Caitlin. From what she revealed, the amount of investment is staggering. Also, Tamara Urquhart doesn't strike me as the sort to get herself involved in something that's going to fail."

"So she's not a stuck-up tart now?" Caitlin asked, replaying his earlier words.

Sidney knew Tamara had left, but still offered a cautionary glance towards the door. "That's no way to talk about my new boss," he said with a grin.

"Eh?"

"Don't worry about it," Sidney said, waving his statement away. "It was just something that came up in conversation." He leaned forward to peel a yellow Post-It note from the screen of his monitor. "Who's this?" he asked, looking at the number written on it.

"Oh yeah. It was somebody who popped in while you were out gallivanting. Some chap who was hoping to have a word with you."

"About?" Sidney asked, having a stretch like a contented cat.

"The missing trophy," Caitlin added.

"Yeah!" he said, perking up. "Has he found it?" he asked in hope rather than expectation.

"He didn't say, Sid."

"What's his name?" Sidney asked, turning it over to see if the name was, perhaps, written on the other side, which it wasn't.

"Oh, sorry!" she said, closing one eye, struggling to recall. "Drexel something-or-other... said he was a private investigator."

"Thanks, Caitlin. I think he's the one the insurance company appointed," Sidney said. "Anyway, you get yourself off, and I'll see you in the morning," he added, reaching for his phone.

"Hi, Drexel, this is Sidney Postlethwaite," he said once the call connected. He listened for several seconds before his eyebrows raised in reaction to what he was hearing. "Several leads, indeed? Well, that's terrific news and encouraging. I don't need to tell you how vital that trophy is for the island so, please, do keep me updated, Drexel. Oh, and great work."

CHAPTER EIGHT – A BARREL OF HOGWASH

Sidney walked over to shut his office door, having a cursory glance up and down the corridor outside before he did so. Once satisfied the building was empty, he returned to his desk, retrieved a silver hip flask from his top drawer, taking a generous slug of the liquid inside.

He scrolled through his mobile phone contacts, easing back in his chair with his phone pressed to his ear.

"Hey, it's Sid," he said, then waited for a response. "Sidney Postlethwaite," he added. "*Sidney Postlethwaite* about the *TT trophy!*" he said, shaking his head. "Oh, I'm pleased you remember me," he added, with no attempt to hide the annoyance in his voice. "Listen, I've just spoken with Drollox," he said before presumably being corrected. "Oh, right. Drexel. Anyway, from what he's just told me, it sounds like he's making real traction regarding the trophy. I thought I should let you know? Also, you won't forget your old friend, Sidney, when all this is over? About how I've been so helpful throughout?"

Sidney listened for a few seconds further, enjoying what he heard judging by the grin emerging. "That's wonderful," he replied. "You scratch my back, and I scratch yours. Marvellous!"

Sidney replaced the phone in his hand with his hipflask. "Cheers!" he said, toasting himself. "It's not turned out to be too bad a day, after all."

CHAPTER NINE
A Song and a Dance

Sam held his mobile phone with a vice-like grip, almost in danger of shattering the screen. "Absolute tosspot," he said, staring down at the display. "Drexel bloody Popek's face is all over Facebook again, Abby."

Abby lowered her binoculars, placing her head through the open passenger window. "He's not found the trophy, has he?"

Sam shook his head. "No, thankfully. But, according to his latest status update, he has just reunited a grateful owner with his missing parrot. The post has over three thousand likes, and the comments are making Popek out to be some sort of modern-day saint. Honestly, that treacherous git is everywhere I look at the moment. I wouldn't mind, but the owner of the parrot is Rupert Templeton. We've worked with his company for the last five years, and it seems that even he's now deserted us for Drexel."

"Every dog has its day," Abby advised, returning to her surveillance.

"Yeah, and he'd probably also find that if it went missing," Sam suggested with a sigh. "Anything yet?" he asked, his eyes following in the general direction of Abby's binoculars.

"Nope," she replied, slowly, not wanting to disrupt her focus. "He's still just sat there, staring. Perhaps he is just out for a nice drive to admire the scenery, after all?"

"Mmm," Sam replied unconvinced. "Sir Barrington doesn't strike me as the type to head out for a drive in the country on his own. I'll bet you a steak dinner that he's here for a cosy meeting with his partner in crime, Quentin Thrumbolt."

Sam and Abby had both been sat in their car, waiting patiently, observing Sir Barrington for two long and particularly arduous days. Those who thought the life of a private investigator was glamorous, clearly hadn't experienced the thrill of sitting in a cramped car for hour after hour, hungry and having to go for a wee in an empty Lucozade bottle (now, not so empty).

Sir Barrington had something of an active social life, they came to realise, with him leaving his house several times, both days. Tailing him, each and every time, was Sam and Abby, hopeful of finding him up to mischief. But... no. So far, his excursions had been relatively mundane tasks and certainly nothing that, say, a master criminal would concern themselves with. The old boy didn't even break a speed limit, although the appearance of his canary yellow corduroy trousers was likely committing a crime somewhere, Sam observed.

They both agreed that the surveillance operation had been a total bust. But, like an angler with an empty net, they talked themselves into one additional effort when Sir Barrington ventured out, once more.

A shower and change of underwear would need to wait, at least for the duration of a further stakeout. This time, Sir Barrington ventured out in a slightly more understated vehicle, a 1960's green Land Rover, with an engine sounding like an old rusting lawnmower. Sam assumed this to be an attempt to remain incognito, but the muddy and uneven farm track where he was now parked up was more likely the reason for selecting a sturdier vehicle, they reasoned.

Baldwin Valley is a rural and relatively quiet area of the island, surrounded on all sides by dramatic green countryside with a reservoir at its heart. It was the unusual choice of destination, up a farm track, in this remote location, that offered Sam and Abby the indication something of interest could be going down.

CHAPTER NINE – A SONG AND A DANCE

Sam's fragile Ford Fiesta wouldn't have had a snowball in hell's chance of navigating the steeply rutted lane and to even attempt it without revealing their presence would have been impossible. Instead, Sam parked up in a position of treelined cover, near to St Luke's church, on the opposite side of the valley. It was a distant view from this vantage point, but with the assistance of Abby's binoculars, they were able to keep Sir Barrington under observation and, crucially, anyone else he might meet.

"Eurgh!" Abby said in abject disgust. "Sir Barrington's out of his car and now having a pee in a bush." She handed the binoculars through the passenger window to Sam. "You can keep watch, Sam. I think I've seen *more* than enough of him today," she said, rubbing her offended eyes.

Sam hopped out of the car, kissed his beloved on the cheek, and assumed responsibility for the surveillance, with him now leaning casually against the passenger door. He pressed the binoculars to his eyes. "You know what, Abby?" he said, adjusting the focus. "Ordinarily, doing this can get a bit boring. Sat in the arse end of nowhere with only the trees and sheep for company. But, it's not like that with you here."

He paused for a few moments before continuing. "What I suppose I'm trying to say, Abby is that any time I spend with you, I enjoy. It doesn't matter if it's in a fancy fine-dining restaurant or, perhaps, trudging through a field full of cow shit following up on a lead. You make me a happier person." Sam smiled, just from the thought of her. "Abby," he added as a follow-up when he didn't receive anything in return. Sam looked through the open window to the driver's seat where Abby had reclined the chair, now snoring gently. "Sleep tight," he said, as it had been an exceptionally long and uncomfortable couple of days. "I've got things under control," he added, offering a salute for no logical reason.

Sam returned his attention to the job at hand, homing in on Sir Barrington who, fortunately, had placed Sir Barrington Jr back into his yellow trousers, now stood looking at his watch.

"Someone stood you up?" whispered Sam, running his eyes across the neighbouring fields and the parts of the farm track unobscured by trees.

It was a little after noon, and Sam's stomach was starting to rumble. "Come on," he said, getting increasingly impatient. Just then he caught a flash of movement in his peripheral vision and, like a sniper, adjusted his stance, training in on the target. His heart raced until he realised it was only a sailor pushing his boat out from its mooring on the reservoir below.

Such was the quality of Abby's binoculars that Sam was able to zoom right in and observe the look of anticipation on the man's face. Sam could now see that several other boats were also being readied. It was, perhaps, a newcomers day at the sailing club as a fair few of the other participants didn't appear overly confident in their abilities with one lady in a furious struggle with her life jacket.

The sailor Sam observed, pushed off from his mooring then immediately stood with assured confidence like a young Lord Nelson eager, it would appear, to have the breeze blowing in both his face and sails. Sam figured this fellow was likely an instructor, out to show the fresh recruits exactly how it should be done. Until that is, the boom sideswiped him, taking him clean off his feet like he was a participant on the TV show *Ninja Warrior*.

Sam chuckled to himself as the hapless sailor plunged, headfirst, into the drink. The subsequent efforts in reboarding his vessel, without success, provided Sam with additional light entertainment. Every time he gripped onto his boat, it tilted towards him, sending him back into the water. The boat acted like a stubborn horse that didn't want to be ridden, and with each failed attempt, the man's strength weakened, resulting in the rescue craft being deployed to offer a helping hand or, perhaps, a gentle shove. "Not for me," Sam declared, returning his attention from whence it came.

"Foxtrot Oscar!" Sam shouted. He darted his head this way and that, but Sir Barrington's vehicle wasn't where Sam had last seen it. Panicked, Sam lowered the binoculars to see if a non-magnified view of the situation would assist and, thankfully, it did. His ears first

CHAPTER NINE – A SONG AND A DANCE

picked up the grumbling sound of an engine which directed his eyes to the vehicle leaving the farm track, rejoining the road.

Sam utilised the binoculars to confirm that the Land Rover was on the move. "Abby," Sam said without breaking his attention away. Sam released one hand, banging it on the roof of his car. "Abby, wake up!"

"I'm awake," she said unconvincingly, climbing out of the car with bleary eyes. "What's up?"

"Sir Barrington's on the move," Sam said.

"Who'd he meet?" Abby asked with a sense of urgency. "What did you see?"

Sam was reluctant to admit he'd been watching a sailor falling from a boat rather than keeping watch. "Ehm, not sure," he replied. "They moved under cover of the trees," he offered by way of explanation.

"Darn!" Abby said, straining her eyes in the direction of the slowly moving vehicle. "Well, is he alone in the car?"

Sam stopped breathing to steady his hands, attempting to answer her question. He followed the vehicle, aware that it would shortly move out of visual range. "He's alone," Sam said once he had a clear view of the passenger seat.

Abby pressed her hands on her hips. "So he did at least meet with someone?" she asked. "As you did say that *they* moved under cover of the trees."

Sam started breathing again, which was fortunate, as he was getting dizzy. "Well... the thing is," he moved to explain. "I didn't, actually... entirely... now you mention it..." he stumbled on, about to confess to his distraction. Until...

"There!" Sam said, using one hand to point across the valley. "There's someone on a mountain bike riding down the same farm track." Sam moved forward a pace. "They're going too fast for me to make out their face. Whoever it is *must* have been the person meeting Sir B?"

"Let's go!" Abby said, jumping into the passenger seat without hesitation.

Sam didn't need to, but he rolled across the width of the bonnet. He'd seen it once in an episode of *Dempsey and Makepeace* and always thought it was something he'd like to do, and, right now offered him an opportune moment.

"What's the plan?" he asked, thrusting his keys into the ignition.

"Dunno," Abby replied. "Just try and catch up with that mountain bike in the first instance. We need to know who Sir B was meeting and why they were doing it in the middle of nowhere. Nice slide, by the way."

"I've secretly been practising," he said, before moving back to the matter in hand. "I'm putting my money on Quentin Thrumbolt being on that bike," Sam said, giving the accelerator a little more pressure than usual. "I'll bet he's ditched his fancy suit and taken to two wheels to put any prying eyes off the scent."

The difficulty for Sam was that the country roads were narrow, often single-track traffic in parts, so gaining speed was a challenge unless you wanted to end up embedded in a grass verge. For that reason alone, a mountain bike was ideal for traversing the Manx countryside.

"There!" Abby said, pointing to a break in the trees. "I caught a glimpse of a bike."

"There's a steep hill up ahead," Sam said. "We should hopefully catch up then, assuming this car can also make it up."

Sam sped through the small village of West Baldwin, receiving an angry shaken fist from a local due to his excessive speed. "Sorry, but I'm on a pursuit," he said, for nobody's benefit as it was only Abby who could hear him anyway.

"They're already halfway up the hill," Abby said.

"That thing's bloody shifting," Sam said, planting his foot to the floor. "We're either following Mark Cavendish, or that's one of those electric bikes?"

Abby took her phone from her pocket. "Try and get alongside, Sam. I'll take a sneaky video of them as we go past."

"Easier said than done," Sam replied, shifting up a gear. "This car's got the pulling power of Quasimodo."

CHAPTER NINE – A SONG AND A DANCE

Gradually, with his engine screaming, Sam gained on the bike, indicated, then when safe to do so, overtook, slowly... eventually...

Abby held her phone to her ear, using the rear camera to discreetly record the target. "Mission accomplished," Abby said, staring dead ahead as they reached the brow of the hill.

"No need," Sam declared. "I know *exactly* who that was," he added, glancing in his rear-view mirror. "Drexel effin' Popek."

"You're sure?" Abby asked, taking a cautious view in the passenger wing mirror to see for herself.

"Yup," Sam said, waving exaggeratedly for Drexel's benefit. "And he's now eagerly extending a middle finger for our benefit," Sam added, returning the same finger-based gesture.

"He must have recognised us?" Abby asked, pointing out the obvious.

"Well, either that or he casually flips the bird to every car that passes him by. Wouldn't surprise me, knowing him."

Sam considered braking sharply so Drexel would, hopefully, power into the back of his car. It slightly concerned him as to how long this remained a genuine consideration.

"Maybe Drexel was just meeting Sir B to update him on the missing bronze busts? You know, like a progress report or something."

"Up a farm track in the middle of nowhere?"

"I know, I know," Abby replied. "I suppose I was just keeping an open mind, but, it does stink a bit, doesn't it."

"I'll tell you what else stinks," Sam offered.

"Us?"

"Yup!"

Smelly, hungry, and tired, Sam and Abby returned to their adorable little cottage. It was a delight, as always, to see the gentle waves lapping the shore on the beach opposite, and the welcome scent of the sea always reminded Sam he was home.

Sam removed the keys from the ignition, resting his head back and giving his neck a gentle rub. "Perhaps I should just go and get a proper job, Abby?"

Abby took hold of Sam's spare hand, giving it a squeeze. "Sam, you're an outstanding investigator and don't you forget it. We just need to get cleaned up and have a bite to eat. Perhaps a power nap, also, and you'll soon be back to your enthusiastic self and raring to go."

Sam appreciated the pep talk, but it didn't lift his sombre mood. "We've wasted what?" he asked. "Nearly forty hours and achieved the grand total of nothing. Well, at least I now know that sailing's not for me. But, aside from that, we're no closer to finding the..."

Sam had a habit of flaring his nostrils when deep in thought and, right now, you could have inserted a ten pence piece up each one with room to spare.

"Sam?" Abby pressed, in reaction to his far-away expression. "Everything okay?"

Sam rattled his fingers off the steering wheel, closing one eye such was the depth of his concentration. "Something's not working out," he declared, after prolonged consideration.

Abby put her hands to her face. "Sam?" she said. "I thought things were good between us?"

Sam didn't respond immediately, his nostrils still in an agitated state. "What?" he said when Abby's words eventually registered. "Oh no," he added, turning to face her. "We're good. We're more than good... *we're amazing*. In fact, Abby, every day I'm with you I feel like I'm a featherweight boxer in the heavyweight division. You are the most perfect thing I've ever had in my life or likely ever will. Trust me, we're fine." With that, Sam leaned across the seat for a kiss. "Well, they are from my side?" he said, smiling to invite a similar assurance that he was hopeful would be heading his way.

Abby smiled. "All good from my side too, Sam. So, if it's not us, then what's not working out?"

"I need to speak with Rupert Templeton," Sam said, reaching for his phone.

"You're not going to shout at him for taking his business to Drexel?"

CHAPTER NINE – A SONG AND A DANCE

"What... no. Of course not. Rupert's six foot three and owns a shotgun. He's not the sort of person you shout at," Sam added, looking up Rupert's number.

"I'll get inside and put the kettle on," Abby suggested. "I also need to jump in the shower, soon," she added, giving her pits a little sniff.

Abby left Sam to make his call, taking a moment to admire the floral display in their modest yet perfectly equipped garden. She caught sight of an errant weed that must have eluded her previous cull earlier in the week. "Gotcha," she said, reaching down, yanking it from its earthen bed in a practised, fluid motion. Unfortunately with weeds, once you spot one, you'll usually find several more of the critters keeping it company. As was the case, just now.

It was a rather splendid location where they lived. What they lacked in internal space was more than compensated for by having the seaside a stone's throw away. Sam often joked that he could be sat on the toilet holding his fishing rod and still be able to catch a fish for his tea, such was the proximity of the Irish Sea. Abby often joked, in return, that she didn't want to know what he did with his rod while in the confines of the toilet.

There was nothing more enjoyable than on a balmy summer's evening, sparking up the BBQ on the beach and partaking in a glass or two of something cold, watching the setting sun.

"Oh god," Abby said, yanking up another weed. "What if we lose this place?"

Abby was ordinarily full of optimism. For her, the glass wasn't half full, but positively overflowing, for the most part. Just then, however, the realisation of a mortgage secured on a failing business suddenly hit her as it had Sam a few weeks earlier. The life she was living and loving, right now, was her perfect slice of paradise and the prospect of losing it was, well, downright horrifying.

"Hey," Sam said, closing the car door, shaking her from her thoughts.

Abby held up a clump of weeds, giving them a gentle shake to illustrate her endeavours and explain the reason why the kettle wasn't boiling. "Well?" she asked.

Sam opened the iron gate, shaking his head in the process. "I knew something was up, Abby. Firstly, as I suspected, Rupert confirmed that Drexel *did* poach his business from us. Rupert was even pleasantly surprised to hear from me as Drexel, the devious tosser, even went as far as to say that we'd retired and planned on leaving the island!"

Abby tore the weeds in her hand in half. "I should have opened my door earlier and knocked him off his bike," she said snarling. "So, I presume there's a *secondly* to follow the *firstly*?"

Sam jumped up, taking a seat on the weathered barrel next to the front door, caressing his chin. "Secondly is a parrot," Sam replied, trying and failing to stifle a yawn.

"The what now?" Abby asked, assuming Sam to be a touch overtired and confused, maybe?

"A parrot," Sam replied, flapping his arms. "Remember that picture I took of the parrot in the back of Drexel's van?"

Abby nodded, encouraging further explanation. "Yes, from when you were out following him."

"Correct. Anyway, on Drexel's Facebook page," Sam continued, "he was recently making a song and dance about how he'd managed to find the parrot and reunite it with its owner in less than forty-eight hours. He was proud as Punch of that fact as I recall."

"That's pretty quick?" Abby said, but unsure where this was heading, exactly.

"Too quick," Sam said, "and the reason I wanted to call Rupert. He just told me that he'd noticed a smashed window and also that the parrot was missing from its cage last Tuesday, yeah. It's some sort of valuable rare breed, so he immediately got Drexel on the case with it. What with his impressive pet recovery rate."

"Yeah?"

"Well," Sam pressed on, "Drexel was on record as saying he'd managed to find the bird on Thursday and, as a result, claimed a reward of one thousand pounds."

CHAPTER NINE – A SONG AND A DANCE

Abby smiled blankly. She liked to offer support, particularly as Sam had been a touch fragile of late, but this conversation appeared to be going nowhere quickly. "Ok-ay. And that means...?"

"Well... I saw the same parrot in the back of Drexel's van on *Tuesday*. Tuesday being the same day as the parrot went missing. Not Thursday as he later claimed."

Abby allowed that snippet to digest for a few seconds before pretty much repeating back what she'd just been told. "Wait, so... the parrot goes missing on Tuesday, but Drexel doesn't announce another mission accomplished to the world until Thursday. Two days later. Even though you know for a fact, he had the parrot in his possession on Tuesday. I have that correct?"

"You are correct," Sam advised.

"Maybe he had his days mixed up?" Abby suggested. "Or you were confused? Maybe you didn't actually see Drexel on the Tuesday?"

"No," Sam said. "I know for sure it was a Tuesday as I... well... I had an appointment," he added, blushing and eager to the move the conversation forward. "It was just after I finished up that I started tailing Drexel."

"And Rupert is sure that it was two days later when the parrot was found?" Abby asked.

"One-hundred percent. So the question now remains, how did Drexel have a parrot in his possession on the same day it went missing?"

Ordinarily, it was Abby summarising an investigation, with Sam following diligently, albeit a minute or two behind. He enjoyed listening out for the cogs working overdrive in Abby's head.

"No way!" Abby said once she'd processed all of the information and the penny finally dropped.

"Yes, way!" Sam replied, really hoping they were both on the same page.

"Drexel Popek must have stolen the parrot in the first place," she added with a gasp loud enough to satisfy the gravity of the situation.

"Or it just happened to fly into the back of his van when he popped into the bakery," Sam added with a hint of sarcasm.

"The crafty bastard," Abby said, unleashing a rarely heard expletive. "What about all the other valuable and exotic pets he's miraculously found lately?"

Sam pressed out his bottom lip, offering a gentle shrug. "It appears that the island's finest pet detective is, in fact, the island's finest pet thief and pocketed a fortune in reward money in the process."

Abby ripped what was left of the weeds in her hand. "He's poached most of our business on the pretence of being an investigative genius! The devious little—"

Sam climbed down from his perch, eyes half-closed from sleep deprivation. "Come on," he said.

"To kick lumps out of Drexel?" Abby asked, spoiling for a scrap, it appeared.

Sam put his arm around his beloved. "Not yet, Abby. He can wait. First, we've got an appointment with the shower because we both stink."

"We could save water and time if we jumped in together?" Abby suggested with a wry smile.

"Your commitment to saving the environment is just one of the many reasons why I love you so much," Sam said, loosening his belt.

Abby stopped on a sixpence, eyes wide and filled with love. She shifted a step closer to Sam, moving her chin closer and nuzzling into Sam's chest. "Can I just put on record how that was some incredibly impressive detective work today! I told you that you were a brilliant detective, Sam Levy!"

"It wasn't half bad, was it?" Sam mused. "Oh," Sam said, raising his finger. "I've got it!"

"Got what?"

"The Seaside Detective Agency in, The Case of the Pilfered Parrot?"

"Mmm," Abby offered. "We'll pop it on the shortlist."

CHAPTER TEN
A Mist Rolls In

Trent Partridge could place considerable strain on knicker elastic from a good fifty metres away. With his mane of jet-black hair swept back in a bro flow and piercing green eyes, he sent knees aquiver wherever and whenever he appeared. This was a man who fell from the rugged good looks tree, hitting each and every branch on the way down. Throw into the mix the fact he was also a multi-millionaire world championship-winning motorcycle superstar, and you pretty much had your perfect specimen of manhood.

Trent wasn't visiting the island to compete, however. Aside from some brief commercial commitments for his sponsors and the race organisers, he was there to spectate alongside the thousands more who had a shared appreciation of this adrenaline-fueled spectacle. The TT could and did attract the biggest names in motorsport as visitors, simply because they wanted to experience and appreciate the mindboggling talent of the racers for themselves.

Riding a missile with over two hundred horsepower around the thirty-seven-odd mile course was difficult enough to comprehend even to those who made their living from the sport, like Trent.

All of the spectators, regardless of racing pedigree, were in awe of the riders. With over two hundred corners on each lap to negotiate, it was a minor miracle that they could even remember what was coming next, let alone covering it at race pace.

THE SEASIDE DETECTIVE AGENCY BOOK TWO

If you enjoyed watching an onboard racing lap on YouTube, you'd know it was a challenge to even keep up with the pace from the comfort of your armchair, what with each new corner approaching you at warp speed.

This wasn't a circuit where you had the safety of gravel trap to slow you down if you had an unfortunate spill. Here, the only things bringing you to a halt were likely going to be, unfortunately, a telephone box, tree, or some other solid and stationary object. It was for this reason the TT racers were revered so much by their racing family and army of supporters alike. They really were a special breed of men and women.

Trent soaked up the paddock atmosphere, relaxed, and with a smile planted on his mush that'd been there since his arrival. The race organisers were keen for Trent to schmooze the many wealthy sponsors in the hospitality area. However, for now, Trent was rather more at home mixing it with the great unwashed, as it were.

There would be time enough, he figured, for the corporate stuff. But, at least for now, he was happy to nurse a pint of lager in a plastic beaker, posing for photographs and autographing whatever was presented before him for signature.

The item presently thrust in his direction was an oversized breast belonging to a tittering brunette called Karen. "Sign this?" she asked, batting her eyelashes as her friend handed Trent a black marker pen to facilitate the request.

Trent handed his pint to Karen's mate, eager and willing to assist. After all, who was Trent to disappoint his adoring public? "I've a funny feeling this signature is going to take me a long time to finish," Trent offered with a cheeky wink, popping the cap off of the pen.

"You can write your phone number on there, also... if you like," Karen added, her eyelashes now fluttering quicker than a bee's wing.

Meanwhile, further up the paddock, someone else feeling a bit of a tit was Sidney Postlethwaite. Tasked with hosting several pre-arranged press conferences, the barrage of snide comments about his general organisational abilities and also the missing trophy was relentless.

CHAPTER TEN – A MIST ROLLS IN

"I-well-that is-what I mean to say is that—" Sidney stuttered, addressing a room of journalists assembled from the global press outlets. Old Sidney was being grilled by one particular sassy journalist who, like a dog with a bone, just wouldn't let the subject matter go.

"Surely," the feisty female journalist countered before Sidney could finish his sentence. "Surely the theft of this trophy has made the Isle of Man TT, and you, a laughingstock, no?"

"Well..." Sidney replied, running his finger under the collar of his blue shirt. A blue shirt that was resplendent with two sweat patches increasing in mass with each and every challenging question. "We're confident of securing the return of our missing trophy, shortly. We've got our very best people on it!"

This declaration prompted another salvo of questions from the baying mob eager, it would appear, to hang poor Sid out to dry.

"Look," Sidney continued, holding his hands out flat in front of him. "It's understandable to only focus on the negative, but... let's not forget that we've still got the racing to look forward to, yeah?"

Sidney ran his eyes around the press room, hoping for a friendly face amongst the frosty audience.

"Yes?" Sidney asked, pointing to the next journalist with his finger in the air.

"Wayne Snapper," announced the young lad, still with his finger in the air. "Road Racing Adventure magazine," he added, by way of introduction.

"My favourite magazine," Sidney replied, perhaps hoping a spot of buttering up would reduce the acerbic tone of the next question.

Wayne was a seasoned professional, however, and not one to succumb to such blatant flattery. "You've secured a visit from Trent Partridge, I understand?"

Sidney relaxed his shoulders a touch in anticipation of turning the conversation to something altogether more positive. "That's correct, Wayne. We're delighted to confirm that our special guest for today's race is none other than the World Champion Motor-"

"Bit desperate, isn't it?" Wayne chipped in.

Sidney's shoulders returned to their previous stress position. "Excuse me?"

Wayne slouched in his seat, chewing his pen causally. "Well..." he replied, with no attempt to disguise the contempt in his voice. "Is this not some sort of desperate, last-ditch effort, to get some positive PR on what's been a bit of an embarrassment? I imagine you've paid Trent a small fortune to secure his appearance, today? Mr Postlethwaite, this has to be a last hoorah to save your job, surely?"

Sidney appeared, for a brief moment, to be contemplating diving over the table to throttle the first journalist he could place his sweaty hands on. But, with his boss sat next to him and several video cameras present, he settled on a more upbeat approach. "Trent Partridge is one of the finest ambassadors in our sport," Sidney replied, collecting his papers together, poised to get the hell outta there. "And Trent's appearance today demonstrates that the Isle of Man TT is the most significant motorsport event on earth. Bar none!"

Now safely in the corridor and free from the vultures inside, Sidney moved his arms like a windmill, eager to get some air circulating around his damp patches.

"That was something of a car crash," Sidney's boss suggested, shaking his head in the process. The minister looked Sidney up and down, continuing with his gentle head shake.

Sidney screwed up his face with his left eye starting to twitch. "You could have jumped in at any time, Minister. That would have been nice. That would have been very nice, in fact. Quite helpful, even."

The Tourism Minister cleared his throat, unconcerned, it would appear, by the man at breaking point in front of him. "Sidney, this is turning into an unmitigated catastrophe for the Isle of Man, and I'm not sure how much I can—"

Sidney placed his palms on the minister's shoulders, cutting him off before he could finish his sentence. "I've managed to secure the attendance of Trent Partridge," Sidney said, tightening his grip slightly, crumpling fabric in the process. "*Trent... Partridge...*" Sidney added with raised eyebrows.

CHAPTER TEN — A MIST ROLLS IN

The minister flicked his eyes towards his shoulder, holding his mirthless gaze until the offending hands were removed.

"Sidney. You couldn't appease that lot, in there, even if you'd secured the services of His Holiness the Pope, riding a Moto Guzzi around the streets of Douglas, naked." The minister threw his thumb over his shoulder, cocking his head a touch. "They're out for blood. *Your* blood…"

"This'll all blow over, Minister," Sidney suggested. "As soon as something else comes along, we'll be yesterday's news."

"Sidney… Sidney… Sidney… You're a man of the world, yes? You know that once the press has their claws embedded in your back, then it's only a matter of time."

The minister didn't appear prepared to elaborate on his statement, instead turning his back, heading for the exit. The minister was content, it would seem, as long as those sharpened claws weren't heading in his direction.

Sidney extended his arms like a crazed zombie strangling an imaginary foe, grinding his teeth in the process.

"See you then!" Sidney called after the minister in an overly cheery tone, quite impressed — but, not surprised — at how the entire shitstorm had been placed entirely at his front door.

"Oh," the minister said over his shoulder, offering up what appeared to be an afterthought. He turned to face Sidney, caressing his jawbone between thumb and forefinger. "Sidney," he said, in a disappointed tone like a parent catching their child stealing biscuits. "Sidney, the TT is, of course, bigger than the two of us. I'm sure you'll agree?"

Which, when translated, meant bigger than just Sidney. No *we* or *us* in this, no sir! Sidney was acutely aware that if/when heads were going to roll, it would likely be the minister swinging the axe towards Sidney's neck.

"Yes, Minister," Sidney replied. "I can assure you that—"

But the minister was in no mood to listen, instead cutting straight across him. "Sidney, without the trophy, you're position is… well… I'm sure you know what I'm saying?"

THE SEASIDE DETECTIVE AGENCY BOOK TWO

Sidney nodded along agreeably. "Of course, Minister. I'm confident we'll have that trophy back, imminently."

The minister looked down to his watch. He often did that when bored with a conversation. "No... more... controversy," he said, slowly and deliberately. "Understood?"

"Understood," Sidney confirmed.

The moment the minister turned his back, Sidney began strangling the air, once again. There was a red fire extinguisher secured to the wall next to where Sidney stood which he stared longingly at. It was all he could do to not rip it off the wall, remove the release pin, and discharge the entire contents over the hyenas in the press briefing room.

"Ahh," he said with a contented sigh.

From inside the press room, he could hear chairs moving, indicating they were all packing up and likely to descend into the corridor any moment. He'd had quite enough of them for one day and so made good his exit, buggering off smartly to his next appointment, via the toilet to dry out his sodden armpits.

"Bastard trophy," he said, kicking the side door open, happily imagining it was Wayne Snapper's larynx his foot had just made contact with.

🔍

Due to poor visibility on the mountain section of the course, the Frank and Stan's Bucket List-sponsored Superbike race had been delayed for a little over two hours. One of the many island charms was the ability for the weather to change in a heartbeat. Glorious sunshine earlier in the day had given way to a heavy cloak of sea mist, resulting in the delay. The officials were, however, cheerily optimistic that a gentle breeze would soon see the fog on its way and permit the racing action to commence.

Trent Partridge had the enviable honour of waving the competitors away and then, after the race, presenting the trophy to the winner. All of which, of course, was a significant PR coup for Sidney & Co, who'd faced something of a challenging few weeks.

CHAPTER TEN – A MIST ROLLS IN

The short delay was a welcome benefit for Trent, due to the challenge he faced completing the short walk to the corporate hospitality tent. At every turn, giddy race fans prevented his progress, keen to have a photograph taken with their hero. The issue Trent faced — something he'd experienced first-hand — was that no matter how long he spent signing autographs, listening to inane anecdotes, and attending to every breast thrust in his direction, there would always be someone he'd end up disappointing. It was a physical impossibility to please everyone, no matter how hard he tried.

He'd enjoyed a marvellous day, so far. But several missed calls on his mobile phone suggested his attendance was required at the glitzy reception. With the drop of a shoulder and an impressive turn of pace, Trent was able to cut a path through the sea of people just as his phone burst into life, once more.

But the sponsors would need to be patient for just a little while longer. Two pints of splendid lager and several autograph-related delays were placing something of a strain on his bladder. He took a cautious glance over his shoulder and apart from a slack-jawed kid gawping in wonderment, the rest of his adoring flock dispersed — likely to secure a seat ahead of the racing action.

"Ah-ha," Trent said, feasting his eyes on the glorious vision of a public toilet sign up ahead. His flies were virtually unfastened by the time he reached the urinal, such was his anticipation of lightening the load, so to speak.

"How do?" he said cordially to the chap stood next to him as Trent Jr was released and put to work. His eyes rolled back in his head due to the sheer relief as the flow intensified. Such was the length of time it took for Trent to declare his mission a success, that at least two more visitors with the same intention, came and went.

With his hands washed, Trent exposed his teeth to ensure they were free from any remnants of his earlier cheeseburger. He sighed in frustration as his phone vibrated, once again, in his pocket distracting him from his oral inspection. "Bloody phones!" he said for the benefit of the footsteps arriving in the toilet block. "Am I right, or am I right?"

Trent flicked his fingers dry on account of the empty paper towel dispenser. "Damn!" he grumbled, noticing water droplets from his digits had landed on his polished black leather boots. Droplets that could give the incorrect impression he'd peed on them. With no towel to absorb the excess moisture, he leaned down, hoping to knock the liquid away with the back of his hand. After two or three attempts, they were as dry as they were going to be. At least until he secured a fabric towel, which he assumed he'd find in the plusher client suite in a few moments.

"Jaysus!" Trent shouted when he returned to full height. "You two scared the living shit outta me!" he said to the two helmet-wearing figures he was now looking at in the mirror, stood either side of him. When no response or movement was received from either, Trent offered an uneasy smile via the reflection in the mirror. "Ehm…" he said, "everything alright?"

Trent's apprehension was justified. The two bookends were dressed in immaculate navy-blue suits with crisp white shirts — their black helmets with a tinted visor simply didn't go with their formal attire. Additionally, for an otherwise empty toilet, the two new arrivals were standing a little too close for comfort, with each of them nearly standing on Trent's feet.

Trent moved to break the silence. "Is it an autograph or some–"

"Trent Partridge?" asked the man on the left of the reflection, trampling over his offer of autographs.

"Yeah… sure," Trent offered without turning, staring dead ahead and flicking his eyes between the two of them. Trent was used to people coming up to him unannounced, but, these two? Dressed as they were, in the toilet and stood motionless, caught him somewhat off guard.

"Who's… ehm… well… asking?" he enquired politely, unsure of the intentions of the two of them and keen not to antagonise.

"You're coming with us," the man on the right said, in a tone that indicated this was not a suggestion, rather an edict.

CHAPTER TEN – A MIST ROLLS IN

Trent offered a nervous laugh. "Oh, is that right?" he said, pretty much wedged between the two of them. "So, what makes you think that I'll—"

"My good friends, Smith and Wesson, insist," came the immediate and forthright response.

Bizarrely, Trent genuinely hoped the firm prod he'd just experienced in his lower back was indeed a gun. As the alternative, in a men's toilet, with two weirdos, simply didn't bear thinking about.

Both men took a step back, allowing Trent some breathing and manoeuvring space. "Let's move, Partridge, and get your hands in the air," said one of the men.

"Move!" insisted the other.

"Okay... okay!" Trent begrudgingly submitted. "But, I can't raise my hands yet."

"What?" asked the man with the gun, giving another prod for good measure. "Why not?"

Trent lowered his head in the direction of his feet. "I can feel a draft... down there. I think my flies are still undone and I'm sure you don't want to do it for me, now do you?" he asked, almost afraid of the answer.

"Do your flies up and don't try anything funny, yeah!"

Shortly after Trent and his associates departed, a face appeared from above the cubicle door. A bald-headed man, advanced in age, peered gingerly over the top of the door like a stabled donkey. His floating head startled the next two men who'd just arrived to make use of the facilities.

Satisfied the gun-toting thugs had indeed gone, he climbed down from the toilet seat on which he'd been perched these last few minutes.

"Oh my god!" he shouted, throwing the door open, wide-eyed like he'd just caught sight of a ghost. "That's absolutely awful," he exclaimed, pressing his shaking hand to his shiny bonce.

"You stunk the place out?" the newest arrival asked, veering away from the now vacant cubicle. "Thanks for the heads-up, grandad. I'll probably leave it for a minute or two."

"It's not that, well... possibly! But, what I mean is... what I'm trying to say is... it's just that... oh my. Just now... right there... Trent Partridge has just been kidnapped, at gunpoint!"

CHAPTER ELEVEN
Brighter than the Sun

The Isle of Man, a sedate little rock in the middle of the Irish Sea, was currently the subject of an unfortunate crimewave, relatively speaking. Ideal conditions, then, for the island's leading firm of private investigators, ready, willing, and able to jump into action at a moment's notice to capitalise on this unexpected uptick.

Sure, cash flow was tight, on occasion. But Sam, Abby, and the team at Eyes Peeled were sure to be rolling in cash before you knew it. After all, it was a boom time for a business such as theirs, and there was absolutely no need to panic about the negative state of the company's bank account. No... no need to panic. None, whatsoever. They were just about to turn a corner, and their overdraft would soon be cleared along with the overdue payments on their rather significant loan.

Well, that is, at least, what Sam had just spent the previous twenty minutes convincing their bank manager was *absolutely* the case. That they'd be back on track, shortly. Sam had even donned a tie for the meeting, and while he portrayed a confident air, externally at least, the truth was that he was starting to panic.

Still, if the PI gig *should* dry up, after the performance he'd just delivered he contemplated applying for an equity card to pursue a career in the performing arts.

The thought of solving the Senior TT Trophy case was tremendously appealing. Very much so. As Sam drifted off to sleep each night, he could imagine his face (along with the rest of the team) plastered on the front page of every national newspaper. They would be lauded as the saviours of the TT. Hell, they'd probably even make a Miss Marple-inspired TV series on the back of their collective endeavours. And the only thing sweeter than receiving the hefty finder's fee would be seeing the dour expression on Drexel Popek's smarmy face behind bars for pet pilfery.

The unfortunate truth, however, was that Sam and Abby simply couldn't devote all of their time and resources to this prestigious — but non-fee-paying — case much longer. That is, if there was any hope of paying the bills and themselves, of course. They could hold out for two or three more days, Sam figured, before they'd need to return their collective efforts to more mundane investigations, such as cheating spouses and the theft of agricultural equipment. Cases that wouldn't result in Sam's face being plastered all over the front pages.

Sam pulled up outside Eyes Peeled HQ, removed his tie, rolling it into a ball, before stuffing it in the glovebox. The place where it'd likely remain until the next wedding, funeral or bank manager's meeting he was required to attend.

"Bloody money!" he moaned but knew a brave face was the order of the day so as not to concern the troops. Yes, a stiff upper lip was invented for challenging times such as this, he reckoned.

Also, it wasn't *all* bad. After all, a potential new case had come in that certainly piqued their interest. The query, in itself, wasn't particularly impressive, but the timing of the call was remarkable. Exceptionally so.

A distraught woman had phoned — in floods of tears — looking for assistance in the recovery of a stolen item. That item being a prizewinning English bulldog called Hercules, taken from her rear garden.

Ordinarily, a missing pooch wouldn't cause too much excitement at Eyes Peeled, if any. However, a valuable, pedigree pooch goes AWOL

CHAPTER ELEVEN – BRIGHTER THAN THE SUN

in the current environment? Well, this had to have Drexel's grubby fingerprints all over it, Sam reasoned.

Proving Drexel's involvement in this pet-related thievery was now the top priority. Discrediting Drexel was the only way they'd win back the business they'd lost to him. It would also prevent any future business from going his way because who, in their right mind, would employ a fraudster. That was the hope, at least. Oh, and the possibility of seeing Drexel in handcuffs was also quite appealing to Sam.

And so inside HQ...

"Hey, Tom," Sam said with as cheery a demeanour as he could muster, falling into his chair. "Where's the rest?" he enquired, what with the office being all but empty.

"Abby and Suzie are digging into the kidnapping of that motorcycle chap."

"Trent Partridge," Sam offered helpfully. "They think it's linked to the stolen trophy?"

"Sure," Tom replied, staring diligently at his monitor. "Not sure why they've both gone?"

"Because he looks like a film star, is why!" Sam leaned forward in his chair, hope etched on his face. "Did you manage to get Popek's address?" he asked, crossing his fingers in anticipation.

Tom winced for a moment before switching it to a smile. "Would I let you down, boss? It's just printing out," he added, pointing to the printer which had just burst into life. "Not only that..." Tom teased further.

"Yeah?" Sam asked, enjoying being teased in such a manner.

"Drexel apparently had a lockup garage registered to him. I thought that might be of interest?"

Sam pushed his heels into the carpet, propelling his chair towards the printer. "Marvellous, Tom. Dare I ask how you managed to...?" he asked, holding the printout aloft with a broad grin.

Tom merely raised one eyebrow in response. His methods were, after all, his methods. "Now, Sam. About this rental car you asked me to arrange..."

"Go on?"

"It's a no-go, I'm afraid. Don't forget it's TT week and every hotel room and hire car is booked up months in advance," Tom explained with a shrug.

Sam released a disappointed sigh. "Drexel knows what cars we all drive, though. He'll be on to me in no time."

Tom tapped the side of his nose, knowingly. "I'm one step ahead!" Tom said, cryptically, rotating his neck like an owl. Sam followed the direction of Tom's eyeline towards the front window of their office.

"What's this? What are we looking at?" Sam asked, standing and now moving to the window which offered a panoramic view over Peel Beach, opposite. Well, ordinarily, at least. But the sorry-looking heap parked directly outside presently obscured any view of merit.

"I don't follow?" Sam said, not following.

Tom flapped his eyebrows several times in quick succession. "Well... you will be *following* in your new chariot for the day, boss!" Tom said, pleased with his genius wordplay.

Sam looked over to Tom and then out the window, once more. "The ice cream van?" Sam asked, returning his attention to the rusting metal bucket blocking his precious view of the beach. He'd noticed it when he parked up, even thinking that it made his own vehicle look good such was its dilapidated state.

"*That* thing...?" Sam asked, taking a step closer to the window, allowing him a complete view of the vehicle.

The chartreuse-coloured van sported an oversized and heavily sun-bleached plastic ice cream cone attached to its roof along with sporadic rust patches all over the ageing bodywork. "You're talking about that... that *thing*... just *there*?" Sam clarified, pressing the tip of his index finger against the glass.

"Uh-huh," Tom replied, smiling. "She's a thing of beauty, ain't she?" he added like a shifty car salesman.

Sam took a moment to run his eyes over the van, which was very possibly brighter than the sun. He joined both sets of fingers on top of this head, cradling his bonce. Staring. Transfixed.

CHAPTER ELEVEN – BRIGHTER THAN THE SUN

"That's inspired, Tom, my old son. Bloody brilliant!" Sam gushed, turning to offer his colleague a well-deserved high five for a job well done.

"I know, right," Tom said, gratefully receiving the praise bestowed on him. "It belongs to my mate, Bob. He's just bought a new van and so..." he added, handing the keys to Sam.

"Drexel will never suspect me in something so utterly obvious," Sam said, gratefully receiving the keys. "I always wanted to drive an ice cream van, Tom. Happy memories."

"Not for me," Tom suggested.

"Oh?" Sam asked, taken aback. After all, everyone loved ice cream, surely?

Tom lowered his head. "My dad used to tell me that when the van played music it meant they'd sold out. I'd hear the music coming up our street when I was a kid, then see all the other children skipping merrily with cash in their hand, ready for their frozen treat. I'd sit in my bedroom, laughing smugly, as I knew they'd sold out because of the music playing."

"Oh..." Sam said, also lowering his head in sympathy. Several long seconds elapsed with Sam not entirely sure how to follow up on this unfortunate childhood memory. Sam returned his attention to the ice cream van parked outside.

"One more thing, Sam," Tom said, thankfully breaking the nostalgic silence, but Sam was still transfixed by his surveillance vehicle for the day.

Tom cleared his throat to attract Sam's attention. "Whaddya think?" Tom asked, his voice sounding more nasal than usual.

Sam moved his attention away from the van, turning, with a simple smile across his contented face.

"*Aaagh!*" Sam screamed, jumping back with his arms shielding his face. "FOR THE LOVE OF GOD, TOM!"

"Calm down, it's just a Latex mask," Tom explained, prodding his cheeks to demonstrate it wasn't really his skin. But that, of course, was completely obvious. Unless Tom had been subjected to a nuclear blast in the last two minutes, that is. "My niece and nephew gave it to me for Christmas last year. It's Captain Jean-Luc Picard from Star Trek."

"*Captain Picard?*" Sam scoffed, tilting his head but failing to see any resemblance. "I'm not sure about Captain Picard, but I *have* just delivered a captain's log in my pants, Tom. Honestly, you should have warned me. I could have keeled over!"

Tom removed the mask, contorting most of his *actual* face in the process. "I thought it'd be a good disguise for you," he said, handing it over to Sam. "Oh, before you put it on, you should wash it down. It's hay fever season, and I sneezed in it earlier. I'm sure I got most of it, but..."

Sam shook his head in wonderment. "Tom, you're on fire today. Seriously, great work!" He took a cautious glance over his shoulder, moving his head closer to Tom so they were positioned like two drunks in a pub declaring their love for each other.

"Tom, it's probably best you don't mention our surveillance strategy, you know... to Abby or Suzie. *Especially* Abby. I think she tends to worry when I go *deep* undercover."

Tom winked an assured wink. "No problem, Sam. Also, I went to the supermarket and stocked up the fridges in the van with an assortment of frozen treats. I wanted it to be convincing in case you were subject to any scrutiny concerning your credentials."

Sam used his sleeve to mop up the saliva dribble pooling at the base of the mask in his hand. "We don't deserve you and Suzie. Honestly, we don't. Tom, as soon as we get some cash in the coffers, you're in for a pay rise, okay!"

"Roger that," Tom said. "Now, I must get on as I've a lead to follow up on my stolen tractor investigation. Stay safe out there! Oh, if you wouldn't mind, please don't turn the van music on when you leave as, well, you know... sad memories."

CHAPTER TWELVE
Greensleeves

The only thing crappier than the bodywork on the van was... well... pretty much everything, actually. Inside there was a sickening odour that smelt like week-old microwaved haddock. The upholstery on the seats had, in parts, given way to naked springs, and the electrics were utterly shot with the dashboard warning lights flashing like a school disco.

The horn would activate at will, and occasionally when Sam applied the brakes, the famous ice cream van chimes burst into life, releasing a thirty-second rendition of "Greensleeves." It was a melody that ordinarily brought a smile to his face, but not now, not after four miles and a mini traffic jam at the Quarterbridge roundabout which required several musical applications of the brake pedal. There was even a low point when he was about to climb out of the van and simply leave it there, idling in traffic. He was wearing a Latex mask so there was little chance he could be pointed out by any witness as the absconded owner.

Although having already completed a half-hour drive, Sam was starting to question the wisdom of donning his mask as early as he had. The handle on the window winder was a broken stump resulting in the cabin being akin to a bread oven in this warm weather. Sam had genuine concerns that his disguise was in danger of melting to his actual face. But, despite all of the minor flaws, it was perfect for his surveillance operation.

Sam had two potential addresses for Drexel Popek, courtesy of Tom's source — a home address, and one for a lockup garage in town. Of course, Sam was aware of a home address for Drexel from their brief time working together, but this new residential address indicated he'd moved on recently. Drexel was astute, however, with Sam reasoning that he wouldn't poop on his own doorstep, as it were. If Drexel was going to harbour stolen animals, it was unlikely he'd court attention by doing this at his primary residence. For that reason, Sam headed to the other address in his notebook, Drexel's lockup garage in the centre of Douglas.

With his face disguised, Sam felt confident enough to drive directly past the address for an initial recce. However, he soon worried he must be at the wrong place as there were no lockup garages at or near the address he'd been provided, only several industrial units utilised as either offices or the occasional retail space.

Undeterred, Sam headed around the block for another pass, rubbernecking as he went.

"Ah-ha," Sam said eventually, slapping his hand down on the steering wheel, which could have been a mistake as a large bolt dropped onto the floor as a result. Sam didn't have a clue what the bolt was holding in or together. He just hoped it wasn't too crucial to his safety or the overall operation of the vehicle.

Sam slowed, which wasn't difficult as the engine had less power than a 60w lightbulb. He crawled along, twisting his neck towards the units on his right. "Branching out, are we?" he asked, catching sight of a tacky-looking sign hung in one of the windows. "Popek, PI," Sam read from the poster with a laugh. "That's original..." he sniffed.

Sam had the benefit of a disguise, but knew he couldn't rest on his laurels. After all, he was dealing with a fellow professional who was aware of every trick in the PI rule book. Sam knew he'd have to use all of his guile to remain inconspicuous, for one little slip-up could blow his cover to smithereens.

Fortunately, a car pulled away, freeing up a parking space at the end of the street. Sam indicated — sending the dashboard warning lights into a tizzy in the process — and, unfortunately, was then

CHAPTER TWELVE – GREENSLEEVES

required to apply the brake pedal if he didn't want to make contact with the vehicle in front. He said a little prayer that the chimes wouldn't kick in, but...

"Soddin' thing!" he admonished the van as "Greensleeves" kicked into life, announcing his arrival to the neighbourhood. He waved to the faces appearing at the windows in the block of flats opposite. Inconspicuous, this was not.

Sam knew from driving by that the offices of Popek, PI were in darkness. And with no sign of Drexel's car either, he figured it was now or never. With the clock ticking, Sam simply didn't have the luxury of waiting for hours on end as he'd done with Sir Barrington as Drexel could return at any moment.

He pulled his Picard mask down, ensuring it sat correctly on his face, popped a baseball cap on his bonce and then, casual-as-you-like, walked over to Drexel's office.

He wasn't entirely sure what he hoped to achieve at this particular time. In an ideal world, he'd simply press his nose up to the front window where he'd see a stolen English bulldog wagging its tail, then rolling over for a tummy tickle. Such an outcome would be all Sam needed to prove Drexel was a serial pet pilferer whose investigative credentials were a fraudulent sham. Yes, such a result would be most agreeable, he thought.

Sam could hear his heartbeat in his ears as he approached Drexel's shop. Rather than immediately stopping for a gawp, however, he kept his face dead ahead, flicking his eyes to his left like he were on a military parade for a crafty glimpse as he passed by. The office was, as he believed, in darkness with no apparent movement inside. He continued his ruse until the end of the block where he raised his hand, muttered something aloud, hoping to give the impression he'd forgotten something hence turning on a sixpence and heading back the way he'd just walked.

Now reasonably confident there was nobody inside (of the human variety) Sam pressed his nose up against the window. He raised his right finger, tapping on the glass, hoping to be greeted by a throaty bark in response to his presence.

"Here, boy!" Sam said, giving the glass another rattle with his fingernail. But the chances of hearing anything were drowned out by the roar of an angry-sounding V8 engine, inches from where he stood. Sam used the reflection on the glass to observe a black SUV directly behind him with a head peering out. "Bollocks," Sam said to himself, fidgeting on the spot. It was Drexel.

Drexel must have assumed the figure stood outside his place of work to be a potential customer and stopped to offer a welcome. "I'll be there shortly," Drexel said, "once I've found somewhere to park."

Sam simply raised his thumb in response. "Bugger off, then," Sam muttered under his breath when the vehicle didn't immediately move away. He panicked. Was Drexel on to him...? Had his cunning disguise been rumbled...? Fortunately, it appeared not, as the expensive-looking vehicle eased away. A flash motor likely funded by the business he'd poached, Sam wondered.

Sam returned, at pace, to the ice cream van before Drexel returned. *Could the stolen dog be in his car?* Sam thought.

"Oh, hello," Sam offered upon approaching the van. For a moment he was concerned there'd been an incident of some sort, as seven or eight people were milling around the area where he'd parked. He quickened his step, just in case his limited first-aid skills should be called upon.

"I think this is him," announced an abrupt woman holding the hand of a young girl. She glanced at her watch with an audible tut. "Five minutes we've been waiting," she said as if this was a terrible imposition. Sam turned as he walked, looking behind himself and wondering who this lady might be talking to.

As Sam reached for the door handle, the cluster of people fell into order, forming an orderly queue by the serving hatch at the side of the van. The tutting woman took the lead, removing her purse from her bag.

"Ehm..." Sam said uneasily. He smiled politely, with all eyes now on him. "Ehm..." he said, once more, widening his smile, but of course this gesture was concealed behind the mask. "Can I help?"

CHAPTER TWELVE — GREENSLEEVES

"A choc-ice and a large Whippy," the woman said having given this some initial thought, it would appear.

"And a Flake!" added the young girl, tugging at her mother's arm. "You promised me a Flake."

"And a Flake," she added to the order on the young'un's behalf.

A young lad further back in the queue was presently hopping on the spot, desperate, it would appear, to get off his chest what he was thinking about. "Mummy, Mummy," he said, shuffling urgently like he was in dire need of a wee. Mum, for her part, was already tuned in to what her little darling was thinking and therefore likely to say. She placed her finger against her mouth, likely assuming Sam had some form of situation that required a prosthetic mask. "Mummy, Mummy," the lad continued, undeterred. "Has that man's face melted?" he asked, staring intently at Sam.

Sam had actually forgotten he was wearing a mask and figured it best if he climbed inside the van to avoid further scrutiny and also the potential of alarming the kids further. It was quite a freaky-looking mask, after all. With the door closed and him now in the driver's seat, Sam hoped the crowd would quickly disperse.

The woman with her cash at the ready wasn't happy, however, by this course of action. She sidled up to the driver's side door — where Sam was doing his best to appear engrossed in something up ahead — and tapped her fingernail on the glass.

"Excuse me," she said, her voice increasing in pitch. "We're waiting to order."

Sensing this lot was going nowhere fast, Sam reached for the window winder before he realised it was a plastic stump and didn't work. "I don't have any ice cream," he shouted through the window with an apologetic shrug.

Sam was trying not to antagonise the situation further as he was still trying to, but failing miserably at, remaining incognito.

"Bugger!" Sam mumbled, noticing that Drexel was now wandering up the street in his direction, alone, without any canine for company.

For one awful moment, Drexel slowed, appearing to join the ice-cream queue. But the several animated and noisy kids in need of a sugar fix appeared to have deterred him, thankfully, with Drexel instead heading towards his office.

"Look!" Sam said, returning his attention to the woman. "I don't have any..." he moved to explain, but then had a moment of glorious recollection to his earlier conversation with Tom.

Sam raised his index finger for the benefit of the angry-looking woman at his window. He climbed into the rear compartment of the van to where the fridges lived. Considering the overall dilapidated, stinking condition of the vehicle, it was a miracle that the fridges appeared to still be operational, although sounding like an anvil inside a washing machine on spin cycle. He could have kissed Tom (and probably would) for having the foresight to stock the fridge with an assortment of frozen treats.

With Sam now stood in the dispensing position, the queue moved forward a pace in anticipation. Sam forced open the filthy sliding glass hatch from which thousands of expectant customers would have been served over the lifetime of the weary vehicle.

"*Mummy*, you *promised* me ice cream!" the delightful young lady nearest the van snapped, stamping her foot like an aspiring Veruca Salt.

"Of course, Tilly-Bell!" Mummy agreed, pacifying her little angel with a gentle head rub. "You!" she said, turning her attention back to Sam. "You were playing your music when you arrived, which got these children all worked up and excited. To now say you don't have any ice cream is completely—"

"Here!" Sam said, fearing a riot was about to break out. Sam grabbed a handful of the frozen ice lollies that Tom had stacked in the fridge. "It's all I've got," Sam added, throwing them one at a time in the direction of the children now jumping on the spot with their hands in the air. "Take them... no charge!"

Needless to say, an ice cream man dispensing free lollies did nothing to reduce the queue. Rather the opposite, in fact.

CHAPTER TWELVE – GREENSLEEVES

Sam soon felt like he was pushing water uphill with a fork. For every happy child licking a lolly, another took their place in the queue just as quick. *Where the hell are you lot coming from?* he thought, until the realisation he was parked near a school at home time offered the explanation he'd been searching for.

With the contents of the fridge soon emptied and several expectant children still stood in front of him, Sam had little option but to lift up and present the two empty cardboard boxes for their inspection. "I'm all out," Sam declared, concerned his mask had shifted position with his recent efforts, not that the hungry kids appeared to notice, either way. "That's it," Sam added, turning the boxes upside down to indicate he wasn't lying and there were, in actual fact, no lollies left.

The remaining stragglers eventually took him at his word, moving in the direction of another ice cream van that'd turned up and parked several metres away, likely hoping to capitalise on school kicking-out time.

Sam was dripping in sweat, flustered, and still hadn't progressed further with his mission. He needed to get inside Drexel's office and to do that, Sam needed to get Drexel *out* of it... but how the hell was he supposed to do that.

Climbing back into the driver's seat, Sam was aware of a figure moving towards the passenger side window. "I'm all out!" Sam said, paying the person little attention and eager to return his efforts to work-related matters.

With his cheeks chafing under the mask, he thrust his lolly-chilled fingers under the Latex to bring blessed relief to his irritated skin. Sam was beginning to question the wisdom of his disguise and, in his mind's eye, could see Abby, hands on her hips, telling him what a foolish idea it was. She was often correct in such matters.

With the assistance of the binoculars, Sam had a quick look over at Drexel's office, which was now illuminated. *How the hell do I get inside that office?*

Sam's thought process was, however, disrupted by the figure which had moved over to the driver's side of the van. "I told you I'm all out!" Sam stressed, climbing out of the van to fully consider his next step.

A stout, shaven-headed man stood directly in front of Sam, blocking his path. He stared up at Sam with a grave expression that didn't translate as somebody in the market to purchase ice cream. In fact, his fierce demeanour also didn't really go with his cheery yellow suit made from an embroidered ice cream pattern. "You're in my space," the man barked, pointing his stubby digit to the ground.

Sam took a helpful step to the left. "Is that better?" Sam asked, trying to move around the man.

"I'm Mr Chill," announced Mr Chill. Although, the snarling lip didn't give the impression he was currently chilled.

"A pleasure..." Sam offered, attempting to ease past Mr Chill, once more. However, each time Sam moved, so did Mr Chill. To the casual observer, they appeared to be getting in a little ballroom dancing practice. "Look... do you..." Sam said, frustrated. "It's just that I've—"

"You're in my space!" the angry fellow countered, increasing in mass as he did. "This patch is Mr Chill's," he continued, referring to himself in the third person. "Look, buddy, are you trying to muscle in on my turf?" he asked, jabbing Sam in the chest. "And what the hell is with that stupid mask. You do know that your nose is half ripped off?"

Sam thought he could feel a bit of a draft in the nasal area. "Look... Mr Chill," Sam said, adjusting his nose. "I'm not here to *muscle in* on your patch. I wasn't even selling ice cream. I was giving it away."

This explanation didn't have the effect Sam hoped it would, and his t-shirt was now gripped firmly in Mr Chill's fist.

"Not only have you nicked my patch, but you're also *giving* the product away? Are you working for Mr Freeze?" Mr Chill asked, tightening his grip and moving his head closer.

Sam, it would appear, had found himself in the middle of an ice-cream turf war.

"It's not my van," Sam replied, now on his tippy-toes due to the upward forces on his shirt.

CHAPTER TWELVE – GREENSLEEVES

"Not your van... Then who the hell sent you here? It was Mr Freeze, wasn't it?"

Sam shook his head in the negative. "No," Sam pleaded, looking around for assistance. He didn't see any, but what he *did* see was Drexel's plush and expensive-looking car parked further up the street.

Even in his distressed state, Sam knew this was too good an opportunity to miss. "Look, Mr Chill," Sam said, struggling for breath. "It's not a move by Mr Freeze. My boss sent me here to muscle in on your patch. Let me go, yeah? I'm just an employee. My boss is the brains of the outfit."

"I knew it!" Mr Chill roared in response. "Who the hell is your boss?" he demanded. "I'm going to stick a Cornetto where the sun doesn't shine when I find him. Where is he?"

"Okay, okay, Mr Chill. He lives around here," Sam replied. "He must have seen you making a fortune and thought he'd walk on in to take a slice of the pie."

"Where does he live?"

Sam placed his hands on Mr Chill's ham-hock fists, gently easing them down and away from his neck. "Okay, fair enough. I know he lives around here, but I'm not exactly sure which address," Sam explained. "But I do know that's his car, over there..." Sam said, pointing to Drexel's flashy motor, resisting the desperate urge to smile.

"That one there?" Mr Chill asked, following the direction of Sam's pointed finger with his eye. "The black one with the shiny alloys?"

"That's the one," Sam confirmed with several eager nods. "He even told me to give the merchandise away for free. Said he wants to put you out of business," Sam confessed, lowering his head in shame. "He's probably hoping to use your cash to pay for that car."

Mr Chill could barely contain his rage. "Is that right? Well, it's time I had a word with your boss."

"But you don't know where he lives?" Sam said, secretly hoping that he knew exactly where this situation was headed to next.

"Oh, I've a funny feeling we'll soon see him when I'm using the bonnet of his expensive motor as a trampoline," Mr Chill replied, stomping towards Drexel's car.

Sam didn't hesitate, reaching into his pocket for his phone. He knew this was his chance. "Tom," he said, once the phone connected. "This is urgent, and I'll explain later. Drexel has his mobile number listed on his Facebook page. He doesn't know your voice that well, so phone him up, right now. Pretend you're a concerned neighbour and that you've seen someone vandalising his car, yeah?"

Roughly thirty seconds or so later, Drexel's car alarm burst into life. Sam dearly wanted to watch exactly what Mr Chill was doing, as it sounded terrific. Yes, very satisfying. But Sam's eyes remained fixed on Drexel's office door, and when it flew open a moment or two later, Sam was off like a stabbed rat.

Sam kept his head down as he sprinted up the street. He crossed Drexel's path, but, of course, Drexel was more concerned with the lunatic performing star jumps on his car.

Sam poked his head through the partially opened door into Drexel's office. "Hello," he called out in case there was anyone else remaining in the office. "Hello," he said again, this time walking inside. His heart was pounding, knowing that Drexel could return at any moment.

Once inside, Sam was disappointed to see no immediate sign of a stolen dog. The office was relatively sparse apart from a desk and chair and several framed copies of Drexel's recent press clippings hanging on the walls. "Bastard," Sam said, looking at Drexel's smug face on the photo closest to him.

Sam crept to the doorway at the rear of the office. "*Woof*," he said, tapping the wood, hopeful of a bark in return. But again, nothing. There was, however, a strong aroma which reminded Sam of the contents of a hamster's cage. "*Woof*," he said again, this time pressing down on the handle. With the door open, Sam fumbled for the light switch as the smell intensified. "Ah," he said, locating and then flicking the switch. Sam could now, sadly, visually confirm there was no

CHAPTER TWELVE – GREENSLEEVES

pooch inside. There wasn't much of anything other than four empty birdcages and a sack of pungent seed.

Sam's heart sank. He knew this was his golden opportunity to expose Drexel for the conman he was, but there was nothing here to incriminate him. Sam could have an educated guess that the empty birdcages were used for pet pilfery, but proving anything was another matter altogether.

"Damn," Sam said, knowing he best get the hell outta there. But he couldn't resist having a little peek at Drexel's notepad, sat there on his desk, all open and alluring, tempting him in. Sam pressed his finger down on the opened page, running his eyes over the handwritten notes. Most of what he read was the initial draft of a press release for the recovered parrot. But then, right there at the foot of the page in block capitals: *QUENTIN THRUMBOLT. 3 PM CASH OFFER.*

Sam used his phone to take a photograph of the notepad. Before leaving, he teased open the top drawer of the desk, just for a sneaky look inside, but nothing of interest only office supplies. Bravely, or stupidly, he pressed on, sliding open the larger drawer below.

"What do we have here?" he said, checking to make sure he was still alone. Sam then opened the zip of the black duffle bag, staring down at the contents. "Ho... ly... shit!" Sam said, moving his head closer to confirm what he thought he'd seen was actually what he'd seen.

"*What the hell are you doing?*" a flustered-looking Drexel demanded, filling the doorway to his office. Drexel had a cut below his left eye and half his shirt missing. "Snooping around my office, are you?" he said, moving closer. "I suppose you're with that deranged idiot I've just had to drag off my car? And what's with the stupid disguise?"

But before Sam could offer any response, Drexel punched him square on the jaw. "Was it you that phoned to get me out of the office?" Drexel asked, moving forward for another attack.

Sam's mask had shifted position from the first strike and was now obscuring his vision, so his retaliatory punch missed Drexel by about nine feet. The momentum from the wayward punch sent Sam tumbling to the floor, with his head coming to rest under Drexel's desk. "Aww," Sam moaned, making urgent adjustments to restore his vision. Drexel grabbed Sam's ankles, making every effort to drag him out.

"Get off me," Sam demanded, kicking his foot out in defence, but this only served to anger Drexel who doubled his efforts. As Sam slid forward, he took hold of a desk leg.

"Get out here!" Drexel shouted, heaving with all his might.

Sam's grip on the desk was starting to give as both he and the desk now edged forward in unison. "Drexel... stop..." Sam pleaded. "It's me, Sam. Sam Levy. I'm wearing a disguise."

Drexel stopped pulling while the voice registered. "What the hell?" he asked, dropping Sam's feet.

Sam used his heels to drag himself out from under the desk. He shielded his face to prevent a further attack, sliding out on his bum like a dog scratching its arse on the carpet.

"What's with the Kojak mask?" Drexel asked, still poised with his fist at the ready.

"It's not Kojak," Sam said, now clear of the desk and righting himself. "It's Captain Picard from Star Trek."

Sam took hold of the mask, ready for the big reveal, but no matter what he did, it wouldn't move over the width of his jaw. "Hang on," Sam said. "It's just a bit stubborn." Placing one hand on the ear and the other on the skull, he pulled upward, but all he succeeded in doing was to twist it, so he was rendered blind, once more. "Oh, sod this," he said, inserting his fingers in the tear by his nose, ripping the mask from his face. The fresh air on his skin was heaven sent.

Drexel watched on quite unsure what was happening. "Sam, what the hell are you doing here? Are you anything to do with the damage to my car and some lunatic calling me Mr Freeze?"

"Why am I here," Sam scoffed as if his presence should have been entirely evident to Drexel. "Why am I here..."

Drexel shrugged in response. "Yes. *Why?*"

"Stolen pooch," Sam put forth. "Sound familiar?

CHAPTER TWELVE – GREENSLEEVES

Drexel tipped his head. "Huh? Seriously, Sam. I'm starting to lose my patience."

"Well then... if a stolen English bulldog doesn't mean anything, then what about a missing parrot?" Sam could see the flicker of a reaction register on Drexel's face. "Ahh, touched a nerve have I? *Pieces of eight, pieces of eight,*" Sam offered in a rather impressive pirate voice. "Yeah, I'm on to you, Popek."

"Wh-wh-What?" Drexel spluttered. "You're talking crazy, Levy. Now get out of here before I phone the police."

Sam smiled, presenting his wrists out like he was about to be cuffed. "Go ahead. You can explain to them about how you managed to find a parrot before it'd even been reported stolen. You received a nice little reward for that, didn't you, Drexel?"

Drexel went quiet, processing his thoughts before replying. "You can't prove anything," he said, laughing the accusation off. "If you go to the police with that, they'll think you're crazy. A crazy, bitter detective who's badmouthing his former employee for taking business away from him. Come on, Sam. Have a little respect for yourself."

Drexel extended his arm in the direction of the door, indicating that Sam had well and truly outstayed his welcome. "I know it hurts, Sam. You know... me taking all of your large accounts, and all. But that's because I'm just a superior detective to you. I'll tell you what I'll do, Sam, in the spirit of friendship. I receive lots of crappy little jobs, missing shopping trolleys and whatnot. Usually, I decline them, but, as a friend, I'll be happy to send them your way. Give a little back, yeah? Plus, I always had a little soft spot for Abby. Well... when I say soft, it wasn't actually soft, it was—"

"Popek, you piece of shit," Sam said, moving towards the desk. He held up his phone to demonstrate he had been and was still videoing their conversation. "I'm onto you and your animal theft scam, and—"

"Prove it!" Drexel snapped back. "All I did was to reunite upset owners with their beloved pets, Sam. You know, this bitter side doesn't become you," Drexel said, staring directly into the camera and, to be fair, was playing a bang-up convincing role. "Does Abby ever ask after me?" Drexel went on, twisting that knife.

"You've very good, Popek. Impressively so. I knew you were a wrong 'un, Drexel, but I didn't think you'd stoop as low as this." Sam grabbed the duffle bag from the bottom desk drawer, unfastened the zip and before Drexel could react, Sam had the contents displayed in his hand. "Oh, the video goes straight to the cloud, so don't think about grabbing my phone."

Drexel was like a rabbit caught in the headlights, shifting uneasily, with Sam unsure if Drexel was either going to hit him or make a run for it. "Not so cocky now, Drexel?"

Sam trained the camera on the hefty Queen Victoria bronze bust in his hand. "Care to give us some commentary, Drexel? I'm sure this video is going to make for splendid viewing on YouTube. You can tell us about how an expensive, stolen bust has ended up in your crappy little backstreet office?"

"You've got nothing, Sam," Drexel scoffed, arrogance returning in spades. "Don't forget, Sir Barrington hired me to find those busts after you'd cocked the case right up. I did what I was paid to do, and I'm sure Sir Barrington will be delighted when I call him tomorrow to tell him I've found one of them."

Sam shook his head, smiling. "I had a feeling you'd throw that one at me," Sam countered. "And you could have probably got away with that lame explanation if it wasn't for this."

Sam placed the exceptionally heavy bronze on the desk then held up a printed email that'd been in the bag alongside Queen Victoria. "Should I read it?" Sam asked, dangling it in front of the camera. "Oh, I think I will…"

Attn: Mr Popek

Thank you for the image of the Queen Victoria Bronze, as discussed. I have several clients who have indicated an interest in the item as mentioned above.
I'll revert soonest.

Best
Quentin Thrumbolt

CHAPTER TWELVE – GREENSLEEVES

Sam placed the printout into his rear pocket, moving the camera closer to Drexel's face. He wanted to capture the gusto disappearing from his mush for posterity.

"Have I missed anything, Drexel?" Sam asked, rather enjoying this now. "Just so you know, my next phone call is going to be to the insurance company and then the police."

Drexel cupped his face in his hands, releasing a pained sigh. He moved slowly towards his chair, placing himself gently down. "Good work, Sam," he offered after a while. "Truly, excellent work."

Sam scarcely dared to breathe. It was everything he could do to stop himself from punching the air. "So, you admit it? You stole the bronze busts?"

Drexel puffed out his cheeks, reaching over and caressing Queen Victoria's face. "I didn't think this cheeky girl would result in my downfall." He then looked directly at Sam. "Turn the camera off, will you? I'll tell you all you need to know. Can you give me a lift home after though, as Mr Chill smashed my windscreen?"

CHAPTER THIRTEEN
The Plot Thickens

Suzie wheeled out their trusty and well-used whiteboard, taking care not to trip on her impossibly wide pink flares. She clapped her fingertips in delight, taking immense pleasure in drawing a massive tick underneath the caricatures she'd previously drawn of Sir Barrington and Quentin Thrumbolt.

"Brilliant work," Suzie said, offering a raised thumb in Sam's direction.

"Yes, superb," Tom agreed. "I'm sure it was all because of the cunning disguise that you secured the result," he offered with a wry smile. "Although you don't appear too chuffed considering you smashed a significant theft ring wide open, Sam. I thought you'd have been doing cartwheels around the room, this morning?"

Sam didn't appear in the mood for celebrating. He sat, running his finger around the rim of his coffee mug, screwing his face up with something on his mind, it would appear. "It's Drexel's car," Sam said eventually. "I know I shouldn't feel guilty, but that lunatic, Mr Chill probably caused about ten grand's worth of damage. Drexel told me it was his dream car. He'd been saving up for years for it."

Abby leaned towards him, extending her arm to give his back a tender rub. "Just remember that Drexel could have put us out of business, Sam. He wouldn't have worried about us, that's for sure."

"I suppose," Sam conceded, lowering his head. "Oh, Tom. I'll be sure to get you a replacement mask, also."

Suzie tapped her pen on the whiteboard to bring the meeting to order. "So... fill us in on all the details, Sam?"

Sam took a slurp of his coffee. "Aww," he moaned, rubbing the purple bruising on his jawbone. "It's where Drexel punched me," he explained. "Though I suppose I did deserve it."

"Sam!" Abby admonished him. "You know I find your compassion to be one of your more endearing qualities, but Drexel didn't think twice about us when he was poaching our clients hand over fist, now did he...?" Abby held her stare, but it wasn't too frosty. Rather like scolding a dog for eating from the table. "So," she continued, shifting her attention to Tom and Suzie who were both eager for a more detailed account of the previous day's events. "According to our friend Drexel, he stole the bronze busts under the direct instructions of Sir Barrington Hedley-Smythe."

"Knew it!" Suzie ventured in. "So our Drexel's extending the remit of his services to grand larceny now?"

"It was blackmail," Sam explained. "A few months ago, Drexel read an article about Sir Barrington's valuable prize peacock and hatched a ridiculous plot to steal it. Figuring there'd be a handsome reward, he'd then simply return it a couple of days later and trouser a nice little payday. Simple. Or so he thought."

"Cheeky bugger," Tom said. "I'm guessing Sir Barrington cottoned on to this little ruse?"

Sam nodded his head as confirmation. "Exactly, Tom. CCTV captured the entire theft. Then, when Sir Barrington miraculously received a call from Drexel offering his services to find his beloved bird, Sir Barrington put two and two together. When Drexel returned the bird safely, as promised, he was then presented with the CCTV footage showing him nicking it in the first place. Sir Barrington threatened to call the police, and from then on, he had Drexel exactly where he wanted him."

"So the theft of the bronzes was all for the insurance?" Suzie asked before adding, "Sir Barrington gets his expensive busts stolen, triggering a generous pay-out from the insurance company. Then, a

CHAPTER THIRTEEN – THE PLOT THICKENS

few weeks later, I'm guessing the stolen items are then sold to Quentin Thrumbolt at a significant discount?"

"Yup," Sam replied. "A nice little insurance pay-out and then a few months later, the stolen items are shipped abroad for another payday. Crafty buggers. Drexel's payment for a job well done was Queen Victoria who I found in his drawer. He was going to sell that on when everything had calmed down."

"And Sam feels sorry for this guy?" Abby added. "Oh," Abby went on, remembering another point. "The insurance company insisted Sir B had to employ a firm of reputable PI's in addition to the ongoing police investigation. And the reason Eyes Peeled were hired… any guesses?"

"Go on, Abby," Tom pressed.

"… Is because Drexel convinced Sir B that we were all utterly useless and wouldn't have a cat in hell's chance of finding the stolen bronzes. But, at least the insurance company would think he was making every effort."

"Cheeky sod," Suzie said. "That's what Drexel told you?"

"That he did," Sam confirmed with a dejected nod.

"I don't get it?" Tom said, not getting it. "Drexel was employed here, with us, when he stole that peacock. Here, with us, in paid employment. So, why do something so bloody stupid?"

Sam sighed a sad sigh. "Drexel was worried about his job, Tom. After several successful cases, he'd had a quiet few weeks and what with being new and all, was concerned that it might be first in first out. He figured a juicy case would help his job prospects no end. But, when Operation Peacock went tits-up, well, that's when Drexel decided to leave. He quit to save our business from any potential reputational damage," Sam added, in a tone suggesting Drexel could actually be a knight in shining armour, rather than a peacock-stealing scumbag.

"I'm calling bullshit on this!" Suzie declared succinctly. "I'm not buying that saving-the-business-from-reputational-damage line. I'll bet he just wanted to earn some extra moolah on the side and got a little greedy. Also, we know he carried on with his pet recovery scam after the peacock, so he certainly didn't learn from his mistakes."

"Have you called the police, Sam?" Tom chipped in.

"Ehm..." Sam said, squirming in his seat like he had a dodgy stomach. "Yes... well. About that. Thing is... I was on the way to... And well... No, not as yet. See I thought Drexel might still be of some use to us."

"Sam!" said an exasperated Abby. "You said you'd phoned them. You confirmed that just before we came into this meeting," she added, pointing to the door they'd walked through only a few minutes earlier.

Tom, for his part, had been chewing the current situation over and interjected at this point. "I suppose..." he began, mulling over his thoughts further before he continued, "Drexel could help us with the Senior TT case. If he was so inclined, of course."

"Exactly!" Sam said, pleased to receive some backup on the subject. He briefly considered a told-you-so glance at Abby but knew it was one he'd regret immediately. "If, as we think, Thrumbolt is somehow involved in the stolen trophy, then Drexel may be able to help us recover it," Sam added. "Drexel and Thrumbolt are already in bed with each other over the stolen busts and likely already trust each other."

"Drexel working with us?" Suzie asked to clarify what she was hearing. "Seriously? Are we even confident that Drexel's not involved in nicking it in the first place? Because that would look just splendid all over the front pages, *PI firm employs disgraced former employee to find the item he stole in the first place.*"

Sam shook his head. "No, he won't be working with us! Well... not in the traditional sense, at least. As no cash will be paid for services rendered. So, more of an unpaid volunteer. And no, he's not involved in the robbery, I'm sure of it. Guys, you should have seen Drexel in the car on the way home. Honestly, he was a broken man. I thought he was going to cry at one point."

"Was that not because of the state of his car?" Abby asked.

CHAPTER THIRTEEN – THE PLOT THICKENS

"Well, that also," Sam conceded, "but I can tell when someone's sincere. Drexel even confided that he thought of us all as his family and that... that... that I was also his inspiration," Sam recalled with a solemn expression. "He just wanted to fit in and made some stupid mistakes along the way. I can completely relate to that. After all, I *am* a leading authority on silly mistakes."

"True," Tom said agreeably.

"Come on, team... let's give him a chance, yeah?" Sam added with a rousing fist shake, rallying the troops like Mel Gibson in *Braveheart*.

Sam stood, walking over to the whiteboard where he pointed to the crude drawing of Thrumbolt that Suzie had illustrated previously. He then looked to each of the Eyes Peeled team in turn. "Guys, just imagine what recovering the trophy would do for the agency," Sam said dreamily. "If Thrumbolt is involved as we suspect, then Drexel is willing to help us recover the Senior TT Trophy."

"And in the process, hoping to reduce any potential criminal sentence for himself?" Tom suggested. "All very chivalrous," he added, with a deliberate rolling of his eyes.

"Exactly!" Sam said, slapping his hand on Thrumbolt's image. "Look," he added, turning to Abby. "I know I was supposed to phone the police... but, what if we have a genuine opportunity to recover the trophy?" he asked, raising his left eyebrow just a touch. "It'd get the business back on track and restore our reputation as the island's primo investigators. Plus, with the reward money, we'd be able to make payroll this month."

"Fine," Abby said. "Today is Wednesday, so we've two days until the Senior TT race. If no progress is made by Friday, we forget all about finding the blasted trophy and go to the police with what we know about the stolen bronze busts, including Drexel's involvement. Agreed?"

"Agreed," Sam said, agreeing most agreeably.

CHAPTER FOURTEEN
A Little Bit of Elvis

Trent Partridge's right wrist was red raw. Cable ties secured his arms behind his back, and each time he attempted to move his hands, the pain intensified from plastic rubbing against bare skin. He'd been successful in releasing his right ankle, so far, but the left one still remained secured to the chair leg. With no available free hands to assist, all he could do was shuffle hopelessly towards a door he could barely see in the darkness.

"Hello," he offered weakly, certain he'd heard some movement. "Is-is-is there somebody there?" Trent went quiet, slowing his breathing. "Hello," he said, once more, but received no response. "LET ME OUT!" Trent yelled, stomping his free foot on the floor.

He braced himself as the sound of heavy footsteps approached. He heard a switch being flicked then a thin beam of light burst through the gap between the door and frame. The illumination caused Trent to grimace as he'd been sat in darkness for what felt like hours.

"Let me out!" Trent demanded as a key rattled in the lock from the other side.

The door eased open, flooding the room with light. "Oi, noisy," said the owner of the voice now stood in the doorway and still wearing a motorcycle helmet to conceal his identity.

Trent narrowed his eyes, turning his head away from the light, which felt like lightning bolts striking in his retinas. "What do you want with me? This is kidnapping!" Trent protested.

"Is it?" the man replied, placing a tray of food on the floor next to Trent's feet. "Shit, I suppose it *is* now you mention it," he added with no attempt to hide the sarcasm in his voice. He held up the snapped cable tie he'd found lying next to Trent's right ankle. "Naughty, naughty," he said, shaking his head, disappointed, it would appear, that his guest would treat his hospitality in such an ungrateful manner.

"I've been tied up in here for hours," Trent said, aggressively, giving the impression he might strike out with his liberated foot. "Look," Trent then added, softening his approach, "I've been in here all night and need, you know, to go to the bathroom. Either that or you'll need to fetch a mop and bucket if you catch my meaning?"

The helmet-wearing man hovered by Trent's feet with a new cable tie poised and readied for use. "Fine," he said, not appearing to relish the prospect of the mop-and-bucket option. He took a penknife from his pocket and also his gun. "I'll cut you free, but no funny business, yeah," he said, waving his weapon for Trent's benefit. "One wrong move and... well, you can figure out the rest."

Trent shook out his arms once released, restoring full blood flow to his digits. "Is it money you're after? I have money. I can pay you. Just... just let me go, yeah?"

"Money," the man said, almost sounding offended at the very suggestion. He continued cutting the remaining tie securing Trent's other ankle. "This isn't about money, Trent. Oh no no no nooo," he said, drawing out the *ooo* like a ghost. "See, I'm your biggest fan, Trent," he added, expelling air through pursed lips, imitating the sound of a motorbike exhaust. "Most people hang up posters, but I like to just kidnap the person instead. I've two popstars locked up in the room next door. I'll introduce you if you like?"

Trent offered a half-smile so as not to antagonise the absolute crackpot before him. Incredibly, as that same crackpot was currently relieving a hard-to-reach itch on his back using the muzzle of his

CHAPTER FOURTEEN – A LITTLE BIT OF ELVIS

gun. "Toilets are the second door on the left. Oh, please do remember what I said about no funny business. You see, I have tendonitis in my knee, and the doctor insisted a don't lift anything heavy. Granted, he didn't explicitly mention dead bodies, but I'm confident that you'd fit in the category of heavy and digging holes would also be considered a definite no-no."

Trent nodded his agreement, now relieved to finally stand, stretching out like a cat in front of the fire. "You're joking... about having popstars next door?" Trent asked.

"Of course I am," the man replied with a laugh. "They escaped yesterday."

Trent didn't have the available bladder capacity for any follow-up questions. With his eyes fully adjusted and the door opened, he could see his prison was, in fact, relatively sumptuous. His earlier arrival had been masked on account of, well... wearing a mask. But now he could see that this wasn't actually the dank hovel which he initially suspected. The hallway was carpeted with plush, deep-pile carpet that sank underfoot and as for the toilet, he'd seen worse in five-star hotels.

"You've got five minutes," the man advised Trent, holding up his gun in case Trent had somehow managed to forget about it during his extensive, four-metre walk from his chair. "I'll wait outside as I really don't want to hear what you're up to, okay? Oh... and just so I know you've not buggered off, or anything, I'd like you to whistle so I know you're still in there."

"I can't really whistle," Trent replied, doubled over, bladder now at bursting point.

"You can't *whistle*? Everyone can whistle, can't they?"

"Not very well," Trent suggested, offering his best effort at whistling, dispelling an impressive quantity of saliva in the process. His lips vibrated, but nothing was sounding like a whistle, rather a rasp, like a child impersonating someone passing wind.

"Sing then!"

Trent stared vacantly at the man, but owing to the tinted visor could see only his own reflection. "Sing what, exactly?" Trent asked.

"I dunno," the man replied with a shrug. "What about Elvis? I always like a little bit of Elvis."

"Fine," Trent said, clearing his throat. "Now, if you don't mind..."

The man cupped his hand near to the position of his helmet-encased ear as a gentle prompt.

"Okay..." Trent replied impatiently, and with that, burst into a somewhat respectable — considering the circumstances — rendition of "Always On My Mind."

Standing watch outside, the man in the helmet tapped his foot, humming along from behind the visor. "Louder," he shouted, rapping his fingers on the door when the initial gusto waned. Then, like pressing the volume button on the radio, the decibel level immediately increased. "Excellent!" he shouted in response. "And don't take too long. Remember, *it's now or never*," he added, chuckling at his own comic genius.

Trent soon finished (the song, not his business) and swiftly moved on to "Blue Suede Shoes."

"You asleep in there?" the man shouted, but as the singing continued, it was something of an illogical question. "Hello..." he said, opening the door with the five minutes due to soon expire. "Your chair is starting to miss you and wanted..." The man lifted his visor, providing him with a clearer view of the bathroom interior. "Oh no you bloody don't!" he screamed, darting forward towards the window. Trent's legs were dangling down from the bathroom window, with his upper half hanging outside in the fresh air. It was commendable how he was still singing with such vigour, considering.

"We're on the second floor, you idiot! You'll fall to your death," the man shouted in an unusual display of compassion for somebody he'd kidnapped only the day before. Trent's ankles were firmly gripped, and a game of tug-of-war ensued. A short-lived game, granted, with Trent registering the fact he was about twenty feet above ground level and the only way he could go, was down.

"Okay, okay," Trent shouted back through the frosted glass. "I'll come back in, just stop tugging me so hard."

CHAPTER FOURTEEN — A LITTLE BIT OF ELVIS

"Ooh, matron!" helmet-man said with a raucous chortle. He was quite the joker, it would appear. "One more pull," he added, giving Trent's legs another heave, and with that, Trent collapsed in a heap on the bathroom floor like a new-born giraffe.

"Now, what did I say about no funny business?" asked the man, visor down, pointing his gun towards Trent's chest. "Look, Partridge. Just have a little patience, yeah. I promise you that you'll be released, unharmed, in the next twenty-four hours if you just play it cool."

"Okay," Trent replied, staring up as he adjusted his trousers. "I just don't understand why—"

"You don't need to understand, Trent. You just need to know that you're part of a bigger picture and if you behave, you'll soon be on your way. Comprende?"

Trent nodded in the affirmative. "Comprende."

CHAPTER FIFTEEN
Another Chocolate Teapot

A metal bin flew through the air like an Exocet missile, coming to rest next to a fragment of the broken desk. A broken desk that would likely still have the imprint of Sidney Postlethwaite's right foot imprinted on it.

"Bastards!" Sidney bellowed, pacing in circles like a crazed bear. Periodically, he'd come to a rest, curl his fingers in a ball and shake his fist, wildly, accompanied by a verbal tirade.

"Ehm..." Caitlin offered cautiously and from the relative safety of her side of the office. "The meeting with the Tourism Minister didn't go too well?" she ventured, grimacing for fear of the reaction she might receive.

"Go well!" Sidney replied, with a sarcastic sneer. "*Go well*," he said once more, shaking his fists to the heavens. "That gormless little peckerhead has only gone and put me on administrative leave. What does that even mean? *Administrative leave*. I'm probably going to end up in some darkened cesspit processing outstanding parking ticket reminders."

"Oh," Caitlin said, for there wasn't too much more she could say that would be of comfort to her *former* boss, right about now.

"I've successfully managed the TT races for years," Sidney said, pacing the floor, once more. "Never has there been even as much as a traffic cone out of place during my tenure. Not one! I've brought this magnificent festival to a global audience, Caitlin. *Global*. And this is what they do to repay me. The gutless minister didn't even have the balls to show up in person. Oh, no... he had his snivelling little assistant, Rupert, meet me to present an email confirming I was being placed on *administrative leave*. That's all the gratitude I receive for running what is, after all, a logistical nightmare and all with a calm and steady hand."

"Well..." Caitlin bravely entered in, raising her pen, twisting it through her hair like spaghetti on a fork. "You *did* lose the Senior TT Trophy on your watch. That is to say, you signed off on the security arrangements. And now, the high-profile ambassador you invited to smooth things over has been kidnapped. You can kinda see why the minister is a little bit pissed off?"

"Thank you, Caitlin," Sidney replied, rolling his eyes. "I thought you were supposed to be on my side?"

"Sidney, you know I am," Caitlin replied, standing and moving around to the front of her desk. She parked her bum down on the surface, offering up a compassionate smile. "I don't know how many ladders you've walked under, or mirrors you've broken lately, but—"

"Have you been on the gin?" Sidney asked, eyeing her suspiciously.

"No!" Caitlin replied, narrowing her left eye. "Ah, well, that's actually a lie as I did have one at lunch. Quite large, also. I'm just saying that you're not having much luck at the moment and anything that *could* go wrong, has."

"*You're* telling *me*," Sidney said, placing his hand to his forehead. "The TT trophy has been nicked, Trent Partridge has vanished into thin air, and it that's not enough, I've just had a call advising that two trucks containing race tyres have gone on a mysterious detour. If we can't locate them, Caitlin, we may as well pack up and bugger off home as there won't be any more racing."

"Well, if you're looking for any sort of a positive, Sid? At least you now don't have to worry about the sponsors pulling out their support left, right, and centre. What with you being on *administrative leave*."

CHAPTER FIFTEEN – ANOTHER CHOCOLATE TEAPOT

"Shysters, the bloody lot of them," was Sidney's considered summary of the present situation. He collapsed into his chair for what would very likely be the final time in his current role. "Soddin' TT trophy!" Sidney mumbled, reaching for his phone. "How can something that big just disappear into thin air?" he asked, looking to Caitlin as if she might have all the answers.

Sidney dialled a number written in his black notebook, impatiently rattling his fingers off the surface of the desk. "It's me," Sidney said once the call connected. *"Sidney Postlethwaite!"* he snapped when his dulcet tones were not immediately recognised. "Where are we up to with the trophy situation as I'm now out on my arse and something of a laughingstock?" Sidney listened for a moment, nodding his head in response to what he was being told on the phone. "Okay, I see. So, you've not the faintest idea where it is, either. Is that what you're telling me?"

Judging by Sidney's bulging eyes, that was exactly what he was being told.

"I've kept you informed of every detail of this case," Sidney continued, speaking through gritted teeth. "I've even shared intelligence from both the insurance company and the police, which I shouldn't have been doing, and yet you've still nothing to go on? Is that what you're telling me, Sam? I'm now out on my ear because you've not been able to find the trophy. Well, that's just bloody marvellous!"

Sidney slammed the receiver down, before picking it up again just so he could slam it down, once more. He looked over to Caitlin, shaking his head in disbelief. "That was Sam Levy from Eyes Peeled."

"I'm guessing... no joy?" Caitlin asked. She was excellent at reading people, after all.

Sidney shook his head. "Nope, sod all."

"What about the insurance company-appointed chap?" Caitlin added optimistically.

"Drinken Popel, or whatever his name is?" Sidney replied, looking for the actual name in his notebook. "Another chocolate teapot!" Sidney added by way of explanation.

"Ah," Caitlin offered, lowering her head.

"Two private investigators, one police force, and collectively, between them all, they've not the faintest clue what's going on, while muggins here," Sidney said, jabbing himself in the chest, "is the patsy who's now out of a job."

Sidney turned in his chair, looking through the window and down on the crowds enjoying the TT catering. "It was my dream job," Sidney said with a sigh. "I love everything about this event and now... now, this. Leaving under a cloud as a laughingstock."

"You're not a laughingstock," Caitlin said with assurance, moving forward to place a hand on his sagging shoulder.

It was at that moment, a bloke wandering towards one of the many burger vans looked up, catching sight of the forlorn Sidney sat there in the window.

Caitlin cringed on Sidney's behalf as the bloke jabbed his mate in the ribs, drawing his attention to Sidney up above them. They both raised their plastic beakers of lager and, filled with enthusiasm, started to chant: "*Where's your trophy gone, where's your trophy gone!*"

"Not a laughingstock?" Sidney said, easing himself up and out of his chair. "Someone's got it in for Sidney Postlethwaite," he added, referring to himself in the third person. "And when I find out who it is..."

Sidney moved a pace closer to the window, raised his right hand, proudly extending his middle finger in the direction of the two lads below who appeared delighted to have triggered such a reaction.

🔍

Sam sat in his car with a bag of chips resting on his lap. He placed his phone on the dashboard with a heavy sigh. "That was Sidney Postlethwaite calling," Sam explained for the benefit of Abby sat next to him.

"I heard," Abby replied, with an impaled chip on her fork hovering next to her mouth. "I think half of the island heard! So, he's lost his job?"

CHAPTER FIFTEEN – ANOTHER CHOCOLATE TEAPOT

"Sounds like it, yeah. I really like old Sid, and was hoping we'd get more work from him if we did a good job on this case. The intel he was feeding us was useful, also."

"I suppose the powers that be were looking for a fall guy, and he was it," Abby suggested. "But at least with Drexel being the officially appointed investigator, we'll still have access to any leads the insurance company or police receive now he's collaborating with us."

"I suppose," Sam conceded, returning his attention to his supper.

Sam and Abby were parked up on Port Erin promenade. The sheltered bay, with its golden sands, was a firm favourite with both sun-seekers and watersport enthusiasts alike. But, on this warm summer's evening, those enjoying a BBQ on the beach and the few remaining paddleboarders wouldn't have imagined, in their wildest dreams, that they could soon be only metres away from a criminal mastermind. Sam had taken this particular parking spot as it provided a clear view of the Cosy Nook Cafe, a hundred metres or so further up the beach, and where Drexel was presently sat nursing a cuppa.

Drexel, for his part, was living up to his side of the bargain. Not only had he revealed, in detail, the interactions with Quentin Thrumbolt to date, but he'd also even managed to secure a face-to-face meeting with the shifty antique dealer at short notice. The prospect of purchasing the Queen Victoria bust apparently an excellent lure to warrant a flight to the Isle of Man.

Sam and Abby's earpieces crackled into life, followed by Drexel's whispered voice. "I'm ready and in position," Drexel said into the concealed microphone in his buttonhole.

"Roger that!" Sam replied, offering Abby a smile. "We've got to get ourselves something like that," he said, admiring Drexel's advanced technology.

"Christmas is coming," Abby replied.

"Tom and Suzie also in position," Tom confirmed over the airwaves, "and we also have eyes on Drexel."

Sam raised his spyglass to the hillside at the far end of the beach. "I can see them," Sam said, waving at Tom and Suzie sat there on a bench, up at the top, like a romantic couple enjoying the view.

"I don't think they can see you, Sam," Abby suggested, using her binoculars to have a quick look for herself. "You're enjoying this?" she asked with a smile. "I can tell. You're like... like a big kid in a sweet shop."

"Damn right," Sam replied. "Surveillance... technology... crime... chips... the woman I love next to me. What's not to enjoy?"

"Ahh. It's nice to know where I am in the pecking order. After chips, no less."

"No..." replied Sam. "What I meant to—"

"Contact!" Abby said into her walkie talkie, moving her attention back to the cafe. Drexel discreetly raised his hand in acknowledgement as a man approached him from behind.

"*He's reaching for something!*" Suzie added, with stress in her voice.

"Scrap that," Abby countered when the man's hand became visible to her. "It's just the waiter, and he's armed only with a notepad."

Sam chuckled with his heart pumping. "You don't get this adrenalin rush working in an office, now do you?"

"Do you think Thrumbolt is going to just spill his guts?" Abby asked, skipping over Sam's question. "I mean... say he *is* a fence for the criminal underworld, do you think he'd be naïve enough to talk about the theft of the trophy in public?"

"Dunno," Sam replied. "But I certainly hope so. Besides, you wouldn't be able to see the wire on Drexel as it's tiny... really small. Honestly, Abby, it's the best quality that—"

"I've told you, Sam. Christmas is coming! You'll have to wait and see what's in your stocking. If you're a good boy, that is."

One hour soon drifted into two, with Drexel now on his third coffee over at the Cosy Nook Cafe. The sun had disappeared until the next morning, having put in an admirable shift, rather like the waiter who also appeared eager to do the same, with no remaining customers, apart from Drexel.

CHAPTER FIFTEEN – ANOTHER CHOCOLATE TEAPOT

"No sign of the target," Tom confirmed, scanning the sheltered bay area from his elevated position. "Drexel, please confirm Thrumbolt has not made contact."

Drexel picked up his phone, checked the display, then offered a shake of the head followed by a shrug. "Sorry, guys," Drexel said into his buttonhole. "Something must have spooked him. Should we call it a day?"

"Roger that," Abby replied. "Disappointing, but get yourselves home. Tomorrow is another day."

Sam and Abby watched on as Drexel drained his cup then moved away as agreed. They maintained eye contact until he reached his temporary hire car, due to his usual vehicle being out of action owing to the unfortunate vandalism.

"Anything?" Abby asked as they both scoured the area to ensure Drexel wasn't being followed.

"Bugger all," Sam replied with a frustrated sigh. As Drexel drove away, Sam lowered his spyglass, picked up his phone, dialling a number he had consigned to memory. "Tom," Sam said. "Drexel's on the move... can you follow him and report back?"

"You don't trust him?" Abby asked.

Sam shook his head. "I don't think I trust many people right about now. Present company excluded, of course."

"Of course!"

Team Eyes Peeled vacated Port Erin promenade with an overwhelming sense of frustration. The no-show from Thrumbolt was a severe blow to their hopes of recovering the trophy. With the blue-riband event due to take place in less than forty-eight hours, time was now very much against them. The only positive from the evening was that Sam was able to spend quality time with his two loves: Abby, and fancy surveillance equipment.

Only... it wasn't just the crew from Eyes Peeled who were on surveillance mode this fine summer's evening, it would appear. Over on the opposite side of the bay, a silver VW Golf sat with its engine purring, the driver watching events unfolding. The male had *also* been listening in on the radio chatter, with his scanner sat on the passenger seat. If Sam was excited by Drexel's surveillance equipment, then this piece of advanced kit would have left him with bulging trousers.

"So," the male observer said, easing his leather driving gloves over each hand in turn, "the plot thickens." He curled each gloved hand into a fist, cracking several knuckles in the process. "Nobody takes me for a fool," he said with a sinister tone. "Nobody!"

CHAPTER SIXTEEN
A Load of Bollocks

Detective Inspector Rump sauntered into the offices of Eyes Peeled with the semicircle of a ring doughnut protruding from his chops. The other half filled his cheeks like a squirrel foraging for acorns. He held up a white confectionary box for inspection, giving it a gentle shake to demonstrate there were still items remaining inside.

"You brought us doughnuts?" Tom ventured, only daring to believe until he received an enthusiastic nod in the affirmative.

"I thought that was just a stereotype?" Abby asked. "You know, about cops and doughnuts?"

Rump placed the box in front of a salivating Tom, removing his notepad as he polished off his sugary treat. "Morning," Rump offered, once his gullet was free from obstruction. "I can't stay long as Hopkins is outside in the car. It's all hands to the pump at the minute after that kidnapping."

"Time to get to the doughnut shop, though?" Tom offered with a belly laugh.

Rump threw him an icy glare. "*Always* time for doughnuts," he said, winking as his expression softened. "Oh-kay," Rump said, moving on, flicking through his notepad. "Needless to say," he began, running his eyes around the room, "you've not seen me today if you catch my meaning," he said, returning his attention to his notepad. "This Thrumbolt fellow you were asking about, Tom."

"Yeah," Tom eagerly replied. "Any news?"

"I've spoken to the guys at the airport who confirm nobody of that name was booked onto any flights yesterday," Rump answered. "Or, for that matter, for the next week. This is the same chap we gave the all-clear to regarding the stolen busts previously, no?"

"The very same," Sam said. "What about the other name we gave you? Derek Popper. Any bites on that one?"

"Ah," Rump replied with a half-smile. "That one I *can* help you with, Sam," he said, referring to his notepad, once more. "There's a reservation in that name on tomorrow evening's flight to London City Airport. Anything we need to know about?" he asked with an air of caution.

Sam shook his head. "No, not just yet, but thanks. We'll keep you fully appraised with progress, but there's just a few things we need to get clear in our own minds first, DI Rump."

"Jolly good," Rump replied, moving towards the doughnut box. "One for the road," he said, pulling out another one for the road, before rejoining Hopkins for the urgent work they had to get back to.

Sam placed his head in his hands, groaning in frustration. "I wanted to trust Popek," he said, slapping his hand onto the desk. "And this is how he repays us."

"You gave him the benefit of the doubt," Abby said. "But you were right to be sceptical. So, now what?"

"Drexel definitely went straight home last night, Tom?" Sam asked.

"Like I said, Sam. Straight home. Suzie and I even parked up near his house for an extra hour, just to make sure he didn't slip straight back out."

"I just don't understand why Drexel would drag us all to a fictitious meeting with Quentin Thrumbolt," Sam said to nobody in particular. "Drexel sat there, at the café, for nearly two hours, in the knowledge that he was going to be stood up. Drexel even pretended he'd spoken to Thrumbolt to confirm his safe arrival on the island. That little conversation was a load of bollocks as Thrumbolt wasn't even booked on a flight in the first place."

CHAPTER SIXTEEN – A LOAD OF BOLLOCKS

"I hate to say it, Sam," Suzie offered reluctantly. "For whatever reason, I think it's safe to say that he's been playing us all along. And just think, Sam. If you hadn't broken into his office last week, you wouldn't have found the bank statement in the name of his alias, Derek Popper. And if we didn't know about the alias, then we wouldn't now know that Drexel Popek is soon to make his exit, stage right."

"With a healthy bank balance if that statement was anything to go by," Tom added and then, "Stage left, innit?" Tom asked, mulling over Suzie's previous statement.

Suzie frowned in return. "I'm not entirely sure, Tom? Either way, Drexel Popek, well, his alias, Derek Popper, is booked on a plane leaving tomorrow night. But why even hang about until then? Drexel must know that we'd shop him to the police over the stolen busts when we realised he's double-crossed us. It just seems a significant error of judgement, and Drexel doesn't strike me as the sort to do something so stupid."

"Unfinished business?" Sam suggested. "It's the only reason. He must have a few loose ends to tie up before he leaves."

"But what loose ends?" Abby asked.

"And, with who?" Tom added.

🔎

"Isle of Man TT Races in Disarray!" and such were the unwelcome headlines emblazoned all over the front page of the local newspapers. To make matters even worse, one of the major US TV networks had now also pulled its support of the event. With them on board, the TT would've been broadcast to an American audience, bringing with it the potential for millions in new sponsorship deals. Not now, however. Who knew that large corporations didn't like to be associated with grand larceny and kidnappings?

Adding to the overall circus, there were genuine fears that the Senior TT would need to be cancelled due to a lack of tyres. The two trucks packed to the gunnels with race-spec tyres that disappeared en route to the island had been recovered, found burnt out in a motorway layby with their precious cargo creating a cloud of rubber for miles around. It was a disaster, and not just environmental, but also for the racing teams on the island. The tyre manufacturers simply didn't have the available capacity to fulfil the order again and without rubber... no racing. A number of the privateer racers often brought their own stock with them, but the factory team riders — those likely to compete further up the leaderboard — were entirely reliant upon this supply being delivered.

Faced with the terrible prospect of cancellation, the unlikely saviour for the Isle of Man TT committee came in the form of the man they'd just sacked, Sidney Postlethwaite. Sidney, who'd accepted the offer of employment from the Isle of Wight was only too happy to release and transport their stock of tyres to assist. Once the appropriate amount of arse kissing had been satisfied by his former boss, of course, in addition to an invite as a VIP guest of honour. It was also the perfect opportunity for Tamara Urquhart to repay the hospitality afforded to her and her colleagues on their recent visit.

Presently, Team Eyes Peeled were desperate to locate Drexel Popek, but nobody knew which hole he was hiding in. Tom and Suzie were tasked with staking out Drexel's known residential addresses, whilst Abby was digging up what she could on Quentin Thrumbolt. Sam had sat in the vicinity of Drexel's office for over two hours, hoping he'd be stupid enough to put in an appearance, which he hadn't. Undaunted, Sam shifted the focus of his surveillance to Sir Barrington's palatial home, figuring Drexel might show up, what with them being thick as thieves, literally speaking.

"What a shambles," Sam said, sat in his car reading the newspaper headlines. He adored the TT races, but even more so, he loved the Isle of Man. Seeing the laughingstock they'd both become was like a knife through the heart for Sam. He threw the paper into the passenger footwell, muttering to himself. The only comfort was that the racing the following day was now going to run as scheduled, even if they didn't have a trophy to present to the winner.

Sam near on shit himself when something banged down on the side of his car. "Hello!" shouted a female voice followed by a tapping

CHAPTER SIXTEEN – A LOAD OF BOLLOCKS

of her ring on Sam's rear window. He was parked up under the cover of trees, remaining incognito, and in no way expecting any visitors in this remote location. Sam shielded his head with his arms fearing an attack, but with no sound of gunfire, broken glass, or even further raised voices to confirm an assault was in progress, he looked to the rear of the car and the source of the voice.

"Ehm..." he said, straightening himself up, offering a wave to his guest who he recognised from his previous visit to see Sir Barrington. Sam wound his window down just a touch so his voice could be heard. As he wasn't sure of her intentions, he remained safely in his car. "Olivia, right?" Sam said.

"Yes. Olivia," she replied, looking down at her heels which had sunken into the soft turf.

"Can... I... help?" Sam asked, confused about why she was stood next to his car.

"Sir Barrington would like to see you if you'd be as kind?" she asked, struggling to free her left foot from the mud.

Sam glanced around the interior of his car, wondering how on earth she knew he was there to even extend the invite. *Has a tracking device been concealed?* he wondered.

Sensing Sam's apparent confusion, Olivia pointed to a CCTV camera inside the boundary wall of Sir Barrington's considerable estate. "We were watching you sat out here," she added. "And I was sent out to request an audience."

"Suuuure," Sam replied, opening the door then stepping out. "Nice day for it," he said, filling a void that didn't need to be filled. "So, you like working for—"

"Please," Olivia said, extending an arm in the direction she'd like him to walk and completely cutting across his small talk.

"Not sure those shoes were the best choice, Olivia?" Sam suggested, eager to press on with the small talk. "There's a little bit of mud on them, and they look expensive. Were they expensive?"

Olivia walked in front of Sam as they approached a wooden door built into the boundary wall. She used her right hand to shield the keypad, securely entered the access code with her left, and with that, they were inside the compound. Sam couldn't help but feel Olivia wasn't quite as amiable as she was on their first meeting. Perhaps it was the mud all over her expensive shoes, he wondered.

Olivia escorted Sam up the white gravel path towards the front entrance of the house where the oil stain from his previous trip was still clearly visible. Unsure of the agenda, Sam reached for his phone. "I just need to report back to base," Sam said. "Just in case I get kidnapped," he added with a forced laugh. However, before he had a chance to dial the number, Sir Barrington appeared at the top of the steps, waving.

"There you are!" Sir Barrington announced in his booming authoritarian tone. "Come inside, dear boy," he said, ushering Sam in.

After the tepid reception he'd received previously, Sam looked over his shoulder to see if there were, perhaps, another visitor who he might be addressing. "He means me?" Sam asked, looking to Olivia for confirmation.

With a nod from Olivia, Sam walked up the staircase towards the imposing oak doors. Sir Barrington sported a broad grin, offering out his hand like he was greeting an old army buddy, which somewhat unnerved Sam.

"We saw you skulking about on the cameras, old bean," Sir Barrington said. "Never off duty, eh?" he asked, tapping his nose in a knowing manner.

Sam smiled, unsure how to reply and as Sir Barrington was deaf as a post, probably wouldn't have heard him in any case. Still, it was nice to be polite.

"Once again, I'm sorry about the mess on the path," Sam offered, following Sir Barrington's lead. "I've had the oil leak fixed, so, it shouldn't happen again."

Sir Barrington whistled a happy tune as he led Sam towards the dining room. "Lovely day," he said, again taking Sam off guard with his cordiality.

In the wood-panelled corridor, Sam slowed a touch, admiring the collection of portraits hanging on the wall. Sir Barrington came to a halt, looking up to the painting that'd caught Sam's eye. "My great

CHAPTER SIXTEEN – A LOAD OF BOLLOCKS

uncle," Sir Barrington explained. "Bad egg," he added. "Roving eye, if you catch my meaning, Pam," he said with a belly laugh.

Sam laughed along like they were two old friends. "Ehm..." Sam said, following Sir Barrington who'd continued on his way. "The name is Sam, Sir Barrington. Not Pam... *Sam*."

Sam dawdled behind. He'd always had a fascination with history and to see those portraits, immortalised in oil, was humbling. Sam didn't say it out loud, of course, but the Hedley-Smythe ancestors were not blessed with good looks.

Amongst the old was also new. The final portrait in the long line was a more modern affair altogether. An impressive painting of Sir Barrington surrounded by what was presumably the current crop of the bloodline hung in a shimmering gold frame. Sir Barrington cut a dashing figure, straddling a handsome grey horse, looking proudly down on his family surrounding the magnificent beast. Sam drifted away, imagining himself aboard a wild stallion, wind running through his fallen-now-restored locks (it was *his* daydream), galloping through the countryside towards the love of his life, Abby.

"Right-ho, Pam," Sir Barrington said, snapping Sam from his romantic reverie. "I've got a wonderful surprise for you. It's simply *marvellous*."

Sam was familiar with the dining room, but what he wasn't sure of is why the hell he was there. Sam looked to Olivia who'd now joined them after replacing her footwear. "Should I be concerned?" he asked through the corner of his mouth.

"You're fine," Olivia replied. "You'll be on your way momentarily."

Sir Barrington clapped his hands, setting his ruddy jowls off wobbling like a bowl of jelly. "Tell me what you see, Pam?"

"No, my name is..." Sam replied, before deciding to give up that battle as a lost cause.

Sam rotated slowly on the spot, running his eyes around the perimeter of the vast dining room. But with nothing obviously jumping out at him, Sam looked to Sir Barrington, following his eyeline for a clue for what he should be noticing. "I don't really..." Sam said, before coming to an abrupt halt as the realisation struck him like a cricket bat in the face. "What the actual..." Sam said, first turning to Olivia who buried her chin into her chest in response. She appeared almost ashamed to be involved in what was unfolding. "What's all this?" Sam asked, glaring over at a grinning Sir Barrington.

"I told you, old bean. Simply marvellous, no?" Sir Barrington moved to the stone column nearest to him, removing a handkerchief from his blazer pocket. "Have you met Queen Victoria?" he asked, giving her face a gentle wipe. "Stunning, isn't she?"

Sam walked the room, stopping at each of the stone columns in turn. Where there was once a bare slab of cold granite was now sat a substantial bronze bust. The full cast was back in situ: Sir Isaac Newton, Sir Winston Churchill, William Shakespeare, and of course, Queen Victoria, whose acquaintance Sam had already made.

"I told you it was marvellous news!" Sir Barrington gushed, like a proud parent. "I just wanted you to be the first to know," he said in his gruff, sergeant-major voice. "Anyway, Pam. Busy day and all..."

With that, Sir Barrington guided Sam towards the door eager, it would appear, for Sam to promptly disappear from whence he came.

"Woah!" Sam said, standing his ground, jaw swinging low. "What the hell?"

Sam shook his head slowly. Deliberately. He moved over, pointing to his old pal, Queen Victoria. "She was stuffed in the desk drawer of a crappy backstreet office less than forty-eight hours ago," Sam said. He moved his face closer to the bust, wondering if, perhaps, she were a twin or a duplicate of some sort. Confident it was the real deal, Sam continued, "I found Queen Victoria in a desk drawer belonging to a crooked PI that *you*, Sir Barrington, employed to steal it for the insurance pay-out along with the others. I've even got him on film confessing to the entire sordid affair."

Sam carried on over to Sir Isaac, giving him a visual inspection before adding, "And then the rest of the stolen items miraculously reappear a few hours before the entire scam is about to come crashing down around you. That's some coincidence, don't you think?"

Sam was beginning to suspect that Sir Barrington's hearing was selective, as he didn't appear to have missed a word that'd just been

CHAPTER SIXTEEN – A LOAD OF BOLLOCKS

said. Sir Barrington puffed out his chest, his cheeks vibrating from the frustrated air being expelled with force. "The bally impudence!" Sir Barrington protested. "I've had men shot for less."

It appeared that Sam's warmer welcome was now disappearing quicker than an ice cube on David Dickinson's sun lamp, with Sir Barrington's agitated state causing concern.

"Oh, *come on*," Sam said, going on the offensive. "This lot," he began, running his hand around the dining room, "all get nicked and then *happily* come back like a homesick salmon." Sam rubbed his chin, frustrated until he had a lightbulb moment. "Oh, I see what's going on, *Barrington*. You and Popek knew the game was up and so simply replaced what you'd stolen. It's brilliant now I think about it." Sam moved to Sir Barrington, circling him like a vulture. "So, what happens next, then? You simply phone the police and the insurance company to tell them there's been a bit of a misunderstanding and that the stolen items have turned back up. Where were they? Did you lose them down the back of the sofa, maybe?"

"Nonsense," Sir Barrington barked in response. "They *were* stolen, but to my immense relief, we were able to locate them before they were likely melted down or shipped off to who knows where."

"We?" Sam asked, fearing he might already know the answer to his question.

"Yes, *we*," responded a familiar voice echoing through the dining room, followed by footsteps making their grand entrance.

"I bloody well knew this little act had your hallmark written all over it," Sam said, as Drexel Popek arrived, grinning like a Cheshire cat.

"*Moi?*" Drexel asked, jabbing his two thumbs to his chest. "There's no *act* about this, Levy. This is simply a situation where a *successful* private investigator has solved *another* case. You should take notes, Sam. You might learn a thing or three." Drexel ran his finger over Sir Isaac's nose with a wry smile. "Oh, Sam," he said as if an idea had just unexpectedly arrived in his head. "I suspect I can read your mind," he said, wiggling his fingers like a puppetmaster. Drexel narrowed his eyes as if reading Sam's thoughts. "Number one. You're going to remind me about Her Majesty in my desk drawer. Number two. You're going to remind me about my confession on video. Number three. You're going to remind me about claiming Sir Barrington paid me to steal them. Have I missed anything?"

"The meeting with Thrumbolt?" Sam replied.

"Ah, about that," Drexel replied, finger aloft. "That was just to waste your time. Funny, don't you think?"

"Very," Sam replied, slow clapping the genius that was Drexel. "And, points one to three?" Sam asked before adding, "You know what, I'm not interested as whatever comes out of your mouth is horseshit anyway," he said. "This... all of it. It's all very clever," Sam said, flicking his eyes between Sir Barrington and Drexel. "So, the original plan has been modified, it would appear. The big payday would originally have been for the insurance company to cough up the full amount for the stolen busts, and you then sell them at a later date. But, with me getting too close for comfort, Drexel, *the investigative genius*, has managed to recover them all just in the nick of time. The insurance company is delighted as it now only has to pay a modest finder's fee, instead. The police won't be too concerned. In fact, they'll probably chalk it up as a positive result for their statistics, and I suppose you two will pocket the insurance reward money between you?"

Drexel returned the slow clap gesture with a feigned expression of shock. "What a wild and vivid imagination you have, Sam. It's a bit sad and bitter if I'm honest. Here I am having reunited a worried owner with his prized possessions, and all you can do is throw mud. For shame, Sam. For shame."

"Well, I must apologise, *Derek Popper*," Sam chipped in, revealing his knowledge of the alternate identity. "So, what's with the flight booking tonight? Was that Plan B if Barrington here didn't go for this latest masterplan?" Sam folded his arms across his chest as Drexel didn't immediately respond. "Cat got your tongue, Popper?"

"I... that is..." Drexel replied, evidently caught on the hop. "I'm a PI, Levy. Of *course* I'm going to have several aliases," he offered with a sneer. "Only an idiot *wouldn't*. Let me guess, Levy. You don't?"

CHAPTER SIXTEEN – A LOAD OF BOLLOCKS

Sam realised he was on a hiding to nothing at this point. For the outsider looking in, Sir Barrington employed a PI to help find his stolen items, with said PI recovering the missing items. Case closed... or at least that's how it could appear. Sam knew this sordid affair was bent as a nine-bob note, but proving it. Well, that was another matter, and Sam figured he'd had just about enough of this case.

"You know what, Drexel... Derek, or whatever you're calling yourself, well done," Sam offered magnanimously. "I'm done here," Sam said, excusing himself, "and it's probably a good idea that I go before I knock Queen Victoria there, right on her royal arse!"

Sam didn't want or wait for an escort, instead walking away without so much as a by-your-leave. He marched through the portrait corridor, stopping for a moment to make sure he'd not left his car keys on the dining room table. The very last thing he wanted to do was walk back in after his dramatic departure. Fortunately, he was spared that ordeal when he felt them in his jacket pocket. "Pompous cockalorum!" Sam said, directing his venom towards the portrait of Sir Barrington astride his horse. Sam held his gaze for a moment longer, conscious he could hear footsteps heading towards him. He whipped out his mobile phone, zoomed the camera onto the painting and snapped an image with a smile emerging.

With a renewed vigour, Sam picked up the pace, skipping down the front steps and onto the white gravel path. "*Marvellous*," he said, admiring the discharged contents of his oil sump, there on the expensive stone chippings.

Sam could feel eyes burning into the back of his head as he walked down the drive in the direction he'd first arrived. "Shysters," he said, kicking out at a smug-looking garden gnome for looking at him cockeyed.

"Ah, the access code," he said to himself, approaching the door at the boundary wall. Fortunately, the security code Olivia used earlier was only to gain access and not required to exit as he didn't fancy a long detour or having to climb the wall, like Jon Snow.

Now clear of Barrington's lair and seated back in his car, Sam loaded up the picture he'd just captured on his phone. Pinching the screen with his thumb and forefinger, he zoomed in for maximum magnification, staring intently at the photograph for several seconds. "Bingo!" Sam said eventually, snapping his fingers, distinctly pleased with himself.

Sam attached the image to a text message, then immediately followed it up with a call to the same number. "Hey, Tom, it's me," Sam said once the call connected. "Yeah, I'm all okay, honest. I've just had a somewhat surreal experience at Sir Barrington's house that I'll tell you all about when I get back. Tom, I've just texted you over a picture which I think you'll find very interesting." Sam waited for a moment until he received verbal confirmation of receipt. "Great," Sam went on. "Look, Tom. Ask the rest of the guys to drop what they were doing with regard to finding Drexel, as I just have. Found him, that is," Sam announced. "No... no... Tom, I'll fill you in with all the detail when I get back in about an hour. Tom, for now, I need you to look into something as a matter of urgency. Hang on, mate. Let me just pop you onto speakerphone so I can get moving as I'm probably being watched, right now."

Sam pressed the speaker button on his phone, placing it into a cradle on his dashboard. "You hear me, Tom?" Sam asked, driving away at pace. Well, as fast as his car would permit.

"Loud and clear, boss."

"Great. Tom, listen. I'm pretty sure I'm on to something big. I need you to start looking into something for me as a matter of urgency. Oh, and you might need to engage the services of DI Rump."

"No problem, Sam," Tom replied. "I'll get on it straight away. Let me know what you want me to do?"

"Perfect," Sam said, offering a cautionary glance in his rear-view mirror in case he was being tailed. "Tom, if I'm correct then this could be a game-changer. What I need you to do is..."

CHAPTER SEVENTEEN
Three Peas in a Pod

It wasn't that the police weren't overly interested in what Sam had to say for himself or listen to his suspicions about who did what with who. Well, that wasn't entirely true. In fact, not true in the slightest. As Sam's other recent tip-offs hadn't borne much fruit for the old bill and what with a stolen trophy and kidnapped superstar to find, police resources were thinly spread at present. DI Rump — acting on his own volition — remained happy and willing to provide support as necessary, but, as for the wider force, they were only keen if Sam had something tangible to present to them, rather than suspicions alone. The police needed something that would help them clear their considerable caseload. It was understandable, of course, as they simply had bigger fish to fry and limited resources to hold the frying pan.

In the office of Eyes Peeled, Tom and Sam had their heads buried in a paper mountain. Tom, for his part, was meticulous, with each pile stacked methodically. While Sam, on the other hand, had commandeered half of the available floor space, with paper strewn everywhere like they'd just encountered a localised tornado. Someone with OCD would be uncomfortable on Sam's side of the office right about now.

"Anything?" Sam asked, crawling on all fours, moving to another bundle of papers.

"Hmm," Tom responded, offering just enough encouragement but not raising too much expectation with the tone of his *hmm*. Tom flicked through page after page like a Blackjack dealer shuffling cards. "Possibly," Tom offered without elaboration.

Sam knew Tom well enough to understand that the response politely meant to leave him be. At least for now, anyway. Tom had a wide and varying skillset, fine-tuned during his career with the police force. An extensive period working in the financial crime unit gave him a forensic approach to company accounts, and an ability to decipher even the most elaborate and complex corporate paper trails. It took a particular character trait to feel at home delving through years and years of financial returns, and that was an attribute that Sam was most certainly not blessed with.

"It's all gobbledygook," Sam declared, slapping down a handful of paper on the carpet tiles. "It may as well be written in Spanish for all it means to me," he added with an exasperated shake of the head.

"I think you're on to something, Sam," Tom replied, pressing his glasses up the rim of his nose.

Sam looked at the disorganised chaos surrounding him. "I am?" he replied, wondering how exactly.

"You are," Tom said, lifting his head, raising his arms for a nice little stretch. "The theory you told me about might be more than just a theory."

"You think?" Sam asked, crawling eagerly towards Tom's desk.

Tom slid over the pile of documents stacked on his desk, filling the space he'd created with a piece of A2-sized white paper he'd been scribbling his thoughts down on.

Sam pushed himself upright for a clearer view of Tom's doodling. "It looks like a family tree," Sam observed. "A huge family tree," he added, moving his head closer to the page, reading the notes.

Tom tapped his pen down on the page. "This structure chart is basically a summary of *that* lot," he said, looking up to the three-foot-high stack of paper next to him. Tom lifted his pen, swirling it around the page like he was stirring his cup of tea. "To understand Barrington Hedley-Smythe's business activities, these circles I've

CHAPTER SEVENTEEN – THREE PEAS IN A POD

drawn represent a limited company that he either owns entirely or partially. Now, each of these companies is relatively transparent in their operations. For example, BHS Estates Limited appears to be responsible for his properties and the associated costs of operating those properties," Tom explained. "This company here," he went on, jabbing his pen down on the next circle, "appears to relate to his classic car collection." At this point, Tom sensed he was starting to lose Sam's attention, likely because Sam was tapping the face of his watch with his fingernail. "Yes, sorry," Tom said. "There is a point to this, I think... Sir B has several legitimate and transparent companies, yeah."

"Yeah," Sam said, reasonably sure he knew what he agreed to.

"Well, here's the thing..." Tom said, narrowing his eyes to build the suspense. "These other companies circled over here have Sir B listed as a director, but the ownership appears, from what I can see, to be nominee shareholders, meaning—"

"Can you summarise?" Sam said. "Only I need to leave soon."

"Okay," Tom said. "In the simplest terms, Sir B owns several companies that appear entirely legit. He also holds several more companies with opaque ownership. Opaque, as it's virtually impossible to identify who all the shareholders are and also what the company actually does. These structures can be used for genuine reasons. But they can also be used by unsavoury people trying to disguise what exactly is going on. Fortunately, however, I've been able to at least identify the directors if not the shareholders."

"Okay, so...?"

"So..." Tom replied. "This company here, BHP Limited, not only has Sir Barrington Hedley-Smythe listed as a director, but also one *Mr Derek Popper*.

"Back the truck up!" Sam shouted. "I *knew* there was something else going on. What about the other person I mentioned? Are they listed on anything?"

Tom offered up a toothy smile. "Yup! Also listed as a director along with Sir B and Derek Popper. Three peas in a pod, you might say."

Sam sat on the corner of Tom's desk, head bowed, gently caressing his chin. "Oh no," Sam said after several seconds contemplating.

"What's up, Sam?"

"Do you have a list of Barrington's properties in those documents?" Sam asked, grabbing his car keys from his desk.

"Sure, but there were quite a few listed in the public accounts, though."

"Grab them, Tom. This case is now a lot bigger than stolen bronze busts and, Tom, I think Abby and Suzie could be in real danger. We need to go now!"

"Roger that, Sam. I'm right behind you."

🔎

"Terry, are you bloody stupid or something?" barked a shrill voice from the rear of the car.

Terry released his grip from the gearstick, raising his hand in submission. "Sorry, skipper," he offered, "it's just that there are so many potholes, so it was a case of swerving or—"

"Not interested," came the curt reply. "Just... just, watch where you're going as I've now a streak of red lipstick smeared across my cheek."

"Sorry, skipper. Will do," Terry replied. He grimaced as a waft of what was likely extortionately priced perfume moved through the cabin of the car, catching him at the back of the throat. His eyes watered from resisting the overwhelming urge to cough. Instead, he pressed down on the walnut button to open the window, diluting the plume with fresh air in the process.

"Are you deliberately trying to destroy my hair?" came the harsh response to the window opening. "Is that what you're trying to do?"

"Ehm, no. Of course not," Terry replied, fumbling for the button, once more. "There we go," he added with the window now closed. He flicked his eyes to the rear-view mirror, hoping to see a glimmer of gratitude in return. Even a faint smile would be appreciated, but nothing. He was likely wondering, right about now, if the money paid was really worth being spoken to like he was pond scum.

CHAPTER SEVENTEEN – THREE PEAS IN A POD

Terry placed his gloved finger on his bald head, rubbing the dried blood, a result of the earlier wet shave. "It's nice here," he observed, enjoying the seaside vista on the winding coastal road.

"Explain to me how you avoid potholes when you're gawping out the window?"

"Sorry, skipper," Terry replied, looking in the mirror with solemn eyes, like a chastised puppy. He moved his Ray-Bans down the bridge of his nose, shifting his attention between the road ahead and the road behind. "I think we might have company, skipper," he said.

"What. From who?"

Terry planted his right foot to the floor, regardless of the potential makeup-smearing for his passenger. The car attracting Terry's eye was three vehicles back. As Terry pulled away, his suspicions were confirmed when the suspect vehicle immediately increased its own pace in response. "That's confirmed," Terry said, gripping the wheel firmly in both hands. "That monstrosity has been following us for fifteen minutes, skipper. You don't see many fluorescent pink convertible Beetles on the road, so it caught my attention. Want me to double back and shake it off?"

"We don't have time," came the immediate response. "And trust me, I don't want my departure from this island to be delayed any longer than is absolutely necessary. Lose them!"

"That'll mean driving erratically," Terry said, with the merest hint of sarcasm. "I thought you wanted me to drive—"

"I don't pay you to think, Terry. Lose them!"

Terry was a professional henchman, a seasoned campaigner — as the multiple scars on his head would attest to — and he simply adored a good old-fashioned car chase. It was one of the many highlights of his job, he would often remark. "Outstanding, skipper," he said, dropping down a gear on the throaty BMW, leaving the pink flamingo on wheels in its wake and a broad smile on Terry's mush.

Ten or so adrenalin-fuelled minutes later and now in the north of the island, Terry slowed up, pulling off the main road and turning onto a gravel track. He took a cautionary glance over his shoulder, pleased to see there was nobody on their tail. "We're here," Terry said, easing to a halt where he turned off his sat-nav. "Nice place," he added, admiring the handsome stone buildings surrounding the cobbled courtyard where he'd parked.

"The door," came the frustrated instruction from behind him.

"Oh... yes. Yes, of course, skipper," Terry said, flustered, jumping out to offer assistance. "There you go," he said, opening the car door offering a hand out of courtesy which was, of course, promptly ignored.

"Keep alert, yes!"

"Of course," Terry replied. "Never off duty," he said, offering a salute for no apparent reason, his eyes scanning the surrounding countryside. "Don't you just love the great outdoors..." he said, but his passenger had moved away, heels clicking off the stone cobbles.

"Come on, then," she snapped, tutting at the complete inconvenience of having to turn her head.

Alerted by the noise of the newly arrived car, curtains were twitching behind the wooden sash windows up ahead. Four separate stone buildings hugged the central courtyard, and it was initially unclear in which direction Terry and his passenger should head towards. Fortunately, the clunk of a lock being unfastened offered them a clue. A further indication came from the door being opened, and then further confirmation when a head appeared from behind it.

"Ahh, welcome!" Sir Barrington Hedley-Smythe boomed, offering a generous wave, walking down the stone steps. "I was starting to worry you'd got yourselves lost." Sir Barrington moved his face closer to the woman stood before him, placing a polite kiss on either cheek.

"We were followed," she replied.

"I lost them," Terry entered in, happy with himself.

"Ah... yes. Very good," Sir Barrington said, looking over both of their shoulders to confirm if they had, in fact, shaken off those who were tailing them. "Anyway," he said, extending his hand, ushering his guests in the direction of the door he'd just appeared through,

CHAPTER SEVENTEEN – THREE PEAS IN A POD

taking another cautionary glance as he did. "Things have taken something of an unfortunate turn, my dear."

"How so?" she replied.

"Well," Sir Barrington said, considering his words as he climbed the steps, "I had a situation with some stolen busts, would you believe," he added with a laugh. "And, unfortunately, this other situation has attracted the attention of a local private investigator, you see."

"No, I don't see. What do stolen busts have to do with me?"

"Ah, well. Tenacious little sod he is," Sir Barrington explained. "He's sunk his teeth into my business something awful. I fear that his investigations concerning my stolen possessions may have inadvertently steered him towards other commercial matters, if you catch my meaning?" he said, wetting his lips with his tongue.

"Uncle!" the exasperated woman said with a scowl. "You're telling me that some country bumpkin investigator is aware of our dealings?"

"Well... very possibly, yes," Sir Barrington said, adjusting his collar. "I somewhat underestimated this Sam Levy fellow, it would appear. He presents himself as something of a buffoon, but I'm starting to suspect that it's just some sort of ploy and that the guy is, in actual fact, an investigative genius. I'm now a touch concerned that he might have been the one in the car following you. He's also probably a master of disguise and could be watching us, right now?"

"Uncle," she said, "the car following us was not the work of a master of disguise."

"No, sir," Terry entered in. "The car was bright pink with what looked like a yellow daisy on the bonnet. Far from being in disguise, that car stood out like a polar bear in the snow with the shits... if you take my meaning, sir."

"Mmm," Sir Barrington replied. "If not him, then who? Perhaps..." he added, almost reluctantly, "perhaps we need to undo what we've done while we still have the opportunity?"

"Utter nonsense," came the immediate rebuff. "Uncle," she said, staring intently, "this project is bigger than the two of us. We simply can't just take our ball back and go home. That just wouldn't do. If we have a private investigator sticking their beak where it's not wanted, well, we just have to make it go away."

"We do?" Sir Barrington asked.

"Of course," she replied. "And, fortunately, we have just the person to help us accomplish that task," she said, looking towards the hulking figure of Terry stood a yard behind her.

Terry smiled, pleased to be involved. "That you do," he said, with a sniff. "Just point me in his direction, and my baseball bat and I will be happy to help him consider the error of his ways."

Sir Barrington cocked his head, cupping his ear. "You're making no sense, man. What's his cat got to do with anything?" he asked, leading them into the kitchen.

"No, no, I said..." Terry began, but rather than repeating the threat, simply smiled.

"Bright pink, you say?" Sir Barrington added, catching Terry off guard with what appeared to be a randomly timed comment with the conversation having already moved on from that point. Terry continued smiling, likely wondering if he should take the fellow for a cup of warm cocoa and tuck him up in bed.

Sir Barrington retrieved his reading glasses from inside his jacket pocket. "Over there," he said, moving to the kitchen window. He pointed furiously in the direction of the narrow road meandering down the hillside a short distance away. "That's a pink car," Sir Barrington said, his visual acuity sharper than his hearing, it would appear.

Terry stopped smiling, taking up a position next to Sir Barrington. He watched on as the car disappeared behind the treeline before coming into view, evidently heading in their general direction. "I hate to say this, skipper, but that's certainly them. That's the same car that was following us."

"But how?" she asked.

Terry ran from the kitchen, through the courtyard towards their car. He crouched down on one knee, running his fingers along the underside of the vehicle.

CHAPTER SEVENTEEN – THREE PEAS IN A POD

"Anything?" Sir Barrington asked, following closely behind with his niece.

"Hang on," Terry said, lowering himself onto his back to gain a better view of the subject matter. "Crafty bastards," Terry said, emerging from under the car with a mucky hand and a small electronic device between his fingers. "They must have placed a tracking device on the car," he said. Terry opened the car door, retrieving what remained of his lunch. He peeled off one side of the sandwich, placed the tracking device inside, then rolled the dough into a tight ball.

"That's not going to stop a tracking device working!" the woman chided him.

"I don't want to stop it working, skipper," he said, throwing the dough ball to the far side of the courtyard, casual as you like. Before the rolling ball of bread had even come to a rest, a starving seagull swept down, polishing off the unexpected treat in one sitting, before taking flight once more.

"Bloody good show!" Sir Barrington said, offering a round of applause in appreciation as the bird soared majestically on high, taking with it the tracking device. Well, that is until the seagull landed back on the chimney stack of his property to enjoy its lunch and admire the view.

"Terry!" the woman said. "That car is going to be here in a few minutes, and we don't have time to play scarecrow. Can you greet our—"

"On it," Terry replied, opening the boot of the car. "I've even brought my welcoming committee," he added, kissing the barrel of his well-used baseball bat. "I'll be sure to make them feel very welcome. Very welcome, indeed!" he added, climbing into the driver's seat with his bat placed on the passenger side for company.

Sir Barrington watched on as Terry drove down the driveway, whistling a happy tune through his opened window. "Scary chap," he whispered, for fear of being heard.

"You get what you pay for, Uncle," came the satisfied response.

"I'm not sure about all this, you know. You're my niece, and I'll always support you. But all this? Private investigators and men with baseball bats. It's all a bit…"

"It'll all work out, Uncle. Trust me on this, and soon our only concern will be what we're going to do with all of the money we make," she said. Moving a pace closer to him, she placed her hand on his shoulder. "Uncle, I hope you've been the perfect host to our guests that you've had to stay with you?"

"What… oh, yes. Very much so," Sir Barrington replied, nodding with jowl-shaking vigour. "All the money," he added dreamily. "You know, Tamara. I always said you were my favourite niece!"

"I'm your *only* niece," Tamara replied, moving in to offer a cuddle. "And I'm going to make us all exceptionally wealthy."

The modest engine in Sam's teenage Ford Fiesta screamed like a Boeing 747 taking to the skies. He kept his right foot pinned to the floor even though he was sure the exhaust pipe was presently only hanging on by a metallic shard judging by the racket.

"Phone them again," Sam said, tearing through the pretty seaside village of Laxey, offering an apologetic wave for running straight through a halt sign, cutting up an irate taxi driver in the process. He was confident it wasn't a friendly wave he received in return, however.

"I'm trying," Tom replied, struggling with his phone in one hand and the other gripping the side of the seat to steady himself. "Both of their phones are switched off, Sam," he said, now using both hands to grip the seat. "Sam, please slow down as a tram is coming," Tom suggested, pointing to the electric tram descending from Snaefell mountain towards the tram station in the village, having to cross over the road in the process. "Stop!" Tom said, panic dripping from his voice. "You won't make it," he added, clearly not fancying a game of chicken with a tram.

Sam reluctantly slammed on the brakes, coming to a snaking halt as the electric tram crossed the road directly in front. The concerned

CHAPTER SEVENTEEN — THREE PEAS IN A POD

tram driver threw Sam a stern look as he tooted his whistle. The passengers in the rear carriages offered a cheery wave to the stationary traffic with most of the waiting drivers eager and willing to return the friendly gesture. Not Sam, however. "Hurry the fudge up," he said through gritted teeth, wiggling his fingers in a token effort of a wave. "What about phoning Rump?" he suggested to Tom.

"And say what, Sam? That we've two colleagues who we suspect are missing because their phones are switched off?"

"Aww," Sam said, slapping the top of the steering wheel. "I'm just worried about them, Tom. Trust me, Abby never has her phone switched off. It once rang when we were... in fact, never mind."

Tom and Sam were headed to the parish of Bride in the north of the island. Well, they would be once the tram permitted their journey to continue. Sam was still frustrated over the entire bronze bust farce but was now convinced that Sir Barrington was even less reputable than he initially suspected and involved in other, broader criminal endeavours.

Tom had worked wonders uncovering a paper trail revealing Sir Barrington owned multiple businesses with their ownership disguised, or, exceptionally challenging to establish. This wasn't the norm for an ageing knight of the realm, they both figured, and warranted further investigation. Throw in the discovery that both his niece, Tamara Urquhart, and Derek Popper — aka Drexel Popek — were also listed on various company documents alongside him, then something just didn't feel right.

It was fortunate, then, that Sam had been invited inside Sir Barrington's house the day before. And even more fortunate that he'd clapped eyes on the family portrait as he had. Having only just read the newspaper article about the tyre-related assistance from the Isle of Wight, Sam was able to recognise Tamara's face in the painting and establish the family connection.

She might have been an innocent party, Sam suggested to Tom, but if she was, she could have chosen less dubious business partners. Unsure if Tamara was involved in the plot to steal the bronze busts or not, the fact she was, at present, on the island (as confirmed by the article in the newspaper) was too much of a coincidence, Sam felt.

As such, Suzie and Abby were dispatched to tail Tamara and rattle a few trees, just to see if anything of interest landed on the ground. Suzie had checked in with Tom earlier, confirming that they'd made contact and were following Tamara, heading north. Nothing more had been heard, however, and their phones were now turned off.

Tom had uncovered the extent of Sir Barrington's property empire on the island, which consisted of thirteen in total. Tom was able to cross-reference three properties located in the north of the island, figuring that Tamara was likely heading to one of them. Two of the properties were holiday let flats and the other, a former farm that was presently being renovated. This was the destination, Tom felt confident, and the destination to where Sam's dilapidated Ford Fiesta was currently headed. Also of significance, as confirmed through public records, was that Sir Barrington had recently remortgaged a number of his properties. The question had to be asked, was Sir Barrington's empire falling down around him or was he simply raising cash to fund new ventures?

"Bloody finally," Sam said, smiling to the small child sat at the rear of the tram pressing his nose up against the glass. "You've a rough idea where this farm is?"

"I don't," Tom replied. "But Google Maps certainly does, so, let's get a move on and try not to kill us both en route."

Sam did as instructed, putting pedal to the metal, releasing an ear-shattering rumble through his struggling exhaust pipe, startling those stood on the pavement opposite.

Also delayed by the tram full of jubilant tourists, was a silver VW Golf. Unfortunately, Sam was too focussed on the road ahead to observe that this car had been tailing them for the last two miles.

"Lead on!" the driver of the Golf said, dropping down a gear and planting his right foot as he took off in pursuit.

CHAPTER EIGHTEEN
No Bloody Signal

"Double-check the soles of your shoes, first," Tom said, casting a suspicious glance at Sam's trainers.

"What? What are you on about?" Sam replied, trying to place his dangling foot into Tom's intertwined fingers. "Are you going to give me a leg-up, or not?" Sam asked, hopping on his standing foot.

Tom looked up from his hunched position. "Of course I am, Sam. It's just that when I was a kid, I gave my mate Lofty a leg-up and the sole of his shoe was covered in dog shit. It took months to get the smell out of my nostrils. I can taste it now, at the back of my throat, even just talking about it. You can understand why I'd be so cautious?"

Rather than labour the point of what appeared to be a painful childhood memory, Sam presented his sole for inspection. "Happy?"

"Climb aboard," Tom offered with a smile, taking the strain with his back resting against the trunk of the tree for support. "Bloody Nora, Sam," Tom wailed when Sam planted his foot down in his hands. "I... can't... hold you for long," he said through a series of pained groans, arms shaking under the burden.

"Just a little higher," Sam said, stretching for the branch evading his outstretched fingers by mere centimetres. "Just a bit more," Sam added, with Tom straining and a hernia a genuine concern.

"I'm trying, Sam, but you weigh a ton."

"It's just a little holiday weight from Abby's good cooking," Sam rebuffed. "Right... nearly there, Tom," Sam said, and then, "Got it," he confirmed, joyfully hanging with one hand wrapped around the branch above his head, swinging back and forth like a chimpanzee. A chimpanzee lacking in agility, dexterity, or absolutely any upper body strength. "Stand clear!" Sam warned a second before his fingers gave way, sending him crashing to the ground. "Help me up," Sam asked, raising his hand, "I think I've broken my coccyx," he added, rubbing the general area of his lower back. After a minute of general whimpering, Sam stood, dusting dried mud and leaves off his jeans. "What now?" Sam asked. "We need to see what's going on inside the farm and that tree would have been the perfect vantage point."

"We could try again?" Tom suggested, glancing up the height of the towering tree, but the collective silence indicated neither were willing or able to risk further injury. Both knew that if they were nine or ten years old, they'd have been up that tree quicker than a rat up a drainpipe, but now... not so much.

A combination of Google Maps and Sam's Fiesta delivered them safely to Sir Barrington's remote farm. Unfortunately, the property was set back from the main road by at least two hundred metres making a visual inspection of the building challenging even using Sam's spyglass. The addition of a single-story wall circling the compound like a medieval castle didn't help matters either.

After their brief, painful, and unsuccessful reccy from the road, they decided that advancing up the farm track was not an option as they'd likely be noticed before reaching the top of the lane and climbing anything wasn't an option, for woeful athletic reasons alone.

Several fields surrounded the farm (as you'd expect) so Sam suggested a detour across the grass to approach the main buildings from the rear, hoping there would be further opportunity for a stealthy approach.

Still stood at the roadside, Tom weighed up the benefits of the field-based approach Sam suggested. "I've got a pantomime cow costume at home," Tom chipped in, having given the matter serious

CHAPTER EIGHTEEN – NO BLOODY SIGNAL

thought. "Wearing that, we could have just wandered casually across the field with you at the front and me at the rear. We'd just need to make sure a bull doesn't take a fancy to us. In fact, for that reason you should probably go at the rear," Tom added, but his attention was moving elsewhere and his expression grave.

"Tom?" Sam said in response to the faraway gaze. "Hello, Tom... wakey, wakey."

"Follow me," Tom instructed, breaking into a rarely seen jog which quickly developed into a full-on sprint. Tom continued running up the road until the next corner.

"What's going on?" Sam asked, puffing his cheeks, following behind without question as a competent partner should. "What have you seen? Is a bull chasing us?" Sam asked, looking back and running sideways like a crab.

"No," Tom said, dropping down on one knee. "Sam, I don't want you to worry," he added, retrieving what he'd seen and the source of his concern, jutting out through a fern bush by his foot.

"What is it?" Sam asked, now caught up.

"It could be nothing," Tom replied, pulling out and holding up a half-metre-long cracked piece of bright pink plastic encasing a yellow indicator.

"That looks like part of a car bumper," Sam said, taking the item from Tom's grasp for closer inspection. Tom didn't speak, giving Sam a few extra seconds to catch up. "Holy shitsticks," Sam added when the penny finally dropped. "That's pink. The same colour as Suzie's car!"

"Now, let's not panic too much," Tom suggested, but the shaking tone of his voice indicated he was, very much, panicking.

Sam spotted several smaller pink shards. He followed the trail of plastic breadcrumbs into the bushes until he happened upon a substantial car-shaped gap, punched through the thicket revealing the precipitous angle of the riverbank.

"Tom!" Sam shouted behind him, clambering down the earthen slope to the swollen river below, with no concern for his own safety.

"Tom. It's Suzie's car, she must have crashed. Phone an ambulance now!"

Tom did as instructed, pacing back and forth with his phone pressed to his ear. "Come on," he said, blood pressure increasing by the second. "There's no bloody signal, Sam," Tom said, checking the display when the call dropped. Tom shifted across the road, hoping a clear line of sight to the surrounding hillside might improve the signal, but no. "Sam, it's no use," he said, the desperation in his voice apparent.

"Don't panic," Sam said with his head emerging through the undergrowth. "The car was empty," he added, a mix of relief, confusion, and mud on his face.

Tom pocketed his phone, moving to offer a helping a hand. "Is there any sign of the girls?"

"No," Sam replied, struggling to gain traction against the greasy surface until Tom really put his back into the recovery effort. "I'm no expert, Tom. But from the obvious damage to the rear of the car, it looks like they were forced off the road. We need to get DI Rump and the cavalry here, right now!"

🔎

Thievery and fraud were terrible enough, but forcing a car from the road was moving into another criminal league, altogether. Sam and Tom were genuinely concerned about what they were potentially walking into. Police backup would have been quite useful, right about now, but with no phone signal and Suzie and Abby missing, the time for action was now, Sam and Tom figured.

And so, the two of them headed through the fields, hoping to approach the farm from the rear, unnoticed...

"How's your leg?" Tom asked, offering a sympathetic smile.

"It's still twitching," Sam said, vigorously rubbing his thigh. "Why the hell would they even have an electrified fence on a disused farm? It's just a complete waste of energy and probably costing them a fortune to operate. Maybe they've got those solar panels or something? Anyway, at least the fence wasn't barbed wire, I suppose."

CHAPTER EIGHTEEN – NO BLOODY SIGNAL

Tom spun around with his hand in the air. "No, it's still useless, Sam," he added, cursing his phone. "There's just no signal up here in the absolute arse end of nowhere." Tom continued to wave his phone through the air with his eyes fixed on the signal strength icon on the screen. "Sam," Tom said with an air of caution. "Without any police backup, do you think we should head back and take a drive to a less secluded spot? At least then we could phone Rump. I don't mean to be dramatic, but they could be armed?"

Sam continued walking with a slight limp and the occasional judder. "Tom, I know exactly what you're saying, and I agree entirely," Sam said, agreeing entirely. "But, by the time we get a signal and wait for the police to arrive, the girls could be, well... I don't even want to think about it. Look, Tom, you should go, yeah?" Sam stopped for a moment, turning to his colleague and friend. "I'll be fine, honest. You head back and find somewhere with some phone signal?"

Tom contemplated the suggestion for a moment before replying. "Nonsense, man! Let's go," he said, sallying forth. "Besides, Sam. It'd take me at least ten minutes to find a signal and another twenty for the police to get here from HQ. And I can't leave you to have all the fun, now can I?

"You're a good man, Tom. One of the best," Sam said, taking a moment to embrace his comrade-in-arms.

"Sam, what the hell was..." Tom said, breaking the embrace, taking a step back.

"Don't panic," Sam said, rummaging in his pocket. "It was just my spyglass," he said, holding it up for inspection.

The two investigators traversed several fields and, fortunately, encountered no livestock to worry them, or for them to worry. It'd been a significant detour, but their rear approach strategy brought them to within close proximity of the farm buildings without, hopefully, being observed.

Sam deployed his spyglass, running his eye studiously over the area. "I... can't... see... any people," he said, scanning the farm. "But, I can see a way in, at least." Sam used the spyglass as a pointer for

Tom's benefit. "That gate there," Sam said, as Tom tucked in behind him to follow the line of his hand.

"Yeah," Tom replied, with one eye closed, staring intently. "I see it."

"We'll go in that way," Sam suggested, picking up speed. "Beyond the gate is a stone path through what appears to be the stable block. At the far end, it opens up into a small courtyard where I could see a black car parked. If there's a car there are likely people, so we should proceed with caution."

"Then what do we do?" Tom asked, following behind. "I mean, what do we do once we've climbed the gate and made it through to the courtyard?" he said with concern in his voice. "I should recheck my phone signal," he added, but the expletive that followed indicated the outcome of that investigation.

Approaching what appeared to be a dilapidated barn with half its roof missing, Sam and Tom stopped for a moment. They pressed their backs up against the stone wall, composing themselves. The gate and their entry point now only a short distance up ahead at the end of the building they were resting up against.

"Right," Sam said, taking a series of deep breaths. He formed a V-shape with two fingers, which he pointed to his eyes and then over in the direction of the gate. And with that, Sam was on the move.

"Wait," Tom said, gripping Sam's sleeve, pulling him back and preventing his progress. "What's with the fingers?" he asked.

"Shh," Sam said, pressing one of those fingers against his lips. "It's what they do in the special forces," Sam whispered. "I saw it in a film. They do that before storming a building, so, if it's good enough for the SAS then..."

"Ah, okay. I just didn't know if you were being rude, or something. Carry on."

Sam took several generous side steps until the gate was in touching distance. Barely daring to breathe, he looked around the corner towards the empty stable block and then retracted his head. "I can't see anybody," Sam said, returning his attention to Tom. "But, I could

CHAPTER EIGHTEEN – NO BLOODY SIGNAL

see that the black car in the courtyard has a cracked headlight and large dint across the front."

"Now we know who forced Suzie's car off the road," Tom said, snarling.

"Let's go," Sam said, making short work of getting over the metal gate with Tom following closely behind. Sam, more proficient at climbing gates than trees, it would appear.

Crouched down, tiptoeing like cartoon villains, the only thing missing was a black bag marked *swag*. "Which one do you think?" Sam asked upon reaching the end of the stable block. The two were now presented with a clear view of the courtyard, but with no apparent sign of life, it was unclear which of the buildings were populated, if any.

It was eerily quiet and without atmosphere, almost like the four-minute warning had been sounded, and everyone had disappeared, quick smart.

Tom tapped Sam on the shoulder, drawing his attention to the closest structure in the left corner of the courtyard. "There's an open window," Tom said, creeping forward in the crouching tiptoed posture that'd served them well, so far. "We can try going in there?" he suggested.

Tom wouldn't ordinarily be considered by many to be overly athletic, but with his colleagues in potential danger, he was across the courtyard and through that window quicker than a discharged bullet. "Come on," Tom said, leaning out and offering Sam a hand. "I think it's the cleaners' room," Tom said, helping Sam climb inside.

"Nicely done, Tom," Sam offered once safely through the window. Sam walked over to and pressed his ear up against the closed door. "I can't hear anybody, Tom. Should we make a move?"

Tom shook his head, rummaging in the cupboards beneath the stainless-steel sink. "Hold up, Sam," he said, moving to the nearby storage cupboard. "We're unarmed, Sam. We don't know what danger we're going to face so I'm just looking for something we can—"

"Like this!" Sam asked, twisting the wooden handle of a mop loose.

"Ah, perfect," Tom said, reaching for the brush near to Sam. "There's some age in these," he said, repeating the same process as Sam. "You can tell they're old due to the weight. Real quality," Tom suggested, now holding up his own liberated wooden handle like a pugil stick. "Yes, most adequate, Sam," he added. "If you were struck by one of these, you'd most certainly know about it."

"Well, when you woke up, that is," Sam countered, pressing his ear up against the door, once more. "Ready?" he asked of Tom.

Sam could feel his heart bouncing against his ribs as he opened the door, weapon poised. Fortunately, the coast appeared to be clear, so he gave Tom the nod before taking several tentative steps forward. It was only a single-story building, but there were at least five doors on this corridor alone. "Blooming heck," Sam said. "Where do we even start?"

"Right there," Tom suggested, heading towards the room at the far end of the corridor. "Look," Tom said, pointing to the carpet, "muddy footprints outside, which would suggest that there's been recent activity through this door."

Sam put his ear to work, once more, listening intently.

"Anything?" whispered Tom.

"I can only hear the pulse in my ear," Sam replied. "Try the door," Sam said, keeping his ear pressed against the wood.

Tom pressed gently down on the brass door handle. "It's moving," he said wide-eyed.

Sam stepped back, preparing to either charge or defend himself. Whichever situation presented itself, he was braced and ready for action.

Tom eased the door open an inch at a time, grimacing for fear of a creaking hinge or something else announcing their presence. When a sufficient gap presented itself, Tom filled it with his head, peering into the room behind the door.

"Sweet Lord," Tom said, immediately snapping his head back, slamming the door shut on what he'd just been a witness to.

"What is it?" Sam asked, taking a firm grip on his wooden handle.

CHAPTER EIGHTEEN – NO BLOODY SIGNAL

Tom swallowed hard. "Sam, there's a blindfolded man in that room tied to a chair. I think he had a golf ball or something stuffed in his mouth?"

"What, like Pulp Fiction?" Sam asked.

"I've never watched it," Tom said with a shrug and then, changing the subject to the matter at hand, "What the hell do we do now? About him?" he asked, throwing his thumb in the direction of the door.

"Maybe he's one of the bad guys?" Sam suggested.

"Tied to a chair?"

"I dunno? Maybe he's into the kinky stuff, and you walked in at the wrong time," Sam countered. "Or, the *right* time? Maybe he was hoping for somebody else to turn up, and, well, you know…"

Tom, ignoring Sam, reasoned the man trussed up like a chicken for the oven presented a minimal threat and so reopened the door, repeating the process of poking his head through the gap for a look inside. Confident the seated chap was alone, Tom pushed the door open completely, moving towards the chair positioned in the middle of the otherwise empty room.

Sam cautiously joined Tom, with the two of them stood in front of the blindfolded man, quite unsure what to make of the unnerving situation.

"Hold this," Sam said, handing his Gandalf staff to Tom. Sam felt for a knot at the rear of the blindfold without success. "A-hah!" Sam muttered to himself. "It's elasticated," Sam explained, plucking the fabric like a guitar string, slapping against the poor fellow's head in the process. "I had an elastic tie at primary school," he added. "People always tugging at it."

Blindfold now removed, the seated man winced. He was evidently distressed with a couple of days' worth of stubble and fear written all over his face.

Sam tilted his head, examining the face staring back at him from the chair. "What… the… actual…" Sam said, releasing the strap which secured the obstacle in his mouth. "You know who this is?" Sam asked.

Tom's jaw swung low as the realisation struck him. "That's Trent Partridge," Tom said, confirming what Sam already likely suspected.

"I knew Sir Barrington was up to his neck in something!" Sam said, reaching the for the cable tie securing Trent's wrists behind his back.

"Wait," Tom said, grabbing Sam's hand. "Don't free him."

"*Why not*?" Sam and Trent both said in unison,

"Look, Trent," Tom said, having a quick look over his shoulder, ensuring they were still alone. "Our friends are in real danger, so we need to find them first. If we release you now and your captors find your seat empty, well, that's going to put us all in danger as they'll know we're here. We'll come back to you soon, I promise! Sam, pop that ball... thing... back in his... what actually is that?"

"It's a miniature basketball," Sam suggested.

"It's a ball you'd give a dog," Trent replied.

"Is it?" Sam asked, intrigued, giving it a little squeeze, producing a shrill squeak. "Oh, aye," Sam said, smiling.

"Please, just phone the police?" Trent pleaded, with his bottom lip wobbling.

"No phone signal," Sam explained, holding his thumb and pinkie finger to his ear in the universal explanation of anybody, anywhere, describing how a phone is used. "Who kidnapped you?" Sam asked, "And why? Was it an old pompous-looking chap with chubby cheeks?"

"I-I-I," Trent stuttered, appearing somewhat dazed by the arrival of his new guests. "I-don't... I'm unsure, that is. The only man I've seen is dressed in black, wearing a motorcycle helmet. I never saw his face. Look, please don't leave me in here, yeah?"

"I'm sorry," Tom said, loosely placing the gag back into his mouth. "I promise you that we'll be back for you, and soon. Just don't mention us being here if anybody comes in for you?"

Sam then placed the blindfold back over the head of a bewildered Trent. "What the hell is going on?" Sam asked, shaking his head. "Why on earth is one of the world's most famous motorbike racers tied up in an old farmhouse. What is Sir B up to...?"

CHAPTER EIGHTEEN — NO BLOODY SIGNAL

"I dunno," Tom replied. "But, whatever it is I really, *really* wish we had some phone signal," he said, sticking his head out into the corridor. "Right. It's clear."

Sam patted Trent on the shoulder. "Back very soon," he said, giving him a gentle squeeze of assurance. "Wait up, Tom," Sam said, grabbing his wooden handle from next to the door. "You know you should watch it," Sam said, once caught up. "It's terrific."

"What is?" Tom asked, twisting his head back in Sam's direction.

"Pulp Fiction," Sam replied.

"Ah. Well, if we get out of this unscathed, we can have a film night around mine."

"Excellent," said Sam. "It's really very good."

CHAPTER NINETEEN
A Funny Place to Take a Nap

Sir Barrington stood directly below a mounted and stuffed moose, holding a substantial glass of whiskey in his shaking hand. "This is an unmitigated disaster," he declared, taking a generous slug and with the reddening of his bulbous nose, it likely wasn't the first. "Tamara, this is not what I signed up for," he went on, rocking his head in frustration.

"Uncle, I've told you it's all under control. These latest developments are just a temporary inconvenience, like a splinter."

"*A ruddy splinter,*" Sir Barrington bellowed, moving towards the crystal decanter for a top-up. "We've got the motorcycling world champion tied up in one building, and now we've managed to acquire two female investigators tied up in the kitchen."

"I told you Terry was proficient at his job," Tamara replied, offering Terry a nod of approval.

Terry offered a bashful reply. "When you enjoy what you do, it's not really a *job*," he said, using his knuckles to polish imaginary medals on his chest.

"Uncle... Uncle... Uncle," Tamara said, in a soothing voice. "If, and it's a big *if*, something were to go sour, then the police won't be looking for us. We've been cautious, and I'm certain you have?" she asked, and then, "You're positive that Trent Partridge has never seen you in person?"

"What... no?" Sir Barrington replied. "I've never met with the chap. In fact, the only person to have any contact with him has always had their head covered with a motorcycle helmet at all times. Also, Trent was blindfolded when he was brought to the farm."

"*Marvellous*, Uncle. Then there's absolutely nothing to tie us to anything unsavoury. And, even if the police should come calling, then I can assure you that it won't be any of us wearing bracelets. Am I right, Terry?"

"Always, skipper," Terry replied, tapping his temple and offering an exaggerated wink. "Let's just say it won't be *our* fingerprints on the weapon, so to speak."

"Yes, very good," Sir Barrington said agreeably. "What about our guests, Tamara? I don't want any blood on my hands, young lady."

Tamara placed her hand over her mouth as if even the merest suggestion of causing physical harm had caused great offence. "Heaven forbid, Uncle. No, so long as our guests behave, then they'll all be released without harm. Once we're at a safe distance with cast-iron alibis, of course."

"*Of course*. But, what about those two women poking their nose into our business and the other investigator, Pam Levy?"

"Uncle," Tamara replied like she was talking to a child. "The investigators can have all the suspicions they want, but they won't be able to link anything back to us."

Tamara turned her attention to Terry, who immediately straightened his back in response. "Terry, our two new guests. Did they see your face?"

"No, skipper. Not a chance."

"Excellent," Tamara replied, moving to the window. "Uncle, why is a man walking up the drive?"

Sir Barrington joined his niece, raising his glass to his lips. He looked down on the approaching figure. "That's my man," he confirmed, polishing off his drink. "He calls around to make sure Trent is well looked after."

Sir Barrington tapped on the window, offering a hand in acknowledgement. The man down below offered a discreet wave as

CHAPTER NINETEEN – A FUNNY PLACE TO TAKE A NAP

he snapped down the visor on his motorcycle helmet. Sir Barrington watched on as the man continued walking towards the building where Trent was presently their guest.

"He's loyal?" Terry asked.

"Hmm," Sir Barrington replied with an indifferent shrug. "He's exceptionally fond of money, so that brings him into line."

"If you need me to have a word with him," Terry added, "I'll be happy to have a gentle chat."

In the building where Trent was secured, Sam and Tom had completed their sweep through the remaining rooms. All were empty apart from supplies being used in the extensive renovations. Fortunately, Tom had caught sight of the helmet-wearing man walking across the courtyard.

"We need to get out of here," Tom said, leading Sam to the window through which they originally entered. "The girls aren't in this building, and helmet head is probably on his way in here to see Trent."

"Why don't we just knock him out?" Sam suggested, hovering by the open window. "There's two of us, and we're both armed."

Tom chewed that idea over before discounting it. "We're dealing with a potentially armed, violent gang of kidnappers, Sam. I'm not sure two wooden handles would count as armed."

"Okay," Sam replied, seeing sense and reconsidering his options. "Which window did helmet man wave to?"

"The one looking down on the entrance lane or track, whatever it's called?" Tom replied. "It was discreet, but I'm certain he looked up and waved to someone."

"He's here," Sam said, watching as the man took a quick look behind him before removing a key from his jacket pocket. "As soon as that front door opens and he's inside, we should move."

Tom took hold of Sam's arm, preventing his departure. "Sam, as soon as we climb through that window we'll be seen, for sure?" he said, the reality of the situation hitting him.

"We can't just sit here all day," Sam pointed out, before drifting away for a moment, eyes glazed over, as a thought ran through his mind. "I've got an idea!" Sam declared, moving away from the window. "Follow me," Sam said, giving an assured nod and heading through the door behind them.

"That's where we've just come from," Tom said, pointing out what Sam would already have been well aware of.

"Trust me, Tom. Just make sure helmet man doesn't see us."

$$\mathcal{P}\,\mathcal{Q}$$

A quick change later, Sam and Tom reappeared at the window, ready to make good their escape, the second time of asking. "The coast appears to be clear," Sam said, taking a look over the deserted courtyard. "Let's go," Sam added, climbing out, left leg first.

"You're sure about this?" Tom asked from behind, in a tone suggesting he wasn't entirely on board with the current plan. But as Sam was already halfway through the window, that was all the confirmation Tom required about how sure Sam actually was.

Once outside in the fresh, country air, Sam straightened himself up, placing his yellow hard hat on his shaven head. For someone trying to remain inconspicuous, the choice of wearing a fluorescent yellow jacket was, well, questionable. Indeed, Tom's trepidation was entirely understandable at this moment in time what with them both being directly in the lion's den, as it were.

"You're good to go," Sam said through the corner of his mouth, prompting Tom to join him on the cobbles where Tom fastened his own fluorescent jacket, also now wearing a yellow hard hat.

"Here," Tom said, handing Sam his broom handle.

"Let's go," Sam said, walking forth with confidence and with absolutely no attempt to conceal themselves.

"Ehm... where. Exactly?" Tom asked, following behind like a duckling chasing its mum.

"I was thinking about the front door," Sam said, spinning his handle with the proficiency of a novice cheerleader.

CHAPTER NINETEEN – A FUNNY PLACE TO TAKE A NAP

The two men had raided the builders' store cupboard and were now providing a rather average impersonation of two burly workmen going about their business. With the former farm subject to an extensive ongoing renovation, Sam reasoned this to be the perfect way to move through the compound without question or interference. As Tom pointed out, however, Sir Barrington had met Sam on several, memorable occasions, so they'd even managed to snaffle a pair of safety goggles to complete their overall disguise. With his baldy head and face partially obscured, it was unlikely that the ageing eyes of Sir Barrington would recognise Sam as the PI proving to be a significant thorn in his side. At least that's what they were both counting on.

Sam marched straight up to the front door, bold as you like, removing a measuring tape from his pocket. He handed Tom his wooden handle, crouched down to the height of the letterbox, extending the tape over the width of the door.

"What are you doing?" Tom asked mouth closed, talking like a ventriloquist.

"It's just in case we're being watched," Sam replied. "With this tape measure, they'll think I am *actually* a builder." Sam continued the pretence for several seconds longer, then pushed open the silver letterbox with his thumb, using the opening to have a look beyond the door.

"Anything?" Tom asked, staring intently at his empty clipboard, doing his best to look like an industrious builder reviewing his notes. Notes that, of course, weren't actually there.

Sam shook his head. "No, I don't see anybody," he said, lowering the letterbox and returning to full height. Sam considered his options for a moment, before deciding the best one was to simply open the door, whistling, and generally acting like he owned the place.

"*Sam*," Tom scolded him.

"What?" Sam asked. "We're builders. When have you ever seen builders creeping about? They usually walk around bold as brass."

Now inside, it was apparent that this was where the bulk of the renovations had so far been undertaken. You could still smell the fresh paint. A wooden corridor ran either side of a central staircase and judging by the elegant décor, the improvements in this section were nearing completion.

"Sam," Tom said, looking down at the cream carpet. "Is that cow dung you've dragged in?"

"I dunno?" Sam replied, lifting his foot. "Could also be horse or sheep," he suggested. "No, it wouldn't be sheep, would it? I'm pretty sure that they dispense those little brown balls that look like Maltesers. Anyway, who puts cream carpet in a farmhouse? It's plain stupid and just asking for trouble if you ask me?"

Sam pressed on, causing some slight additional staining as he did so. "You try the rooms on the left side of the corridor, and I'll do the right," Sam suggested, reaching for the handle on the door nearest to him. A cursory glance of the area inside offered no sign of Abby and Suzie, and so he moved to the next.

"Sam!" Tom said from the other side of the staircase. "Sam, come over here."

Sam took a firm grip on his wooden handle, unsure what to expect but ready for the unexpected as his training had taught him. Tom took a step towards Sam, presenting what he'd found in the palm of his hand. "Recognise this?" Tom asked.

Sam pinched his fingers around a snapped silver bracelet. "That's Abby's," Sam said, moving it closer to his face for further confirmation. "I bought her that for her birthday last year."

Enraged at how it was no longer being worn on his beloved's wrist, Sam moved from one door to the next in quick succession, but behind each, was greeted only by empty frustration.

"This is the last room on this floor," Sam said with Tom keeping up the rear. Sam opened the door, poised, ready to defend himself should the need arise. "It's the kitchen," Sam said for the benefit of Tom cosying in behind him.

"This is the size of my entire house," Sam said, walking through the L-shaped kitchen, scanning the room for clues. "They're not here," Sam said, smacking the wooden handle onto the stone tiles in frustration.

CHAPTER NINETEEN – A FUNNY PLACE TO TAKE A NAP

"In there," Tom said, tipping his head in the direction of a door leading off the kitchen. "It might be a utility room or something? But judging by the money spent on this place, it'll probably be a separate annexe to store Sir B's wine collection?"

Sam threw the door open, extending his weapon like he was readying for a joust. "Abby!" Sam shouted, sprinting forward. "Tom, the girls are in here."

Suzie and Abby were both sat on the floor, back to back, knees tucked into their chest with tape securing them to each other. A further generous application of tape had been put to use on their hands, ankles, and mouths. Sam first gripped the black tape covering Abby's mouth, ripping it off in one fluid movement.

"*Holy macaroni,*" Abby said, with a perfect red-raw strip forming below her nose. "Have you left any lips on my face," she asked with her eyes streaming.

"At least you don't need to worry about having a moustache now," Sam joked, kissing her cheek. "I was so worried," he added, turning his attention to Suzie, performing the same manoeuvre as he'd done on Abby. "Are either of you hurt?" Sam asked, looking them both over.

"We're fine, Sam," Abby replied. "Suzie had a gash on her head from the car crash, but other than—"

"Well, well, well..." said the owner of a deep voice stood in the doorway which his broad frame all but filled. "Not interrupting anything, I trust? Only it's quite the party you appear to be having. I can go and get you some peanuts and prosecco if you'd like?"

"Who the hell are you?" Tom asked, pointing his pole towards the man at the door.

"Take it easy," came the immediate reply, "or I'll take that from you and stick it right up your—"

"That's the man who forced us from the road," Abby said, cutting him off mid-threat.

"Terry's the name," Terry said, with a broad smile. "And you two are very naughty girls. You both promised me you hadn't seen my face earlier, which is why you remained unhurt. Mind you, I had a feeling you might have been lying if I'm honest. I've got a sixth sense for that sort of thing."

Without warning, Tom brought his wooden handle down on top of Terry's head where it broke in two (the handle, not Terry's head) with a crisp snap. Tom stared at Terry — who was built like the side of a house — hoping he'd soon keel over unconscious, but no, he was perfectly upright if not a little perplexed.

"Well, that's not very polite..." Terry said, wiping a small trickle of blood from his temple. "There was me about to get you some peanuts, and you go and—"

"Have *that!*" Tom shouted, striking Terry with the remaining piece of broken wood still in his hand. It landed on the exact same spot and this time Terry's eyes rolled a touch, as he rocked back and forth like a giant redwood being felled.

Tom stepped back for fear of the big lump falling directly on top of him, but as he did, Terry lurched forward, catching Tom with the sweetest left hook directly on the point of his chin.

"Tom!" Abby screamed, as her friend and colleague was sent flat on his arse.

Sam scrambled to get to his feet, but the revolver now pointed directly at his head kept him in check.

"Now you've got me in a bad mood," Terry said, shaking his head. "Here we were having a nice little get-together when you all had to go and ruin it. And now I'm going to have to change from Plan A to Plan B which creates extra work for me. It's selfish on your part if I'm completely candid."

"Plan B?" Abby asked.

"Sure," Terry replied. "It's just like Plan A apart from... Ah, I'm not going to lie to you. It's completely different if I'm honest. With Plan A, you get to walk away, eventually. You might have all been tied up for several hours until I escaped along with my employers. But, now you've seen my face, I can't exactly do that, now can I? Anyway, you're all intelligent people, so I probably don't need to spell out the key amendments between the two plans, in detail?"

CHAPTER NINETEEN – A FUNNY PLACE TO TAKE A NAP

"I've forgotten what you looked like already," Abby said, closing her eyes. "There, I can't even see you now, and I don't even remember your name, Terry. I promise."

Terry released a gentle laugh. "I like your style, young lady. It's a shame as Plan B is always the worst part of the job. Well, when I say *job*, it's not really a job when... ah, you don't need to hear about my career observations. Not now, anyway."

Terry paused as a shrill noise increased steadily in volume. It sounded rather like a screaming baby that'd inhaled helium. "Whhaaaaaa!" the noise continued until it reached a crescendo when a foot burst through the air, connecting with the back of Terry's scarred head.

Terry staggered forward, causing his gun to discharge a round into the wall opposite.

"What the..." Terry said, rubbing the back of his head. He turned to face the door of the utility room, eager to see what or who had struck him so hard. Terry stared, not really believing his eyes as a scrawny streak of piss stood in the doorway, topless, adopting a Bruce Lee pose.

"Am I concussed?" Terry asked, but who the question was directed towards was unclear. "I must be concussed," Terry concluded, "because all I can see is an emaciated Bruce Lee impersonator. Who or what are you supposed to be?" Terry asked, gun hanging casually by his waist.

"I'm Adrian Fitzherbert. Guardian of History," Adrian replied. As he said the *ory* in history, Adrian's arms flailed in a blur, releasing a nunchuck that'd been secured in his waistband behind his back.

Terry was struck that many times, in quick succession, that he must have thought he'd been assaulted by a revolving door.

"Whhaaaaa!" Adrian added, sheathing his weapon back down his half-mast trousers, fists clenched, mission accomplished.

Terry remained upright and conscious for several more seconds, but the giant redwood had received a crippling blow of the axe, so to speak. Terry's eyes rolled back in his head a moment before he collapsed unceremoniously in a crumpled heap, fortunately, not using Tom to break his fall.

Sam didn't immediately speak as he was processing what he'd just been a witness to. "Ehm..." he said after a brief contemplation. "Excellent work... Adrian?" Sam stared intently at the semi-naked man, cocking his head, trying to place the face. "Bloody hell," Sam said, "you're the night watchman from the museum?"

"Director of security!" Adrian replied, and Sam certainly had no intention of doubting his credentials on the matter.

Adrian moved to the fallen thug, placing his foot on the man's barrel chest like a big game hunter. "Take my picture?" Adrian asked, handing his mobile phone to a bemused Sam.

"Yeah, of course," Sam said with an awkward laugh.

"I need you to take my picture with the other guy, also," Adrian added with a sniff.

"Other guy?" Sam asked.

Adrian threw his thumb over his shoulder. "Yeah, some guy in a black helmet is presently lying in the middle of the courtyard counting sheep."

"You mean literally or figuratively...? I only ask because we *are* on a farm," Sam said, eager to clarify.

"Where is she?" Adrian asked, ignoring Sam's question and moving to the cupboards. "Where is she?" he asked, once more, throwing door after door open. "She has to be here," he said in desperation.

"Who?" Sam asked, looking around for who he might be talking about.

"I think it's under that white sheet," Abby offered, nodding in the direction of the washing machine.

Adrian took a grip of the fabric, licking his lips in anticipation. He paused, like he was praying to the good Lord above, and then eased the sheet up, slowly, barely daring to believe. "Oh my princess," Adrian said, falling to his knees. "I've come for you, my princess. Each night before I fell asleep, I swore I'd return you to your rightful home, and here I am," he added, as a solitary tear fell down his cheek.

CHAPTER NINETEEN – A FUNNY PLACE TO TAKE A NAP

"Well," Sam said, "I guess we know where the Senior TT Trophy is."

"Sam," Abby called over. "Sam..."

"Yes, my beloved," Sam replied.

"Are you going to help Tom up?" Abby asked as her groggy colleague attempted to push himself up on his elbows without much success. "And, I think that might also be his tooth next to your foot?"

Sam took possession of Terry's discarded gun before offering Tom a hand up. "Come on, buddy. At least you'll get to see the tooth fairy tonight."

With Tom safely seated on a stool, Sam unwrapped Suzie and Abby, using the same tape to truss up the unconscious, but breathing, Terry. "Do you think he's okay over there?" Sam whispered, as Adrian tenderly embraced the trophy like a lover, sobbing gently.

"Well, it was stolen on his watch, so, maybe he just takes his job seriously?" Abby suggested.

"I think we should leave the two of them alone," Sam said. "They look like they need to be reacquainted. Come on, there's a couple of things I need to do."

"Such as," Abby asked, casually picking up Tom's extracted tooth.

Sam closed one eye running through his mental shopping list of things to do. "In no particular order," he began, "I need to release Trent Partridge, and then—"

"Wait, what?" Abby said. "Trent is *here*?"

"Sure is," Sam replied. "I'll fill you in on that one later. Then, after that, I need to find a landline and phone the police. Then... in fact, no. I was going to suggest looking for Sir Barrington. But, I'm guessing those squealing car tyres I just heard, are him and his adorable niece making a sharp exit."

"They won't get too far," Suzie suggested, looking Tom over.

Sam nodded in agreement, walking through the utility room door. "Oh," Sam continued, raising his finger as a further thought entered his head. "We need to find out who the man in the black helmet is," he said. "Although... I've got a sneaking suspicion I know exactly who it is."

Sam, Suzie, Abby, and a weary Tom, headed through the farm building and out to the courtyard. As Sam suspected, the dinted black BMW had gone, leaving a generous skidmark on the cobbles such was the driver's haste to leave.

"I'm guessing that's Adrian's car over there," Sam said, pointing at the silver VW Golf. "Maybe his arrival and the sound of gunshot spooked Sir Barrington and Tamara?"

"He's quite impressive with his fists," Abby suggested, standing over the collapsed, helmet-wearing figure in the centre of the courtyard.

"It's all in the training," Sam suggested with a confident shrug. "I can do all that," he added, chopping his hands through the air like he was slicing carrots.

"Yeah, okay," Suzie said with a smile, looking down as the man on the ground released a pained groan.

Sam leaned over, placing his index finger under the darkened visor. "Wakey, wakey," Sam said, lifting up the visor, revealing a portion of the face beneath. "Hello, Drexel," Sam said. "That's a funny place to take a nap!"

CHAPTER TWENTY
A Thief in the Knight

A Thief in the Knight

Crooked nobleman charged alongside niece with theft, kidnap, money laundering and fraud

By Wayne Snapper

Sir Barrington Hedley-Smythe, along with his niece, Tamara Urquhart, have today been charged with fraud, money laundering and three counts of kidnap - including the motorcycle World Champion, Trent Partridge - and, additionally, the high profile theft of the Isle of Man Senior TT Trophy.

It's alleged that the Brazen Burglars, as they've been described, were involved in an elaborate plan to tarnish the global reputation of the famous Isle of Man TT races for their own benefit. Urquhart, in her senior role with the newly formed Isle of Wight TT, had invested heavily in the new venture alongside several other investors, including her uncle.

By damaging the reputation of the Isle of Man TT, the pair hoped to secure valuable sponsorship as well as a portion of broadcasting revenues as companies moved to distance themselves from the negative publicity and potentially invest in their new Isle of Wight event.

To undermine the iconic Isle of Man TT, it's alleged that Sir Barrington, in his role as trustee of the Isle of Man's Manx Museum, was able to share floor plans and security details to an accomplice, Drexel Popek, to orchestrate the daring heist. Mr Popek – one of several known aliases – is now understood to be of interest to European law enforcement, with several outstanding arrest warrants under his various alter egos. Mr Popek is said to have perpetrated the theft by breaking into the museum in the early hours of the morning once he'd bypassed the alarm system.

The gang are further accused of conspiring to hijack several trucks transporting vital logistics for the event, including over one million pounds worth of race specification tyres and fuel which were later destroyed in an arson attack.

If the plan proved successful, it's believed the potential revenues could have been worth several million pounds each year to the gang and caused irreparable damage to the Isle of Man TT in the process.

Speaking exclusively to this journalist, DI Rump of the Isle of Man Police said: "Were it not for the tenacious actions of the Eyes Peeled Detective Agency, as well as Manx Museum head of security Adrian Fitzherbert, their audacious plan would have likely succeeded."

"The recovery of the Senior TT Trophy was a key priority," said Sidney Postlethwaite, the reinstated Head of Isle of Man Motorsport. He went on to say: "It's one of the hardest earned trophies in worldwide sport and, for many, a symbol of courage, tenacity and pride. We're humbled and grateful to welcome her back in time for this year's race."

Mr Postlethwaite – who was initially forced to resign over the incident – was understood to have taken up a role heading up the Isle of Wight TT. Despite this, Mr Postlethwaite worked tirelessly with the team of investigators to secure the timely recovery of the trophy. He added: "The Isle of Man TT is where my heart was and always will be. Not only is it the greatest sporting spectacle

CHAPTER TWENTY — A THIEF IN THE KNIGHT

on earth, bar none, it's the ultimate test of man, woman and machine. My heart was heavy at the prospect of leaving, so, I thank the Tourism Minister for inviting me back to drive this magnificent event forward."

It's a spectacular fall from grace for Sir Barrington, who was arrested, along with his niece, aboard a fishing boat leaving Douglas. Following a tip-off, the two have been remanded in custody at the island's jail in Jurby.

At the time of going to press, no comment has been received from the Isle of Wight racing committee.

"The greedy bastards!" Suzie declared, drawing an impressive green tick the length of her whiteboard in the offices of Eye Peeled HQ.

Sam, for his part, took great delight in having read aloud the main lead story on the front of the local newspaper. "I think we came across rather well," Sam said, slapping the paper down on the boardroom table with a satisfied grin. "And I do quite like that they mentioned our case name, Brazen Burglar," he added proudly, looking around the room.

"That I originally came up with, if you recall," Abby was happy to remind him.

"Though perhaps it should be *Burglars*, plural, now?" Suzie entered in.

"Mmm," Sam said with a shrug. "For me, the thief was Popek, so I think I'll stay with *Burglar*, for now."

"Boss," Tom said, scrolling through his phone, giddy with excitement. "Boss, I've just been looking at the UK press, and even the tabloids have picked the story up." Tom lifted up his phone for the rest to see. "They've even managed to get a picture of Sam and me in our yellow hard hats," he added to the others, proud as Punch.

Abby leaned over the table for a closer look. "Fab!" Abby said. "Although, Tom, your smile kinda looks like a piano keyboard, what with your missing tooth."

"Lazy tooth fairy didn't turn up last night, either," Tom replied with a piano keyboard laugh.

"Well, team," Sam said, leaning back and placing his feet on the surface of the table. "It's a hard-earned victory, but I can't help being frustrated with myself."

"For wearing that t-shirt?" Abby quipped.

"No," Sam said, looking down at his favourite Take That t-shirt. "For not picking up on the signs earlier on. For that, I apologise."

"What signs?" Suzie asked, glancing at the whiteboard where she'd previously scribed all of their case notes to date.

"The misfiring engine," Sam replied, with a disappointed shake of his head. "When the trophy was first nicked, an eyewitness said they were woken by the sound of a misfiring engine, near the museum. That must have been when Sir B was playing at the getaway driver for Drexel."

"Oh, yes," Abby added, eyes narrowed and deep in thought. "We were right behind Sir Barrington's green Land Rover at one point during the investigation. Now you mention it, I even recall you saying that it sounded like a rusting lawnmower at the time."

"You can't blame yourself for that one, Sam," Tom said. "Hercule Poirot wouldn't have picked up on that."

Sam offered a sigh in return. "Perhaps," Sam said. "I also can't help blaming myself for employing Drexel... Derek... Lexington... whatever bloody name he was using. He had more characters than a West End play, that guy."

Sam went quiet, presumably waiting for shouts about how he shouldn't blame himself for such a calamitous error and how it could've happened to anybody.

"What?" Abby asked with a grin when Sam looked her way with sad eyes. "Sorry, Sam. You *can* take that one on the chin, my love. You were the one that assured us background checks weren't required."

"I know," Sam said. "Who would have known he was a career thief on the run from the authorities and with multiple arrest warrants outstanding."

"Ehm..." Tom ventured in. "I think that's *exactly* what the background checks would've picked up, boss."

CHAPTER TWENTY — A THIEF IN THE KNIGHT

Sam tucked his chin into his Take That t-shirt. "You can have that one," Sam conceded and then moved direction away from what he did or didn't do. "I'll bet Quentin Thrumbolt didn't have a clue about how close he was to being caught up in this mess."

"So," Suzie said, drawing a line through Quentin's name written on the whiteboard. "We're certain he had no involvement in any of this?"

Sam shook his head. "None. Quentin was genuinely only involved in a legitimate purchase of two grandfather clocks to aid Sir B's cash-flow. Drexel must have thought it sensible to have another potential suspect to muddy the waters should the need later arise. Which it did, as it turned out."

"But you found paperwork between the two of them about buying the Queen Victoria bust, no?" Tom asked.

"Yes. But it was just a general enquiry at that stage, nothing serious," Sam explained. "Quentin had no idea anything had been stolen so, in his mind, it would have all been above board. He said he'd have picked up on anything untoward when he completed his extensive due diligence if the deal progressed. Something I should take note of, I know…"

"Ah…" Tom offered almost apologetically. "I might have had a *friend* hack into Quentin's email server, you know, when we thought he was a wrong 'un. I should probably remove that?"

"That would be nice," Sam said. "Although, if this friend of yours wanted to have a quick nosey at *Drexel's* emails to see what else he's been up to, well…"

Drexel Popek, Derek Popper, Lexington Hardcastle, Winthrop Ogilvy, and Eustace Constantine were the aliases that the police — as confirmed by DI Rump — were currently aware of. Unbeknownst to Sam (as he couldn't be bothered to complete background checks) Drexel was a career fraudster operating in several affluent holiday resorts throughout Europe. He was linked to timeshare scams, fraudulent travel agents, bigamy, and wholesale VAT fraud. With the net closing in on him, Drexel settled on a sharp exit to a sleepy island in the middle of the Irish Sea while things calmed down. Still needing to earn a crust, however, a chance job advert for a trainee PI offered him the perfect cover to satisfy his criminal desires during his time on the island. For a short while, his sideline of stealing items — including precious animals — only to return them for the reward money, proved lucrative. Exceptionally so, as evidenced by the handsome contents of his bank balance which the police were eager to seize. It would also now be a bunfight by the various authorities over which jurisdiction would lock him up first.

Drexel had been quite happy to continue with his petty thievery. Why wouldn't he be? It was good money, and he was regularly lauded as a hero. Until that is, he was coerced into a change of career direction. After successfully reuniting Sir Barrington Hedley-Smythe with his prized peacock — and trousering the substantial reward — his nefarious tactics and the fact he'd stolen the bird in the first place, were uncovered on Sir Barrington's CCTV. By having his collar felt by the Old Bill, Drexel knew he would have been facing deportation and facing severe jail time and was, therefore, happy and willing to do anything to avoid that outcome.

It was a chance encounter and fortuitous for Sir Barrington. Facing crippling debts for the upkeep of his extensive property empire and coupled with the substantial amount he'd already invested in his niece's new business empire, Sir Barrington needed a cash injection, and fast. The theft of the valuable and heavily insured bronze busts offered him a solution, and, for Drexel, a renewed taste for more significant and lucrative criminal endeavours.

For his further assistance in stealing the trophy and then kidnapping Trent, Drexel was given a shareholding in the new Isle of Wight business. A partnership that would have set him up for life to see out his days relaxing by the beach, drinking rum from a coconut being served by exotic beauties. Well, that was the plan, at least…

"You know," Sam said reflectively, "I kinda liked Drexel, you know."

"We all did, Sam," Tom offered. "Don't feel too bad as he took us all for fools."

CHAPTER TWENTY – A THIEF IN THE KNIGHT

"He would've continued to be a helluva private detective for us," Suzie added. "He was superb at the legitimate work he did. Still, at least with him out of the way, hopefully, the clients he poached will come back to us? We might even need to advertise for a new PI," Suzie suggested. "You know, for the increased workflows," she added optimistically.

"Mmm," Sam said knowingly. "About a future vacancy," he added, sitting upright. "I think I might have a candidate," Sam confided, looking to Abby, who didn't seem surprised by this revelation.

"Oh?" Tom asked. "Who do you have in mind, DI Rump?"

"Not just now, but maybe when he retires," Sam said. "The person who enquired about any open positions has impeccable credentials and is as tenacious as they come. And, there are not many folks who can also lay claim to being a *Guardian of History*!"

"Adrian Fitzherbert?" Tom said, with a wry smile. "You know," he went on, "he's good at what he does if not a little... unorthodox."

Sam nodded his head, reaching for his coffee. "You're not wrong there, Tom. Adrian was so eager to find the trophy that he's been following anybody and everybody involved in the investigation. He's not slept for days, apparently. So, when we were on surveillance, *we* were being surveyed, by Adrian. He also said our technology was easy to hack, so, we should look to upgrade."

"You just want to play with new gadgets, Sam," Suzie suggested. "Be honest!"

"Well... okay then," Sam confessed.

"So, is that how he knew we were in Sir Barrington's farmhouse?" Tom asked.

"Yup. Thank god Adrian was trailing us because if he hadn't taken out Terry, I'm not sure what would've happened."

"We'd all be dead," Suzie suggested bluntly.

Sam swatted that suggestion away. "*Pfft*. I was just about to disable Terry," Sam said. "It was only that Adrian arrived just before I was about to deliver a crippling blow. It's lucky for Terry, in fact, that he's going to be behind bars for some time and not crossing my path, anytime soon."

"Whatever," Abby said, though not in an unkind way. "Promise me one thing before you employ Adrian?"

"Anything, my love."

"Don't forget to complete the background checks this time!"

CHAPTER TWENTY-ONE
Shift It!

Conditions were glorious for the hotly-anticipated Senior TT race. The crowds were out from first light, with thousands of giddy fans filling every available inch of the near thirty-eight-mile course, cramming into and vying for the optimum viewing spots. There was a party atmosphere on the Isle of Man, and with the safe return of the trophy, a palpable sense of relief for anybody who had engine oil running through their veins.

With race time rapidly approaching, a throaty hum wafted through the air at the TT Grandstand, with race teams making final adjustments to their machines or getting engines to temperature. One of the many joys of the Isle of Man TT was the opportunity to get so up close and personal with all the action. It was something you'd rarely find in any other sport of this scale and just one of the numerous reasons that folk continually returned, without fail, like a homing pigeon with a decent sat-nav.

An unassuming metal gate separating the paddock area and the pit lane was always a popular area for the fans to mill around. Because it was through this very spot that a good number of the riders would make their way from their motorhomes, tents — or whatever else they were sleeping in — to their bikes, sat waiting for them on Glencrutchery Road. These heroic men and women would then soon accelerate away to their first test of many: a stomach-churning descent of Bray Hill at over 180 mph. A small number of spectators, armed with the appropriate passes, were also permitted entry through the hallowed gate. Here, they would enjoy unrivalled access, floating around the starting grid with the riders, dignitaries, TV crews, celebrities, and all of the other guests stumbling about in a state of wonderment and apprehension.

Access passes were, for that reason, highly desirable, and it was probably easier to find a juggling unicorn than locate any spares for the day's action.

Which is precisely why Sam, Abby, Tom, and Suzie had such a spring in their step as they approached the gate, walking straight past the congregation stood either side of the path. Sam happily thrust his pass — secured on a lanyard around his neck — in the direction of anybody who gave him a second glance. Including the security guard he was now stood before.

"Old Sidney did us a good turn with these passes," Sam said, looking over his shoulder to Abby. It was clear from her broad grin that she was also relishing the occasion, although, in a slightly less gloating manner than Sam. "Mind you, we did save his bacon, somewhat," Sam added.

Tom, for his part, was also enjoying the temporary VIP status, with at least two kids stood beside the walkway tugging on their parent's arm, enquiring if Tom was, perhaps, one of the racers whose autograph they should obtain. His reverie was soon obliterated, however, when the father of one such child was heard to remark: "Who, *that* fat bastard, Charlie? I shouldn't think so, son."

Yup, life was splendid right about now, and the contented expression on Sam's face grew exponentially when they walked out and onto the starting grid, mere inches from the idling motorbikes. "This is amazing," Sam said, shuffling through the crowds towards bike number one, parked up on its stand, only a few feet behind the magnificent starting arch. "You think they'd mind if I jumped on board for a photo?" Sam joked. At least Abby hoped it was a joke.

The world's sporting press were also in attendance in their droves, with journalists and TV crews almost outnumbering the mechanics lovingly tending to their bikes. Sam caught the eye of one such TV

CHAPTER TWENTY-ONE — SHIFT IT!

cameraman who was gawping directly back at him, making Sam feel somewhat uneasy. The man with a camera resting on his shoulder nudged his mate, pointing in Sam's direction. He, in turn, then nudged his mate and seconds later, a herd of journalists sprinted towards Sam's location like a baying mob.

Sam took a precautionary step back, panicking, as he'd not rehearsed anything to say about his dramatic involvement in the recovery of the Senior TT Trophy. Still, he'd come up with something, he figured. He cleared his throat, but as the gaggle approached, Sam was unceremoniously shifted aside, with the group continuing on.

"Shift it, slaphead," shouted one particularly abrasive backmarker armed with a microphone at the ready.

Sam turned to see where the pack of hyenas were headed, and the answer was soon evident. No longer an unshaven, dishevelled wreck, Trent Partridge strutted onto the starting grid like a catwalk model. Lowering his Ray-Bans, just a touch, he held a hand out, bringing the press pack to a controlled halt as he ran his hand through his immaculate hair. "Mr Partridge," came the collective cry, with each journalist eager to get the inside scoop on his high-profile kidnapping.

"You thought they were coming for *you*?" Abby asked, putting a supportive hand around Sam's back.

"What... no..." Sam replied with a sigh. "Yeah, a little bit. Do you mind if we move further away, only my masculinity is struggling to cope with being in such close proximity to Trent?"

"What, leave right now...?" Abby replied, reluctantly, her attention obviously elsewhere. "I'm just kidding!" she added, returning her full attention to Sam. Raising up on tiptoe, she planted a kiss on the side of this cheek. "I love you," she said, "and I'm so proud of you for all you do."

"We do make a hell of a team, don't we," Sam said, misty-eyed. "You know, I've got a funny feeling this year is going to be pretty special for Eyes Peeled."

Trent Partridge walked through the assembled media, heading directly towards the Eyes Peeled team with several journalists in tow. Sam, Abby, Tom, and Suzie smiled politely until Trent scooped them all into his arms. "I owe you everything," Trent said. "Thank you," he added as several microphones were thrust in front of him.

"Who are they, Mr Partridge," one journalist shouted. "Can we have a comment?"

Trent stood in the middle of Team Eyes Peeled — Tom and Suzie on one arm with Sam and Abby on the other. Trent directly addressed the media circling around them with a relieved, humble smile. "These beautiful people are the private detectives who secured my release," Trent said, welling up. "I owe them everything," he added.

"After the race," Trent said, turning his attention away from the cameras. "Would you do me the honour of joining me in the hospitality suite as my guest?" Trent asked, looking at Sam & co.

"Well," Sam replied, puffing his cheeks out like there were several other options on the table when, of course, he was salivating at the very prospect. "I dunno about that, Trent. We were going—"

"*We'd love to*," Suzie, Tom, and Abby said, collectively cutting Sam off.

"Seriously, thank you," Trent followed up, looking at each of them in turn. "And, if there's ever anything I can do for you, just name it."

"Anything?" Suzie joked, with a cheeky, hopeful grin.

Trent laughed. "I should get back to the press before they drag me away, kicking and screaming. But I'll see you soon, yeah? We can have a drink or three."

Suzie admired Trent's impossibly tight trousers as he walked away, very much hoping that *anything* was going to be on the menu in the hospitality suite later.

Sam couldn't resist taking the opportunity to appreciate the view from standing directly under the starting arch, looking out at the clear tarmac stretching out in front of him. It was difficult to comprehend that in twenty minutes or so, the grid would be cleared apart from the riders lining up, single file, waiting for their tap on the shoulder from the race official, sending them on their way at the start of their race. So, this was his last chance…

CHAPTER TWENTY-ONE — SHIFT IT!

"Come on," Sam said, taking Abby by the hand. He walked towards the arch — currently fenced off with a velvet rope — staring dead ahead, trying to look as inconspicuous as he could for the patrolling stewards who'd possibly prevent his access.

"What are you doing?" Abby asked, being pulled behind. "Sam...?"

"Abby, it's not every day we're going to be able to stand under the starting arch, minutes before the Senior TT begins," Sam said.

Sam and Abby moved under the velvet rope without delay. It was a special moment for Sam as this was the very spot where so many of his heroes roared away from over the years. "It's pretty special," Sam said, eyes wide like a child on Christmas morning.

"I think a steward is coming this way," Abby said through the corner of her mouth.

"Remember when I told you that I saw that parrot in the back of Drexel's car?" Sam randomly said, ignoring her warning.

"What?" Abby asked, tilting her head. "That's a bizarre thing to recall, right now?"

"I know, but bear with me on this, Abs. It was the day I finally figured out Drexel was a lying scumbag."

"Yes, I remember," Abby said, "but—"

"I told you I was absolutely certain it was a Tuesday as I had an important appointment on the same day. That's how I was so confident about what day it was."

Abby narrowed her eyes, wondering where this was all going, but before she could speak, Sam took her hands in his.

"Abby," Sam said, looking deeply into her eyes. "I love you," he said, dropping slowly down on one knee, maintaining eye contact all the while. "The appointment on that day was that so I could buy this," he said, reaching into his pocket.

Abby placed her hand over her mouth as the realisation struck her. "What... the..."

"Abby," Sam said, looking up at her. "Would you do me the enormous honour of becoming my wife?" he asked, presenting the ring for her inspection, before slipping it on her outstretched finger.

"Yes," Abby replied, without hesitation, fighting back the tears. "Absolutely nothing on this planet could make me happier than becoming Mrs Abby Levy."

"Right, you two," the approaching steward barked. "What the hell do you think you're doing?" he said, tut-tutting. "This is most unorthodox," he said, reaching in his pocket, but for what wasn't exactly obvious.

"I-I-was," Sam moved to explain, but the steward simply walked straight past him, several paces further down the empty road where he turned to face them both.

"I know exactly what you were doing you romantic old sod," he replied. "Your friends over there," the steward said, pointing out Tom and Suzie jumping on the spot like a pair of loons, "told me to get my ass over here, quick smart, and take a picture of the two of you under the arch. So, here I am. Now, hurry up and kiss her will you, before you get me fired."

"I love you, Abby," Sam said, standing upright.

"Back 'atcha, Sam."

The grinning steward raised his phone. "Watch the birdie!"

"Only if it's not a racing pigeon," Sam joked, pulling Abby in close.

"Or a peacock," suggested Abby, glancing at the shimmering diamond on her finger.

"Or the parrot... We could go on all day," Sam added. "Here's to the future, Mrs Levy."

The End
(But, they'll be back!)

Also by the Author

If you've enjoyed this book, the author would be very grateful if you would be so kind as to leave feedback on Amazon. You can subscribe for author updates and news on new releases at:

www.authorjcwilliams.com

J C Williams
Author

authorjcwilliams@gmail.com
@jcwilliamsbooks
@jcwilliamsauthor

And also, if you've enjoyed this book, then please check out the author's other offerings!

The *Frank 'n' Stan's Bucket List* series:

The Lonely Heart Attack Club series!

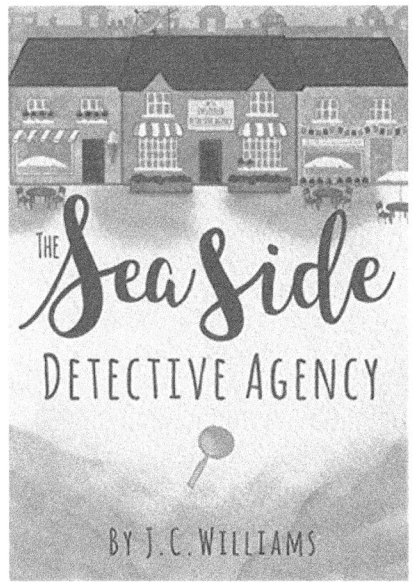

And the first in *The Seaside Detective Agency* series (above), and also *The Flip of a Coin* and *The Bookshop by the Beach* (below):

You may also wish to check out my other books aimed at a younger audience...

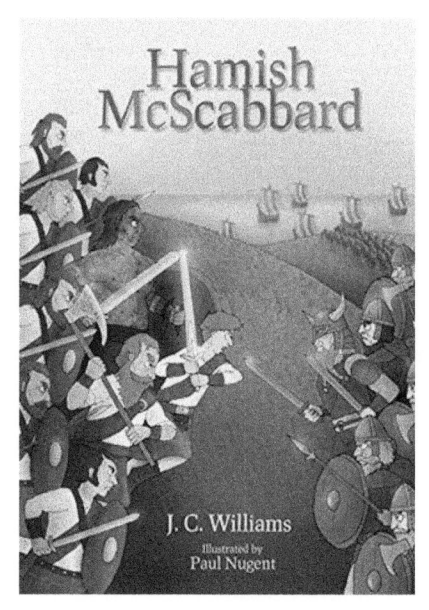

All jolly good fun!